SUGAR COOKIE MURDER

Hannah bent over to examine the large lump of fur. The animal she thought she'd seen was really the expensive fur coat that Martin's new wife was wearing. The only other animal in sight was the reindeer sugar cookie that was broken near Brandi's feet, along with the pieces of a Christmas tree cookie, and a bell decorated in red and green icing. Brandi must have taken several cookies from the dessert table and come out here to eat them. The big question was, did she also take the antique cake knife?

Hoping that she'd just slipped and fallen, Hannah reached down to tap Brandi on the shoulder. "Brandi? Do you need help getting up?" she asked, shaking her a little harder and wondering if she should go for help.

Hannah certainly wouldn't risk moving Brandi, but she'd taken a first aid class in college and she knew there was a pulse point just under the jawbone on the side of a person's neck. The collar of Brandi's coat was in the way and Hannah pushed it back. This caused the coat to fall open and Hannah gave a strangled gasp as she caught sight of Brandi's chest.

"Hannah? Are you out there?" Edna called from the kitchen.

"I'm here."

"Did you find the knife?"

Hannah glanced down at her mother's valuable antique knife, buried to the hilt in Brandi's too-perfectly-proportioned-to-be-natural chest. "I found it . . ."

Books by Joanne Fluke

Chocolate Chip Cookie Murder

Strawberry Shortcake Murder

Blueberry Muffin Murder

Lemon Meringue Pie Murder

Fudge Cupcake Murder

Sugar Cookie Murder

Peach Cobbler Murder

Cherry Cheesecake Murder

Published by Kensington Publishing Corporation

JOANNE FLUKE

SUGAR COOKIE MURDER

A HANNAH SWENSEN
HOLIDAY MYSTERY WITH RECIPES

KENSINGTON BOOKS
www.kensingtonbooks.com

KENSINGTON BOOKS are published by

Kensington Publishing Corp.
850 Third Avenue
New York, NY 10022

All Kensington titles, imprints, and distributed lines are available at special quantity discounts for bulk purchases for sales promotion, premiums, fund-raising, educational, or institutional use.

Special book excerpts or customized printings can also be created to fit specific needs. For details, write or phone the office of the Kensington Special Sales Manager: attn: Special Sales Department. Kensington Publishing Corp., 850 Third Avenue, New York, NY 10022. Phone: 1-800-221-2647.

Kensington and the K logo Reg. U.S. Pat. & TM Off.

ISBN 0-7582-0682-8

First Kensington Hardcover Printing: October 2004
First Kensington Mass Market Printing: October 2005
10 9 8 7 6 5 4 3 2 1

Printed in the United States of America

This book is for Haley, Rachael, and Madeline.

Acknowledgments

Thank you to Ruel, my in-house story editor.
And thanks to our kids who say things like, "You should make a cookie that tastes like German Chocolate Cake." *(I've almost got it, and it'll be in the next Hannah book!)*

I'm grateful to our friends and neighbors:
Mel and Kurt, Lyn and Bill, Gina and the kids, Jay, Bob M., Amanda, John B., Dr. Bob and Sue Hagaman, and to everyone who came running when I said I was testing potluck recipes for this book.

Thank you to my talented editor, John Scognamiglio, for his constant support.
Editors don't come any better than John.
And thanks to all the good folks at Kensington who keep Hannah Swensen sleuthing and baking to her heart's content.

Thank you to Hiro Kimura, my cover artist, for his incredible artwork.

Big hugs to Terry Sommers and her family for critiquing my recipes and for letting me use their family recipe, Aunt Grace's Breakfast Muffins.
Happy Birthday, Terry!

Thanks to Jamie Wallace for shepherding my Web site
MurderSheBaked.com

Thank you to Laura Levine (she writes the Jaine Austen mysteries),
Helen Kauffman, and Charlene Timms, for the title suggestions.
They were all great, and you may see them in print yet.

Thanks to Merle and Tracy for information about
Alzheimer's, and to Doris Hannon for asking about
"Hot Stuff" and "Silver Fox."

A big hug to all my e-mail and regular mail friends who
share their feelings, their baking experiences, and their love
for Hannah with me.

Chapter One

It was a meatball, a really big meatball, and it was rolling out of her closet. It stopped a few feet from the end of the bed, and that was when she noticed its eyes and its face. The eyes stared at her in abject disappointment, and two tears of gravy rolled down its fat bumpy cheeks. It looked so miserable Hannah wanted to reach out and give it a hug.

"You forgot me," the meatball said, "and I'm an entrée. And from what I hear, your entrées aren't that good."

"Yes, they are. We've got . . ."

"I'm doing my best not to take this as a personal insult," the meatball interrupted her, "but you know I'm a lot more delicious than your mother's Hawaiian Pot Roast. What really makes me mad is that you left me out, but you put in four of your sister Andrea's Jell-O molds. Well, it doesn't take a rocket scientist to dump a can of fruit in some Jell-O. If you want her name in the cookbook, you ought to teach her to cook."

What was the meatball talking about? No ordinary mortal could teach Andrea to cook! Her sister was firmly entrenched among the ranks of the culinary-impaired. Hannah sat bolt upright in bed, prepared to give the Swedish treat a piece of her mind. But there was no longer a round, brown entrée with the delectable scent of mushrooms and beef positioned in front of her closet or at the foot of her bed. With the exception of

Moishe, who was curled up at her feet sleeping peacefully, she was alone.

Hannah blinked several times, and then the truth of the situation dawned. She'd been dreaming. The talking meatball had retreated into whatever corner of her mind had created it, but the message it had delivered remained. Hannah had goofed big time. She'd forgotten to include Edna Ferguson's recipe for Not So Swedish Meatballs in the packet to be tested at tonight's potluck dinner.

"Uh-oh," Hannah groaned, feeling around under the bed for her slippers. When she'd wiggled her feet inside the fake fur lining, she patted the mattress to wake the orange and white tomcat who'd been her roommate for the past year and a half. "Come on, Moishe. Time to wake up and smell the kitty crunchies."

Moishe opened one yellow eye and regarded her balefully. Then the phrase "kitty crunchies" must have registered in his feline brain, because he jumped off the bed with an athletic grace that Hannah could only envy, and padded down the hallway at her side as she headed for the kitchen.

Once Moishe had been fed and watered and she'd poured herself a cup of strong coffee, Hannah sat down at the kitchen table that was on the cusp of becoming an antique and considered the problem of Edna Ferguson's meatballs. Since the whole thing was her fault for forgetting to include them, she'd have to find time to test them herself. One thing for sure . . . Edna wouldn't be the soul of understanding if she couldn't find her favorite recipe in the cookbook.

Hannah glanced down at her coffee mug. Empty. And she didn't even remember drinking it. If she showered and dressed right now, before she was fully awake, the lure of a second mug of coffee would make her hurry.

Before the second hand on her apple-shaped wall clock had made twelve complete revolutions, Hannah was back in the kitchen. Instead of her robe, she was wearing jeans and a dark green pullover sweater. Her feet were encased in fur-lined, moosehide boots to stave off the chill of the first cold week in December, and her towel-dried hair was already springing up into a riot of red curls.

"Coffee," Hannah breathed, pouring a mug, inhaling the fragrance and taking the first steaming sip, "is almost as good as . . ." but before she could decide exactly what it was almost as good as, the phone rang.

"Mother!" Hannah muttered in the same tone she used when she stubbed her toe, but she reached for the phone. To let the answering machine get it would only delay the inevitable. Delores Swensen was relentless. If she wanted to talk to her eldest daughter, she'd keep on calling until she was successful.

"Good morning, Mother," Hannah forced a cheery note into her voice and sank down in a chair. Conversations with Delores had been known to last as long as an hour.

"Good morning, dear. You sound like you got up on the right side of the bed," Delores replied, matching Hannah's cheery tone and raising her a cliché. "I know this Christmas potluck has been a lot of work for you and I called to see if there was anything I could do to help."

Warning bells went off in Hannah's head. When Delores tried to be this helpful, she had an ulterior motive. "That's nice of you, Mother, but I think I've got everything covered."

"I thought so. You're so organized, dear. Did I tell you that Luanne found an antique silver cake knife with a prove-nance that dates back to the Regency period?"

"No, you didn't," Hannah said, getting up to pour more coffee and stretching out the phone cord to within an inch of its life. Luanne Hanks was Delores and Carrie's assistant at Granny's Attic, the antique store they'd opened right next to Hannah's bakery, and she was a genius at finding valuable antiques at estate auctions.

"I thought you might want to use it tonight. It has a lovely old-fashioned Christmas tree on the handle."

"Didn't you say it was Regency?"

"That's right, dear."

"But I didn't think they had Christmas trees in Regency England."

"They didn't. But don't forget that the Regent's family was German. And since this particular knife was used at court, it's decorated with a German Christmas tree."

"I'd love to use it," Hannah said. "It'll fit in perfectly."

"That's what I thought. When I showed it to Winthrop last night, he thought it would be appropriate to cut a cake from the period."

Hannah frowned at the mention of her mother's "significant other." She had no basis in fact, but she had the inkling that "Winnie," as her niece Tracey called him, wasn't precisely on the level. She'd asked Norman Rhodes, Carrie's son and the man she occasionally dated, to check Winthrop out on the Internet. Norman had done it, but he hadn't found anything shady about the British lord who was visiting Lake Eden "for a lark."

Hannah pulled herself back to the problem at hand. "I think using the cake knife is a great idea, but as far as I know, no one is bringing a cake made from a Regency recipe."

"Yes, they are, dear. You're forgetting about Lady Hermoine's Chocolate Sunshine Cake."

"Lady Hermoine?" Hannah's voice reached a high note that would have shocked the Jordan High choir director who'd assigned her to the second alto section. "Who's Lady Hermoine? You *know* that's my original recipe!"

"Of course I do, but there's a slight problem, dear. You see, the knife is very valuable. I didn't want to let just anyone use it, so I fibbed a bit."

"What's a *bit?*"

"I said that Lady Hermoine's Chocolate Sunshine Cake originated a lot earlier. If it'll make him happy, is there any harm in letting Winthrop think the recipe's been in our family for hundreds of years?"

Hannah sighed. She didn't like lying even when it was for a good cause, and Winthrop's happiness wasn't high on her list of good causes. "Your fib won't work, Mother. My cake uses frozen orange juice concentrate and that certainly wasn't around back then!"

"That's all right. Winthrop won't notice. And on the off chance he does, I'll say the original recipe called for orange marmalade." Delores gave a sigh and when she spoke again, her voice held a quaver. "That's all right, isn't it?"

Hannah thought about it for a second or two and then she caved. That little quaver in her mother's voice always got to her. "All right, Mother. I won't lie if Winthrop asks me straight out, but as long as he doesn't, I'll play along."

"Thank you, dear! And now I'd better rush. Carrie's picking me up in ten minutes and I still have to do my makeup."

Hannah said her goodbyes and hung up, but the moment she placed the phone back in the cradle it rang again. "Mother," she muttered, grabbing for the phone. Delores often called back immediately if she'd forgotten to say something she felt was important.

"What is it, Mother?" Hannah asked, not bothering with a greeting. She had to leave her condo soon or she'd be late for work.

"I'm not your mother," a male voice replied, chuckling slightly. "It's Mike."

Hannah sat down in her chair with a thunk. Hearing Mike Kingston's voice always made her knees turn weak and her heart beat faster, but she took a deep breath and tried to ignore it.

"I called to find out who's testing my pâté tonight."

Hannah took another deep breath and fought her urge to cave in without a whimper. Tall, rugged, and more handsome than any man had a right to be, Mike wasn't easy to deny. "I can't tell you. You know the rules. The recipe tester has to remain anonymous. Otherwise there could be hard feelings."

"But I really need to know. I might have forgotten to put something in the recipe."

"What?" Hannah asked. She remembered Mike's recipe and there were only two ingredients.

"I need to make sure I wrote down horseradish sauce and not just horseradish. If the tester uses straight horseradish, it'll be too spicy for some people."

"No problem, Mike," Hannah's response was immediate. "You specified horseradish sauce."

"But how do you know, unless . . . *you're* testing it!"

Hannah groaned softly under her breath. Mike was the head detective at the Winnetka County Sheriff's Department, and he'd picked up on her blunder right away. "Uh . . . I can't confirm or deny that."

"Of course you can't, but thanks for putting my mind at ease about that horseradish sauce. How about tonight? Do you want me to pick you up?"

"I think it'd be better if we met at the community center. I'm going to leave work around three, head home to get dressed and pick up the food I'm bringing, and get there early to make sure Edna has all the help she needs in the kitchen."

"Okay. I'll see you there."

Was that a sigh of relief she'd just heard in Mike's voice? "You sound happy that you don't have to pick me up."

"It's not that. I'd pick you up if you needed me. It's just that Shawna Lee asked me if I'd take her to the party."

Hannah closed her eyes and counted to ten. Shawna Lee Quinn had been Mike's secretary in Minneapolis and he'd convinced her to follow him to Lake Eden. She'd landed a job at the Winnetka Sheriff's Department and Mike had found her an apartment in the complex where he lived. He insisted that they were just friends, and Hannah had done her best not to be jealous, but it was difficult to stave off the green-eyed monster when the Southern beauty who'd been crowned Miss Atlanta called Mike every time her car wouldn't start.

"Hannah? Is something wrong?"

Hannah took a deep breath and forced herself to be calm. "Correct me if I'm wrong, but I thought we had a date."

"We do. I'm just giving Shawna Lee a lift there, that's all. She's meeting someone and she's got her own way home."

"Oh. Well . . . okay," Hannah said, hoping that the person Shawna Lee was meeting would show up and she wouldn't turn out to be a third wheel on their date.

"You're really a nice person, Hannah."

"What brought *that* on?" Hannah asked and immediately wished she hadn't. She'd broken one of her mother's cardinal rules: *If a man compliments you, don't argue with him. Just smile and say thank you.*

"Shawna Lee told me you accepted her brownie recipe for the cookbook."

"That's right. The person who tested it thought her brownies were really good."

"But you had the power to veto it and you didn't."

Hannah hoped Mike would never find out how close she'd come to relegating Shawna Lee's recipe to the circular file. As the "author" of the Lake Eden potluck cookbook and the head of the cookbook committee, Hannah had the power to accept or reject as she saw fit. The only thing that had stopped her in Shawna Lee's case was the fear that someone might find out and accuse her of being petty. "Of course I didn't use my veto. Why would I veto a perfectly good recipe?"

Mike chuckled, and Hannah felt her toes tingle. It was an intimate chuckle, one that should be heard up close and personal, not transmitted over telephone wires. "Have you tasted those brownies yet?"

"Not yet." Hannah's eyebrows began to knit, but she

stopped in mid-frown. The magazine she'd paged through in the supermarket line had warned that frowns caused wrinkles in women over thirty, and she'd passed the three decade mark a couple of months ago.

"They're the best brownies I've ever tasted, and I've tasted a lot. I told Shawna Lee she should call them *hot brownies.*"

"Hot brownies?"

"Yeah. *Hot* as in *'terrific'* not *hot* from the stove. You know what I mean?"

"I get it."

"Anyway, they're definitely hot, and if I work it just right, I might be able to talk her into letting you add them to your menu, especially if you call them Shawna Lee's Brownies. What do you think about that?"

"Impressive," Hannah said, envisioning the anvil she'd like to impress into the top of Mike's head. Bake Shawna Lee's brownies for *her* shop? Not a chance!

Five minutes later, Hannah was still sitting at her kitchen table, staring down into her half-filled and rapidly cooling coffee mug. *Hot brownies. The best Mike had ever tasted.* The slow burn she'd started to do when Mike had first uttered those words had grown into a sizable conflagration. If Mike liked hot brownies so much, she'd give him hot brownies. They wouldn't be "hot" as in "terrific." And they wouldn't be "hot" from the stove. Her brownies would be "hot" as in "five-alarm-chili-hot" and she could hardly wait to hear Mike yowl when he bit into one!

Chapter Two

"Hi, Hannah," Lisa Herman called out as she came in the back door at The Cookie Jar. "It's really snowing out there. I had to brush off the whole top of the . . . what's *that?*"

Hannah glanced up at her young partner and started to laugh. Lisa looked absolutely horrified at the sight of the box of brownie mix Hannah had just upended into her bowl. "It's brownie mix."

"I can see that. But why are you using it?"

"Mike called me this morning and he told me all about Shawna Lee Quinn's brownies. He said they were *hot* as in *terrific.* I thought about it after I hung up and I decided I should make him some of my *hot* brownies."

"Okay. But I still don't understand why you're using . . ." Lisa stopped speaking as Hannah picked up an open can of diced jalapeño peppers and dumped them into the bowl. She blinked a couple of times as if she couldn't believe her eyes, and then she laughed. "I get it. *Hot* brownies."

"Very hot. And I didn't want to waste time and effort baking something that Mike's going to trash ten seconds after he tastes it."

Lisa picked up the empty can and took a sniff. Then she immediately grabbed for a paper towel to dab at the tears that were beginning to run down her cheeks. "One sniff and my eyes are watering. Those must be some really potent peppers."

"Florence said they were," Hannah named the woman who owned the Lake Eden Red Owl grocery. "She told me she put one can in a pot of chili and it was so hot, nobody could eat it."

Lisa hung up her coat, switched from her boots to her shoes, and headed for the sink to wash her hands. "Are you going to call Mike and have him come here to taste them?"

"No way! He's armed, you know. I'll just run them out to the sheriff's station and leave them for him."

"Anonymously?"

"That would be my choice, but he's a good detective. He'd figure out who sent them. I'll just drop them off at the front desk and come straight back here."

"Sounds like a wise decision," Lisa said, rolling her apron up at the waist and tying it in place by wrapping the strings around her twice. She was petite, and the chef's aprons were designed for someone Hannah's size. "What do you want me to do first?"

"You can check the cake in the cooler. I need to see if the raspberry Jell-O is set."

"Raspberry Jell-O?"

Hannah glanced up at Lisa. It was clear from the expression on her face that she was thoroughly mystified. "It's Andrea's recipe for Jell-O Cake, and it needs two different colors of Jell-O. She got it in late, but I promised I'd bake it and test it at the party tonight."

"So you're going to put it in the cookbook?"

Hannah sighed deeply. "I'll have to include it if it turns out all right. It's a family obligation, you know?"

"I know all about family obligations. I barely managed to keep Dad from submitting his father's catfish bait recipe."

"He should have done it. I would have put it in."

Lisa's mouth dropped open in shock. "You're kidding!"

"No, I'm not. Tell him I want it. As far as I'm concerned, every book needs a sprinkling of humor."

"Even a cookbook?"

"Especially a cookbook. All the recipes are so precise. I miss those days when it was a pinch of salt, a smidgen of pepper, and a snippet of parsley. Of course that was before Fanny Farmer standardized level cooking measurements."

Lisa turned to Hannah with surprise. "I didn't know Fanny Farmer did that! And she was from Minnesota! So was Betty Crocker."

"Actually, Betty Crocker wasn't from anywhere. It's the name General Mills came up with to market their first cookbook. But General Mills is based in Minnesota so I guess you could say they both came from here."

"Good. I love it when important people besides Sinclair Lewis come from Minnesota."

Hannah blinked. What Lisa said was a jump in logic. "You've got something against Sinclair Lewis?"

"Not really. I realize he's important, but his books are depressing. I'm already living depressing. My mother's dead, my dad's got Alzheimer's, and the wedding's off."

"Whoa!" Hannah pushed Lisa down on a stool at the workstation and made an end run to the kitchen coffeepot. This was a crisis. "What's this about the wedding? Did you have a fight with Herb?"

"Of course not. I love Herb and he loves me. That's not the problem."

"What is?" Hannah filled two mugs, put one down in front of Lisa, and sat down on the opposite stool.

"It's a matter of timing. Herb and I talked about it last night and we both agreed to call off the wedding."

"For good? I mean, you don't have to tell me if it's too personal, but . . ."

"It's not personal," Lisa interrupted her. "And no, it's not off for good. We just decided to wait to get married until everything's settled with Dad."

"He's okay, isn't he?" Hannah felt a quick jolt of fear. Lisa adored her father and she'd given up her college scholarship to stay home and take care of him.

"Dad's fine. It's just that Marge found a new doctor for him, a really good neurologist, and he was accepted in a new drug-testing program. It's some kind of cocktail thing, three drugs that work together to boost a brain-signaling chemical that improves memory. Dad's all excited about it, but the only thing is, the study starts this coming Monday and it lasts for two months. Herb and I didn't think it was fair for us to get married in the middle of the program, especially since we'll be switching houses and all."

"That makes sense," Hannah said, breathing a sigh of relief. As far as she was concerned, Lisa and Herb made a perfect couple. And Herb's mother, Marge Beeseman, was really stepping into the breach to help with Lisa's dad. She was giving them her house as a wedding present and she was moving into Jack Herman's home to become his caretaker. And even though Marge was a widow and Jack was a widower and they used to date in high school, no one in town was saying boo about the living arrangements. "So when do you think you'll get married?"

Lisa looked down at her engagement ring and gave a little smile. "We're shooting for the middle of February. That's when Dad's test program is over. But instead of a big wedding, we're just going to run down to the courthouse."

"Not fair," Hannah said, getting up to stash her crock full of meatballs in the cooler and making a mental note to take it down to the community center at noon and let it cook until time for the party.

"What's not fair?"

"Your dad told me he was looking forward to walking

you down the aisle. And Tracey's all excited about being your flower girl. Not only that, your bridesmaids already ordered their dresses."

"I know." Lisa looked worried. "Herb and I talked about that and we decided we'd pay everybody back. It's the right thing to do."

"No, it's not."

"It's not?"

Hannah shook her head. "Nobody would take your money, and that's not the point anyway. Everybody's looking forward to seeing you marry Herb. Why don't you just postpone the wedding until the middle of February?"

"I always wanted to get married on Valentine's Day," Lisa sounded wistful, "but it's impossible, Hannah. I want to be with Dad while he's going through the clinical trials, and I won't have time to make all the arrangements."

"No problem. Just ask Andrea to do everything for you. She loves to plan weddings."

"But she'll be busy with the new baby."

"No, she won't. She told me she hired 'Grandma' McCann to come in during the week, just like she did when Tracey was born, and Al gave her three months maternity leave. Andrea's going to have nothing but time on her hands, and she'll be so bored, you'll be doing her a favor."

"Do you think so?" Lisa's smile was pure golden.

"I think so."

"It would be just wonderful if all we had to do was show up for the ceremony. That's my idea of a perfect wedding. But . . . are you sure Andrea would be willing to take on a big job like that?"

"Wild horses couldn't stop her," Hannah said. "I'll call her just as soon as we're through here."

"Is Andrea coming to the party tonight?"

"I hope so. She's got an appointment with Doc Knight

this morning and she's going to try to talk him into letting her go."

"I've got my fingers crossed for her. She's probably going stir-crazy at home with her feet up on pillows. I want to work right up until they rush me off to the delivery room."

Hannah turned to give Lisa a sharp look. "Are you trying to tell me something?"

"Of course not! Herb and I aren't even married yet."

"Marriage isn't always a prerequisite for parenthood."

"Maybe not for some people, but it is for me," Lisa said. "I'll get that cake and see if the Jell-O's set."

Hannah kicked herself mentally as Lisa ducked into the walk-in cooler to retrieve the cake. It was clear that she'd stepped over the line into an area Lisa didn't want to discuss, and this was her partner's way of changing the subject.

"The Jell-O's set," Lisa announced, carrying the cake to the workstation. "Do you want me to finish making it for you?"

"That would be great. The recipe's on the counter."

Lisa set down the cake and glanced through the recipe. "This sounds really good."

"It is. Andrea always makes it for Tracey's birthday. It's the one time of year she uses her oven."

"It must be strange having a sister who doesn't cook."

"Not really," Hannah said with a shrug. She'd gotten quite accustomed to being the baker in the family. Delores didn't "do" desserts, and Andrea avoided the oven with a passion. The only other member of the family who showed signs of inheriting Grandma Ingrid's love of baking was Hannah's youngest sister, Michelle. She was constantly calling Hannah for recipes to try out on her college roommates.

Lisa stuck some water on to boil and opened the lemon Jell-O packet. "When I'm done with this, I'll do the baking for the day. You can concentrate on the recipes you have left to test for tonight."

Hannah gave her a grateful smile. Lisa was only nineteen, but she was more responsible than others who were twice her age. Hannah had never regretted the day, only a little over a year ago, when she'd offered her diminutive assistant a partnership in The Cookie Jar.

Once the baking was done and Hannah had returned from her run to the sheriff's station with the brownies for Mike, Lisa and Hannah settled down in the back booth of the coffee shop with fresh mugs of coffee.

"So what did Mike say when you gave him the brownies?" Lisa asked.

"He wasn't there. I just wrote a quick note, put them on his desk, and came straight back here."

"I wonder what time we should start hiding."

Hannah laughed. "Not before noon. I checked with Barbara and she thought he'd be out in the field all morning. If he does come back early and he charges in here, he'll be so bowled over by your decorations, he'll forget all about being mad."

"You like them?"

"They're even better than last year. I never would have thought to paint Christmas designs on the mirror with Glass Wax and powdered tempera."

"It's just an idea I got from a magazine. When you wash it off, it cleans the mirror at the same time."

"Well, it makes the whole place look fantastic." Hannah glanced up at the silver and gold streamers Lisa had hung from the ceiling and admired how nicely they fluttered as the ceiling fans whirred softly overhead. She'd even hung mistletoe from the pull chains, a little extra that Hannah hadn't noticed when she'd first seen the decorations. "It's a good thing Moishe isn't here."

"Why?"

"Because mistletoe berries are poisonous for cats. So are poinsettia leaves."

"I didn't know that!"

"Most people don't. Christmas is very hard on cats, especially if their people don't know how dangerous it is. Sue told me Dr. Bob had three feline patients last Christmas who almost died from eating tinsel. It gets tangled up in their insides and causes all sorts of problems."

Lisa just shook her head. "Maybe it's a good thing Herb wants us to get a puppy."

"Not necessarily. Poinsettias and mistletoe are poisonous for dogs too, and tinsel's not good, either. And then there are the glass balls that people use to decorate trees."

"A dog might bat at them and break them?"

"Yes, and swallow some of the pieces. And then there's chocolate. A lot of people leave a box of chocolates out on a coffee table for guests. That's perfect dog height, and too much chocolate can kill a dog."

"That's a real pity," Lisa sounded very sympathetic. "At least if we eat too much chocolate, all we get is hyperactive. And that reminds me . . . we'd better stoke up on the chocolate tonight, because we have to be on our toes."

"Why is that?"

"Martin Dubinski got married in Vegas, and he's bringing his new wife to the Christmas party."

"Uh-oh," Hannah groaned. "Shirley submitted her Poppy Seed Cake recipe for the cookbook and it's being tested tonight."

"That's what I mean. The ex-wife and the new wife. It's straight out of a soap, especially since Shirley wants Martin back."

"She does?" Hannah was surprised.

"I think so. At least that's what I heard."

"I wish I'd known that before! Now I feel really guilty about going out with Martin."

"You went out with Martin?" Lisa looked positively mystified. "Why did you do *that?*"

"Mother. But it was only once. Tell me what you know about Martin's new wife."

"Well . . ." Lisa paused to take a fortifying sip of coffee. "She's a Las Vegas dancer named Brandi Wyen. Get it?"

"Brandywine. I get it. How did Martin meet her?"

"I don't know for sure, but what I heard was he married her just five hours after he flew to Las Vegas for a conference."

"That doesn't bode well. What else?"

"Before Martin and Brandi flew back here, he took her to a furrier and bought her a twenty-thousand-dollar coat so she wouldn't be cold."

Hannah groaned again, envisioning the old cloth coat Shirley had worn for the past three years because she hadn't been able to afford a new one. "Do you think there'll be fireworks at the party tonight?"

"It's a pretty safe bet, especially since there's another woman in the picture."

"Another woman?" Hannah was mystified that even one woman would be attracted to Martin, much less three! He was a nice enough man, but her date with him had been boredom personified. Why he'd thought she'd be interested in discussing the newest tax laws was beyond her!

"I stopped in to see Janice Cox at Kiddie Korner after I dropped Dad off at the Senior Center," Lisa explained. "She went to school with Martin's secretary, Laura Jorgensen. Janice said Laura didn't exactly confide in her, but she was pretty sure that Laura was in love with Martin."

"Oh, boy!" Hannah breathed, almost wishing that she had gone on for her doctorate and was now teaching in a rarified academic atmosphere that was hundreds of miles from what would probably happen when Laura and Shirley met Martin and Brandi. "I guess it's a good thing that Laura has an accounting class at the junior college tonight."

"Not anymore. Janice said Laura's class was cancelled and she's going to be at the party to make sure that whoever tested her Smothered Chicken did a good job."

Hannah just shook her head. It was a disaster in the making, perhaps even another *Titanic* on a slightly smaller scale. "At least we can get one thing settled before the crockery starts flying." Hannah stood up and headed for the phone by the cash register. "I'm going to call Andrea and ask her if she'll handle your wedding arrangements."

"Tell her she can have complete control of everything. I'll go along with whatever she wants to do."

"That'll sweeten the pot." Hannah started to grin as she punched in the number. "If I know Andrea, she won't be able to resist."

Andrea sounded chipper when she answered the phone. "Hi, Hannah."

"How did you know it was me?"

"I just got a new cell phone with built-in caller I.D. It's a very important tool for a real estate professional."

"No doubt," Hannah said, grinning a little. Andrea always had state-of-the-art electronics, and she always said she needed it because she was a real estate agent. "I called to tell you that Herb and Lisa have to postpone their wedding until Valentine's Day."

"That's too bad. Hang on a second, will you?" Hannah hung on and waited for several seconds. Then Andrea came on the line again. "Sorry about that. So why are they postponing the wedding?"

"Jack Herman's been accepted in a test program for a new Alzheimer's drug. Lisa and Herb want to wait until the trials are over."

"That makes sense. So why did you call me?"

"Lisa needs to spend all her free time with her dad and she won't have time to arrange the wedding. She'd love it if someone else would take charge and I thought maybe you might . . . hold on a second." Hannah put down the phone and motioned to Lisa. "I think I hear someone knocking at the back door. Can you go let them in?"

"Sure."

"Sorry, Andrea." Hannah directed her attention back to the phone. "Someone's at the back door and Lisa went to let them in. It's probably Mother or Carrie."

"No, it's not."

"How do you know?"

"Because it's me."

"What are you talking about?" Hannah was thoroughly confused, especially because her phone had suddenly developed a strange new echo.

"Turn around, Hannah. Lisa just let me in and I'm standing right behind you."

Chapter
Three

H annah whirled around and practically bumped into her hugely pregnant sister. Andrea was standing there grinning, her cell phone to her ear. Despite the fact that she was almost as big around as she was tall, Andrea still managed to look glamorous. She'd arranged her shining blond hair in an elaborate twist, her make-up was perfect, and she'd draped a forest-green cashmere scarf over her fawn-colored coat so artfully, she could have been the cover model for a maternity fashion magazine.

"You can hang up now, Hannah," Andrea said.

"Right." Hannah hung up the phone and hurried to take her sister's arm. "Come with me. You'd better sit down. I'll get another chair so you can put your feet up."

"I don't need to put my feet up. Doc Knight lifted every single one of my restrictions and gave me the green light to resume normal activities."

Hannah glanced at Lisa, who looked every bit as shocked as she did. "But I thought he told you to take it easy until the baby was born."

"He did . . . but that was then, and this is now. When he tested me this morning, he said he can't wait much longer for me to go into labor. I'm overdue."

"What does *that* mean?" Hannah asked.

"It means I should have delivered last week, or maybe even the week before. Doc says I'm getting too big, and that's not good for the baby." Andrea shrugged out of her coat, handed it to Hannah, and pointed at the middle of her wine red maternity dress. "See?"

Hannah's eyes widened. She'd seen Andrea at the beginning of the week, but now it looked as if her normally petite sister had swallowed a large beach ball.

"Doc's giving me until next Friday," Andrea went on. "If I don't have the baby by then, he'll put me in the hospital and speed things up."

"How is he going to do that?" Lisa asked.

"You don't want to know. As a matter of fact, *I* don't want to know, so I didn't ask. I'm just hoping that if I move around enough, the baby will decide it's time to get born."

"Horseback riding," Lisa suggested.

"What?" Hannah turned to her with a puzzled frown.

"That's what my mother used to do. If she went past her due date, she just went out to my grandfather's farm and went for a ride. She said that always did the trick."

Hannah laughed and shook her head. "Thanks for telling us, but I don't think this is the time for Andrea to hone her equestrian skills."

"That's right, especially since the one time Bill took me riding, I fell off. I'd much rather drive around town, but first I need coffee. I haven't had a good cup of coffee for weeks! And then I need some chocolate to give me energy. After that, I want you to give me something to do."

"Like what?" Lisa asked, as Hannah went off to get the coffee and cookies.

"Like . . . that's up to you, but there's absolutely nothing for me to do at home. Grandma McCann was just in to clean and get the nursery all ready."

"How about decorating for Christmas?" Hannah suggested. "Once you have the baby, you might be too busy to put up the tree and everything."

"It's already up and the house is all decorated. Lucy Dunwight organized the whole thing with a couple of the other kindergarten mothers and we had a party at my house. They did everything and the kids helped them. All I had to do was supervise from the couch."

"That's nice," Hannah said, setting a mug and a napkin containing two Twin Chocolate Delights in front of her sister.

"So I have absolutely nothing to do. And I just thought that since tonight's the Christmas party, you might have a last-minute recipe you don't have time to test. I need to stay busy."

"Thanks, Andrea, but I think we've got it covered." Hannah gave Lisa a warning glance that was meant to remind her that Andrea was among the ranks of the cuisine-challenged.

Lisa just smiled, ignoring Hannah completely. "Hannah's right. We've got everything under control here, but I ran into Edna this morning and there's something she really needs for the party."

"Really?" Andrea took a sip of coffee and swallowed with obvious pleasure. "Why is your coffee so much better than mine?"

Hannah just shrugged, biting back the obvious answer. Freshly brewed coffee from freshly ground beans was bound to be better than instant coffee made in a microwave.

"So what does Edna need?" Andrea turned to Lisa again. "Whatever it is, I can make it. I'm not a very good cook, but I've got all day to get it right."

Hannah came close to groaning out loud. Any dish that Andrea prepared was bound to fail through no fault of its own.

"It's not food," Lisa explained. "Edna said people always

forget to bring serving spoons and I promised to find someone who could round them up for her."

"I can do that. It's absolutely perfect for me. I'll canvass
house to house and while I'm at it, I'll pass out calendars for
Al. He's got a really good one this year. It features twelve of
the best homes sold through Lake Eden Realty, one for every
month. And I sold ten of them!"

"I'm surprised it wasn't all twelve," Hannah said, grinning at her sister. Andrea was so good at talking people into
things, she could probably get desert nomads to buy kitty litter. "So how about Lisa's wedding? Will you take care of the
arrangements?"

"Was there ever any doubt?" Andrea turned to Lisa with a
laugh. "All you have to do is give me the guest list, and tell
me your favorite color and your favorite flower. You can
leave everything else up to me."

"Thanks, Andrea. This really means a lot to me." Lisa finished her coffee and stood up. "I'm going to start decorating
those sugar cookies we baked for the party. Call me when it's
time, and I'll open."

Once Lisa had gone through the swinging door to the
kitchen, Andrea leaned across the table. "If you give me two
more cookies and a refill on the coffee, I'll tell you what I just
heard."

Hannah wasted no time getting what her sister wanted.
Andrea always exacted payment for the latest Lake Eden
gossip. "If it's about Martin Dubinski's new wife, Lisa already told me."

"That's old news. If you were a real estate professional
like me, you would have heard about it yesterday."

"Yes, but do you know about the twenty-thousand-dollar
fur coat?"

"Twenty-*two* thousand," Andrea corrected her. "At least
that's the way I heard it. But what I've got to tell you is new
news, not old news. And it's going to knock your socks off."

"Okay. What is it?"

"It's about Shawna Lee Quinn!"

"What about her?" Hannah took a deep breath and held it, hoping that her sister's gossip didn't include Mike.

"She's leaving town tonight."

"You're kidding!"

"Would I kid about something that important? Bill called me from the station to tell me. There was a death in the family and Shawna Lee's going back home to Georgia."

Hannah curbed her impulse to cheer at Shawna Lee's impending absence and did her best to react to the gravity of the situation. "I'm sorry for her loss. Who died?"

"Vanessa's husband. And from what Shawna Lee told Bill, it wasn't unexpected."

"Who's Vanessa?"

"Shawna Lee's younger sister. They're less than a year apart and they were really close growing up. Vanessa's husband was an octogenarian."

Hannah's eyebrows shot up. Shawna Lee was in her middle twenties, and it seemed unlikely that her younger sister would marry a man who was sixty years her senior. "Her husband was in his eighties?"

"That's what octogenarian means. Shawna Lee told Bill that they'd been married for a little over a year before he died."

Hannah didn't comment. It could have been a love match, but the term *gold digger* came to mind. She was trying to figure out a polite way to pose the question, when Andrea nodded.

"I know what you're thinking and you're right. He was a *rich* octogenarian and he owned a whole string of home improvement stores. Vanessa inherited everything and from what Shawna Lee told Bill, it amounts to a lot of money!"

"How long is Shawna Lee staying?"

"I don't know, for sure, but Bill asked her when he gave her the standard form to fill out."

"Yes?" Hannah asked, holding her breath. She hoped it was a good long time.

"She said she wasn't sure, that she'd been homesick for her sister and her family and she could hardly wait to go home for Christmas, even under these sad circumstances. She also promised to call him in two weeks to let him know whether she'd be coming back to her job . . . or not."

"You mean there's a chance she won't come back?" Hannah could hardly believe her good fortune.

"That's what it sounds like to me. Bill has to hold her job for a month. That's a union regulation. But after that, the job can be posted at the sheriff's discretion."

"And Bill's *discretion* will be right away?"

"It will be if I have anything to say about it! I feel the same way about Shawna Lee as you do, and her sister sounds like more of the same. I mean . . . I suppose it's unfair of me to judge her when I've never even met her, but think back to when you were twenty-three."

"Okay." Hannah thought back to her college days and she remembered the efficiency apartment she'd rented in a crumbling stucco building six blocks from campus. She'd fixed it all up with low-cost decorations, and it hadn't seemed to matter that if she took longer than a three-minute shower, she'd run out of hot water.

"You were young and you had the whole world ahead of you, right?"

"Right."

"And you dated guys your own age, or a little older, right?"

Hannah shrugged. "I would have, if they'd asked me."

"Good enough. Anyway . . . there you are, surrounded by all these good-looking guys your age. Would you have fallen in love with a sick old man in a wheelchair?"

Hannah did her best to think of a scenario that would fit the situation, but she came up blank.

"I didn't think so," Andrea said, interpreting Hannah's silence as assent. "Vanessa married him for his money. There's no other explanation. Let's just hope she shares all that cash with Shawna Lee and both of them stay put in Georgia!"

Chapter Four

It wasn't until the predictable eleven-thirty break that Hannah remembered Mike's brownies. When she did, she let out a gasp that made Lisa rush to her side in alarm.

"It's okay," Hannah reassured her. "I just remembered Mike's hot brownies, that's all. I'd better call him and tell him not to eat them."

"You mean because Shawna Lee's leaving town and you don't have to compete with her anymore?"

"That's right. The green-eyed monster made me start the brownie wars, and I'm a little embarrassed."

Lisa shrugged. "I don't see why. Mike deserved it. He still deserves it. He didn't have to suggest that you serve Shawna Lee's brownies in here!"

"True, but I think I'd better keep the peace if I want a date for tonight."

"There's always that," Lisa said with a grin, "especially since you bought a new outfit. Why don't you call Barbara before she goes to lunch? She can snatch the brownies off Mike's desk and toss them, and he'll never have to know anything about it."

"Good idea." Hannah headed for the phone. A moment later, she had Barbara Donnelly, the head secretary at the sheriff's station, on the line.

"Hi, Hannah." Barbara sounded glad to hear from her. "All ready for the party tonight?"

"I'm ready. How about you? Your Irish Roast Beast's being tested, you know."

"I know. I've been on pins and needles about it all day. Did you hear about Shawna Lee?"

"I heard. Bill told Andrea and Andrea told me."

"Some wives around here are going to be mighty relieved, that's all I have to say. And at least she won't be flirting with your guy anymore."

"Which guy?"

"That's a good one!" Barbara said with a laugh. "I forgot for a minute that you had two guys."

"I'm not sure I've got either one of them, but I do need to talk to Mike."

"He's not here, Hannah. He came in about an hour ago, but before he could even hang up his jacket, he got a call to go out again."

Hannah took a deep breath and asked the important question. "I put a package on his desk this morning. Do you happen to know if it's still there?"

"Hold on a second and I'll check."

Hannah heard a click, and she found herself listening to a tape of winter driving tips, read by someone who sounded as if he had a cold. She already knew about carrying a candle and matches in a coffee can so that if she was stuck in her car, she could heat the interior and melt snow for drinking water. The announcer was just pontificating about the wisdom of putting a twenty-pound sack of kitty litter in the trunk for traction when Barbara came back on the line.

"It's gone, Hannah. Mike must have taken it with him."

Hannah had all she could do to keep from groaning. It would be bad enough if Mike tasted the brownies at work in front of the other deputies, but if he bit into one when he was alone in his cruiser, navigating an icy patch of highway, he might just end up in the ditch. "Do you know when he'll be back?"

"I don't think he will be, not today. He's coordinating with two other law enforcement agencies, and that means conferences and meetings all afternoon. He'll probably go right home when he's through. He could call in, though. If he does, do you want me to give him a message?"

"No, that's okay. I'll see him tonight. Thanks, Barbara."

Hannah did her best to grin and bear it as she dashed to the community center with Edna's meatballs. She got back just in time for the noon rush, when dozens of people wanted their after-lunch cookies and coffee. Hannah manned the cash register and took care of the take-out cookies customers ordered, while Lisa waited tables. It was a system they'd worked out together. Things were just slowing down again when Hannah looked up to see a familiar face at the door. It was Norman, and he was carrying something in a Granny's Attic bag.

"Hi, Norman!" Hannah greeted him, smiling warmly. Norman certainly wasn't movie star handsome, with his slightly thinning brown hair and stocky frame, but Hannah considered him one of the most attractive men she'd ever met. He had an open, friendly look about him and his sense of humor meshed with hers perfectly. As Delores and Carrie were fond of saying, especially if they'd just come from one of their Regency romance group meetings, Norman and Hannah made a perfect match.

Hannah waited until Norman had hung his parka on the coat rack near the front door and taken a seat at the counter. "Coffee?"

"Of course. You make the best in town. And a couple cookies of your choice. I'm in the mood to live dangerously."

"Dangerously?" Hannah turned and glanced at the glass serving jars behind the counter. "How about a Cherry Bomb?"

"What's that?"

"It's one of Grandma Ingrid's recipes and I'm trying it out for the first time today."

"I'll be your guinea pig," Norman declared, twitching his nose.

"That's exactly what the guinea pig at Kiddie Korner does!"

"I know. Janice Cox called me with a dental emergency on Wednesday when Mr. Whiskers got a seed stuck between his front teeth."

"Did you make a house call?" Hannah asked, realizing she hadn't talked to Norman in a few days.

"Of course. Mr. Whiskers is fine now. I got the seed out."

"How did you do that?"

"Very carefully. And very quickly, too." Norman glanced at the cookies Hannah placed in front of him. "They look like little white bombs with a red fuse."

"The fuse is a cherry stem. That's a little square of dough wrapped around the cherry and then baked. And the reason they're so white is because they're dipped in powdered sugar. You're supposed to pick them up by the stem and eat the bottom part."

"Okay," Norman said popping the white part into his mouth and chewing. "They're good! The cherry sort of explodes when you bite into it, so Cherry Bomb is a good name."

Once Norman had tasted the second Cherry Bomb and pronounced it as good as the first, he set the Granny's Attic bag on the counter. "Your mother sent this over for you."

"What is it?"

"Her antique cake knife. She asked me to bring it to you for safekeeping."

Hannah opened the bag and drew out an elaborately carved wooden case. "Have you seen it?"

"Yes, it's beautiful. Take a look."

The carvings were lovely, and Hannah admired the box for a moment. Then she lifted the lid and gasped as she saw the knife. "It's gorgeous! And it's not what I expected at all."

"What do you mean?"

"It's narrower than the combination cake knife and server I'm used to seeing and it looks a whole lot sharper."

"Your mother said it was especially crafted for the court by a well-known sword maker of the period."

"No wonder it looks so sharp! The Christmas tree on the handle is beautiful and I just love the colored stones they used to decorate it."

"Those *colored stones* are small blue and yellow sapphires, rubies, and emeralds. And the star at the top is a perfect diamond. I think you'd better put it away in a nice safe place."

"I will," Hannah said, closing the lid of the box reverently. "I suppose it's very valuable?"

Norman glanced around, but no one at the counter was paying any attention to them. "Yes, if it's genuine. And everyone at Granny's Attic, including Luanne, thinks it is."

"Thanks for telling me." Hannah slipped the box back in the bag and secreted it behind the counter. "I'd better keep it under wraps until it's time to cut the cake, or someone might use it to carve the turkey."

"I don't think that'll be a problem. I'm bringing the turkey, and it's Rose's recipe. She swears it's so tender it practically falls off the bones."

"Rose's turkey is great," Hannah said, glancing out the window. Her eyes narrowed and she gave a deep sigh. "You might know it! It's starting to snow. It's a good thing that Minnesotans aren't afraid of a little winter weather. Unless it turns into a full-scale blizzard, they'll still show up for the dinner and stay for the dancing."

"Of course they will. Nobody wants to miss the feast."

Hannah had just refilled Norman's coffee mug when the phone rang. She reached out to answer it. "The Cookie Jar. Hannah speaking."

"Hello, Hannah. It's Kurt Howe."

"Hi, Kurt," Hannah said, hoping that nothing was wrong. Kurt was her editor at Savory Press, and the last time he'd called, he'd asked Hannah to get the cookbook recipes ready several months before the due date in the contract she'd signed. "You're not going to move up the deadline again, are you?"

Kurt chuckled. "No, but I do have a question about one of the recipes you submitted."

"Which one?"

"Fudge Cupcakes. Are you sure it's baking soda?"

"Baking *soda*?" Hannah began to frown.

"That's what it says."

"Hold on a second." Hannah motioned for Lisa and asked her to run to the kitchen to get the master recipe list. Then she turned back to her phone call. "Lisa's checking on it right now, but I think it's supposed to be baking powder. Baking soda would make them puff up too high in the oven and then they'd fall like craters."

"That's what my publisher thought and I told her I'd check with you."

Hannah took the three-ring binder Lisa handed her and glanced down at the Fudge Cupcake recipe. "It's baking powder, Kurt. One and a half teaspoons of baking powder."

"That's what we thought."

"I'm really sorry about that," Hannah said, her cheeks coloring in embarrassment. "I proofread all those recipes before I sent them to you, and that mistake got right past me."

"It happens, especially when you know how it's supposed to be written. You read right past the error and don't notice it. But that's only one of the reasons I called. I'm driving in for the Christmas dinner party."

"That's great! Then you can taste the recipes yourself!"

"I'm looking forward to it. I just got off the phone with the staff photographer. I wanted him to come along to take some food photos and some candids of the crowd for the cookbook."

"That would be perfect, especially if he can get a picture of Mother's antique cake knife. It's gorgeous, Kurt, and we're going to use it to cut one of the cakes."

"That would have been a great photo."

"Would have been?"

"That's right. Our photographer can't make it, and that means we may have to re-stage some of the food photos."

"Maybe not," Hannah said, glancing over at Norman. "I know a local photographer and I'm sure he'd be willing to take some photos of the party for you. Hold on and I'll ask him."

Norman nodded at Hannah before she could even ask. "Tell him I'll be glad to bring my camera, but I don't have any experience with food photography. I know it's highly specialized."

"I heard that," Kurt said in Hannah's ear. "Tell him anything he gets is all to the good. I'm going to leave the office early. If the traffic's not terrible, I should get to Lake Eden around five or five-thirty. Where will you be?"

"At the community center. We're closing the shop at three and I'll be there early to help Edna in the kitchen."

"Better tell him it's snowing here," Norman reminded her.

"I heard that," Kurt responded before Hannah could tell him. "Maybe I'll leave a little earlier than I planned, just to be on the safe side. See you tonight, Hannah."

Hannah was smiling when she hung up the phone and turned to Norman. "Do you have time to run back to Granny's Attic for a second before you go back to the dental clinic?"

"Sure. What do you need?"

"It's only fair to tell all the contributors that our editor is coming to the party. But I really don't have time to call everyone."

"So you want the mothers to call for you?"

"All they have to do is make one call. They're part of the Lake Eden gossip hotline. It's like a telephone tree. If they call one person, that person calls another couple of people. And then those people call other people and before you know it, the whole town knows. I figure that if you get to Mother and Carrie by one, everyone in Lake Eden will know before one-thirty at the latest."

Chapter
Five

"So how do I look?" Hannah asked, turning around for the benefit of her I-couldn't-look-less-interested-if-I-tried roommate, who was perched on the back of the couch.

Moishe glanced her way for a moment, but then he went back to staring at the television. Since Hannah had tuned it to one of the animal channels and they occasionally showed documentaries about flightless birds and small furry rodents, she guessed she couldn't blame him. Basic instinct was compelling. It was the reason why Moishe was hoping for easy prey, even if it turned out to be pheasant behind glass screen.

Hannah had also relied on basic instinct when she'd dressed for the party tonight. She was wearing the most alluring outfit she owned, a brand new cobalt-blue knit dress with a flared skirt that emphasized her figure plusses, all one of them, and minimized her figure minuses, all four of them, not counting the biceps she'd developed from lifting fifty-pound bags of flour and sugar. As usual, Claire Rodgers at Beau Monde Fashions had urged her to try on the dress, and, as usual, Claire had chosen well. One look in the mirror, and Hannah said she'd take it without even asking the price, something that would be risky in a shop where she didn't get a hefty discount for owning the business next door.

"I'm so glad you approve," Hannah said, realizing full well the folly of asking her resident feline a fashion question . . . or any question at all other than, "Are you hungry?" or "Would you like another kitty treat?"

"Your food bowl's full and you've had your vitamins. I'll be leaving now, if that's okay with you." Hannah shrugged into the black coat that acted like a magnet for orange and white cat hairs, and picked up the ridiculously small purse Claire had insisted she buy to go with the dress. She grabbed her gloves and the bag containing Mike's pâté, tossed several more salmon-flavored treats shaped like little fish toward the couch, and informed the cat, who still wasn't interested in anything except the television screen, "I may be late. You don't have to wait up."

As she stepped outside, testing the door to make certain it locked behind her, Hannah found herself wishing she'd worn a ski mask, or at least a knit cap. The air was frigid, and it would be even colder by the time she came home tonight. She hurried down the outside stairs, thankful for the roof that the builder had designed to keep them free of snow, navigated an icy patch of sidewalk, and then went down the six concrete steps that led to the underground garage, barely missing bowling over her downstairs neighbor, Phil Plotnik.

"Sorry, Phil," Hannah apologized as he steadied her on her feet. "You don't have to say it. I really ought to watch where I'm going."

"I wasn't going to say that. I was going to remind you to unplug your truck."

"Thank you! I always forget when I'm in a rush, and I've already totaled two cords this winter."

"I'd better make sure it doesn't turn into three." Phil reversed his direction and walked her to her truck. "What's your record?"

"You mean in one winter?"

"Right." Phil went to the line of electrical outlets specifically designed for plugging in the head bolt and dipstick heaters that were so necessary during a cold Minnesota winter, and unplugged Hannah's extension cord.

"Seven. It was the first year I bought my truck. I just couldn't seem to get used to unplugging it. Are you coming to the Christmas party tonight?"

"Wouldn't miss it. Sue wants to get a picture of Kevin in front of the Christmas tree. We tried to do it last year, but he was too young to sit up. She's going to order some of those photo cards to send to the relatives."

"They're bound to like that. Thanks for helping me, Phil. I'll see you all later at the party." Hannah was smiling as she climbed inside her candy-apple-red Suburban with the vanity license plate that read COOKIES. Her taxman claimed that the plate and the gold lettering on the sides that advertised The Cookie Jar constituted a write-off.

As Hannah drove up the ramp and along the narrow road that wound through her condo complex, lights winked on in several of the units. It was only four in the afternoon, but the shadows of the pine trees on the snow had darkened from lavender to indigo blue, and the horizon would soon be indistinguishable. Hannah switched on her headlights. At dawn and dusk visibility was poor, and even at the slow speeds that were posted in the complex, it was possible to have an expensive fender-bender.

In the few minutes it took Hannah to exit her complex, darkness fell completely. She turned left onto Old Lake Road, switched on her wipers to deal with the snow that was striking her windshield, and tuned her car radio to her favorite local station. The news on the hour was just ending and Rayne Phillips, KCOW's meteorologist, was in the process of wrapping up his weather report.

". . . chance of snow flurries later this evening. Presently, we have clear skies with temperatures ranging in the teens across Winnetka County. It's a beautiful night, folks. Get out there and enjoy it."

Hannah grumbled, turning up the speed on her windshield wipers to handle the rapidly falling snow. "You're an idiot, Rayne. If you just look out the window, you'll know it's already snowing!"

Edna Ferguson looked surprised as Hannah stepped into the kitchen at the community center. "What are you doing here so early? I didn't expect you before five."

"I thought maybe you could use some extra help." As Hannah stashed Mike's pâté in the refrigerator, she noticed that Andrea's Jell-O Cake was already there on a shelf. "Lisa was here?"

"Come and gone. She said she had to rush home to get dressed. She dropped off the sugar cookies, and they're just beautiful."

"Lisa's a whiz with a pastry bag. How about Andrea? Did she bring you the serving spoons?"

"She did, and I don't know how she does it, as big as she is. That sister of yours is really something."

"You mean because of the serving spoons?"

Edna shook her head so hard, her tightly permed gray curls bounced like springs. "That too, but mostly because of the decorations. The decorating committee was here when Andrea came in, and she asked as nice as pie if she could help. It was just the Hollenbeck sisters. Bernice Maciej was supposed to come too, but her back was acting up. Anyways, they didn't want to let Andrea help at first, her being in the condition she is and all. But then she said she'd call a couple of her friends to do all the lifting, and they admitted they could use the help. You should have seen the whirlwind once those younger gals started working. Why, they finished it all in less than two hours, including the eighteen-foot-tall Christmas tree!"

"That's Andrea. She really knows how to get things done with a couple of phone calls."

"She did more than that. I tell you, I almost dropped my teeth when I saw her up on the ladder, putting the angel on top of the tree."

Hannah was glad that she hadn't witnessed that particular folly. She doubted that Doc Knight had realized the full ramifications when he'd told Andrea to resume her normal activity.

"Go turn on the lights and have a look." Edna motioned toward the door. "It's just beautiful!"

Hannah went back out into the dining room. Only a few lights had been on when she'd come down the stairs, and she hadn't really noticed the decorations. She flicked on the bright lights and blinked in astonishment at the wonders her sister had accomplished.

There were four long tables at the front of the banquet hall, each covered with a different color tablecloth and sporting a large centerpiece of poinsettias, pine boughs, and gold Christmas balls. Stuck inside each one was a hand-lettered flag on a candy cane pole. The red table was for appetizers. It said so right on the flag. The gold was for entrées and sides, the silver was for desserts, and the green was for salads, soups, and breads. Another table, covered in red and green plaid, had been set up with coffee, tea, and a cooler that would contain bottles of milk, water, and juice.

More long tables were set up in a geometric pattern around the room, each decorated with Christmas tablecloths sporting snowmen, Santas, Christmas trees, holly, and snowflakes. Three centerpieces, scaled-down versions of the ones that were on the food tables, were placed equidistant down the middle of each table.

Hannah glanced up and was surprised to see that a canopy

that had been woven overhead from red, green, gold, and silver crepe-paper streamers crisscrossed in an intricate pattern. Everything was lovely and festive, especially the Christmas tree that resided in what her Regency-enamored mother would have called *pride of place* in the center of the room. Hannah walked over to switch it on and actually gasped as thousands of miniature bulbs lit up in a rainbow of colors.

"It's gorgeous, all right," Hannah announced to the empty room, turning to walk back to the kitchen. Andrea had done a superb job today, and it was good to have her back in the mainstream of life in Lake Eden. They'd never been close growing up, but working together to investigate the murder that had earned Andrea's husband his detective badge had taught them to appreciate each other, at least when they had a common problem to solve.

Hannah crossed her fingers, a habit left over from childhood, and wished that the Christmas buffet dinner would be a huge success. And then she headed back to the kitchen to see if she could lend a hand until Edna's work crew arrived.

Forty minutes later, Hannah took up her position at the foot of the stairs. She'd been shooed out of the kitchen by Edna and her minions, and sent here to greet the people who were soon to arrive. Soft Christmas music was playing over the sound system, something that sounded suspiciously like a late-night-television, not-sold-in-stores Christmas collection available for nineteen ninety-five plus seven ninety-five postage and handling, and if you called within the next five minutes, you got a second CD free.

"Hi, Hannah." Kirby Welles, the Jordan High band teacher, was the first down the stairs. He was followed by the Jordan High Jazz Ensemble, ten members in all. The boys were dressed in red satin jackets with black pants and the girls were wearing green satin dresses.

"You look great!" Hannah said, admiring the new outfits each student had bought for the occasion. The jazz ensemble was scheduled to play for the dancing that would take place after dinner and to provide music during the dessert course. "What do you need, Kirby? I'll help you set up."

"I've got it covered," Kirby said, flashing teeth that just might have been whitened by Norman. He was a well-muscled bachelor in his middle twenties, and over half of the female population at Jordan High had visions of dating him. "I was down here this morning to arrange everything. All we need is folding chairs. We brought everything else with us in the school van."

Hannah directed Kirby to the area beneath the stairs where the extra tables and folding chairs were kept and hurried back to her post. She was just in time, because Kurt Howe was the next to arrive.

"Hi, Kurt!" Hannah called out, greeting him before he'd even started to descend the stairs. "I'm glad you made it."

Kurt hurried down the steps. "I would have been here sooner, but it started snowing when I hit Elk River, and that slowed me down. Something sure smells good in here!"

"That would be food," Hannah said, taking his arm. "Everybody knows you're coming, so let me introduce you to Edna and the ladies in the kitchen before they gang up on us out here. And then I'll get you a good place to sit and we can wait for Norman. He should be here any minute and you can cue him in on what shots you want him to try for tonight."

Once Kurt had met the kitchen staff, Hannah settled him at a table and served him a relish dish that was typical of Minnesota cuisine. It was a small bowl with crushed ice in the bottom and it was filled with celery sticks, carrot sticks, radishes, and dill pickle spears. A second small dish, special

fare for tonight's party, contained pickled green beans, mushrooms, beets, and baby onions.

Hannah had just explained that the contents of the second
dish of appetizers were all homegrown and pickled in farm
kitchens, when Norman came down the stairs with his camera bag slung over his shoulder. He was carrying a box
wrapped in Christmas paper, and Hannah thought he looked
very dashing in a tan suede jacket, black turtleneck sweater,
and black pants, with his fur-lined parka draped over his
arm.

Norman came straight over to Hannah and hugged her a
few seconds longer than some older and more conservative
Lake Eden residents might say was appropriate. Then he
handed her the box. "This is for you. It's an early Christmas
present, and Claire thought you might want to wear it tonight."

"Thank you, Norman," Hannah said, and wasted no time
opening the box. Inside was an appliquéd Christmas sweater
that perfectly matched her dress. "I love it! It's gorgeous!"
Hannah slipped it on immediately and turned around so that
Norman could see.

"It looks even better than Claire said it would." Norman
gave her another hug and then he turned to Kurt. "Hi, Kurt.
Good to see you again."

"Same here," Kurt said, patting the chair next to him. "Sit
down and have some of these appetizers with me."

"I will in a second. I just have to go hang up my parka."

"I'll take it," Hannah said, taking Norman's parka before
he could step away from the table. "I want to dash into the
ladies' room and look at my new sweater in the mirror. And
you need to talk to Kurt about what sort of photos he needs."

After Hannah had hung Norman's parka in the long, narrow cloakroom and admired her new sweater in front of the
ladies' room mirror, she went back to her post at the foot of
the stairs. Her next few minutes were spent greeting several
dozen Lake Eden residents and telling them where to deliver

casseroles, bowls, and platters. She was about to dash back to the kitchen to grab a mug of coffee when Mike arrived with Shawna Lee.

"Hi, Hannah!" Shawna Lee walked gracefully down the stairs balancing a platter, something Hannah wouldn't even have attempted, especially in four-inch high heels. "I really hope I did these right. I followed the recipe exactly."

"I'm sure they're just fine," Hannah said, hoping that her words would be prophetic. She'd given the blond secretary one of the easier recipes, Susan Zilber's Spinach Rollups. Once the spinach had been cooked and drained, there was no other cooking involved.

"I hope they make the cookbook. The only thing I did different was I cut them on the slant. I think they took better that way."

Hannah glanced down at the platter Shawna Lee was holding. It was covered with plastic wrap and the rollups looked just fine to her. "They're very attractive."

"I know. And they're good, too. I tasted the end pieces when I cut them off."

"Cook's prerogative," Hannah commented, smiling at Shawna Lee. She could afford to be charitable now that her rival was leaving town. "Just take them in the kitchen and give them to Edna. She'll see that they get out to the right table when it's time to serve. And tell her what we should do with your platter after it's washed."

"Oh, Mike can take it home for me. He's got the key and he knows where it goes in the cupboard."

Hannah saw red, and that made her forget all about being charitable. Only a frequent visitor to Shawna Lee's kitchen would know where her dishes belonged. Visions of intimate candlelight dinners and early breakfasts danced through Hannah's mind and made her long for retribution.

"I'm really sorry I can't stay for the dinner," Shawna Lee interrupted Hannah's contemplations of double homicide. "I just know it'll be wonderful! But I've got a ten o'clock flight and I have to be at the airport two hours early. Mike's taking me. Isn't that nice of him?"

"Nice," Hannah said, putting on a smile that wouldn't have fooled anyone except perhaps a brand-new acquaintance with a severe visual problem.

"While you're in the kitchen, why don't you see if the coffee's ready?" Mike suggested, giving Shawna Lee a little push in that direction. "I could use a cup before we hit the road."

"Cream, two sugars, right? Except in the morning, when you don't take cream."

"Right." The moment Shawna Lee had left, Mike turned to Hannah. "I need to talk to you about those brownies."

Hannah gulped slightly, glad that she had witnesses just in case this turned ugly. "Look, Mike. I'm really sorry about . . ."

"I haven't had a chance to taste them yet," Mike interrupted her, "but I wanted to thank you in advance. That was really nice of you, Hannah. I would have opened them right away and had a few, but it's been a totally impossible day. I just put them in my drawer so the other guys wouldn't snitch them and I never got back to my desk."

Hannah nodded, but she hadn't really listened to anything Mike had said beyond the first sentence. "So . . . you haven't had a chance to taste the brownies?"

"Not yet. They're still in my center desk drawer. Do I have to refrigerate them or anything? Or will it be all right if I leave them there until tomorrow?"

"They'll be fine in the drawer. Absolutely." Hannah gave him what she hoped was an innocent smile, her mind already working on a way to retrieve them before Mike had the chance to take the first bite. "I'm sorry you're going to miss the buffet."

Mike slipped his arm around her shoulder and gave her a little hug. "What do you mean? Just keep a chair warm for me. I'm going to drop Shawna Lee off at the airport and come straight back. Maybe there won't be much food left by the time I get here, but there's no way I'm going to miss my first Lake Eden Christmas party with you."

Chapter Six

Once Mike and Shawna Lee had left, each carrying a large frosted sugar cookie for the trip to the airport, Hannah went back to her greeting duties. She could hear the wind whistle every time the upstairs door opened to let in another group of hungry arrivals. If there were children in the group, they squealed in excitement as they spotted the miniature Christmas village in the lobby of the community center. The Jordan High shop class had made it as a holiday gift to the city of Lake Eden three years ago, and they kept making improvements and adding structures to the basic design. Last year George Baxter's students had put in lights that twinkled from the windows. And this year, his senior boys had built three churches with stained glass windows that were exact replicas of the three churches in Lake Eden. Pam Baxter, George's wife and the home economics teacher at Jordan High, had decided to help with the project. Her girls had made tiny wreaths for the doors and decorated the windows of the stores.

"Hi, Aunt Hannah," a familiar voice called out.

"Hello, Tracey." Hannah gave a big smile as her niece came down the stairs. Andrea and Bill's daughter was dressed in a dark green velvet jumper with a white lace blouse for to-night's festivities, and with her shining blonde hair tumbling down in a mass of natural curls, she looked just like a Christmas angel. "Where's your mother?"

"She's still talking to Mrs. Beeseman and Mr. Herman in the lobby. Aunt Lisa and Uncle Herb are there, too."

"You didn't want to stay and talk?"

Tracey shook her head. "It was boring, all about fur coats, and diamond rings, and some kind of drink."

"A kind of drink?" Hannah was stymied. What did fur coats and diamonds rings have to do with a kind of drink? Unless . . . "Do you mean brandy?"

"That's it! Anyway, Mommy said I could go downstairs and mingle until she got here."

"Your mother told you to *mingle?*" Hannah wondered if her five-year-old niece knew what the word meant.

"Not like that exactly. She said to go talk to the people I know. But that's *mingle,* isn't it?"

"It is," Hannah assured her, impressed, as always, with her niece's vocabulary. "Norman's around here somewhere, and he's taking pictures. You should go say hello to him."

"I will. I like Uncle Norman. How about Uncle Mike?"

"He'll be here later. He's taking Shawna Lee Quinn to the airport."

"In his new yellow Hummer?"

"That's right."

"Uncle Mike took Daddy and me for a ride. It bounces a lot, but you probably know that since he takes you out on dates. Which one do you like best? Uncle Norman's? Or Uncle Mike's?"

"That depends on how far I'm riding," Hannah said with a grin.

Tracey had just left to find Norman when Andrea came down the stairs. She looked lovely in a deep purple velvet maternity pantsuit, and Hannah was relieved to see that she was holding tightly to the rail.

"Hi, Hannah. What's up?"

"Nothing. Martin and his new wife haven't arrived yet."

"Maybe they're not coming. That would be good as far as Shirley's concerned, but I'm dying to get a good look at her. Do you suppose she'll wear gold spandex and glitter in her hair?"

"I doubt it. She's probably perfectly nice."

"With a name like Brandi Wyen?"

Hannah thought about it for a moment and then she smiled. "Point well taken. Is Bill here?"

"Not yet. If he gets held up, I'm supposed to save him a piece of Jell-O Cake. It's his favorite thing that I bake."

"It's the *only* thing that you bake."

"Well . . . there's that, too. See you later, Hannah. I'm going to see if I can round up Tracey. She's probably in the kitchen trying to talk Edna into letting her help."

"She'd probably do better than some of the help Edna's had over the years." Hannah smiled, watching her sister set out for the kitchen. She was just thinking about how pregnant women resembled sailing ships in a high wind, when she heard voices at the top of the stairs.

Hannah put on the best smile she could muster, but since she'd been meeting and greeting for well over thirty minutes, it was beginning to wear a little thin around the edges. Then she caught sight of the couple coming down the staircase and her smile gathered lumens until it was full wattage.

Hannah greeted the mayor and his wife and then dissolved into a burst of spontaneous laughter, despite her effort to keep a straight face. Mayor Bascomb's tie was splendiferous. It was the old-fashioned wide type and the background was studded in red sequins. A green felt Christmas tree was tacked to the front, and it actually lit up with tiny colored lights that flashed on and off. "Great tie, Mr. Mayor."

"Steffie found it out at the mall. Runs on one of those little disk batteries they use for cameras." Mayor Bascomb tucked his wife's arm through his and patted her hand. "She's the world's best shopper, aren't you, honey?"

Stephanie Bascomb gave a very nice smile, but Hannah noticed that it didn't reach her eyes. She also pulled her hand away from her husband's, and Hannah concluded that there was trouble in Lake Eden's first family. The Bascombs would put on the appearance of connubial bliss for the crowd of constituents that had gathered for the party, but it was all for show.

"Lovely dress, Mrs. Bascomb," Hannah said, admiring the white wool dress with white-on-white embroidered snow-flakes forming a border around the hem and the neckline. Tiny snowflake earrings made of small diamonds twinkled at her ears, and Hannah suspected the worst. It was a well-known fact that Stephanie Bascomb bought herself an expensive new outfit every time she thought her husband was cheating on her. And this time she'd bought diamond earrings, too.

"Thank you, Hannah," Stephanie said, shrugging out of her coat and handing it to her husband. "Hang this up for me, Richard. I want to see if they need any help in the kitchen."

Hannah just shook her head as the mayor trotted obediently to the cloakroom while his wife headed off to the kitchen. She'd been in the kitchen enough times to imagine the scene that would ensue. Stephanie would offer to help. Edna would say that was so nice of her, but she sure wouldn't want Mrs. Bascomb to get that beautiful dress mussed. Once these polite proprieties were fulfilled, Stephanie would leave, and the scorecard would be even. The mayor's wife would get credit for the offer without doing anything, and Edna would get credit for keeping Stephanie out of the kitchen so that the ladies who were there could gossip about whether Mayor Bascomb's eye was roving again.

A few minutes later, relief arrived in the person of Barbara

Donnelly, who said Edna had sent her to take over as greeter. Hannah was on her way to the table where Norman and Kurt were still in deep discussion about the photographs Kurt wanted for the cookbook when she spotted one of the possible combatants of the night. Shirley Dubinski was sitting at a table with her ex-mother-in-law, Babs. While they hadn't gotten along that well when Shirley and Martin were married, it appeared that the shock of Martin's surprise marriage had brought them together. Shirley and Babs looked tighter than thieves.

"Hi, Babs," Hannah greeted the woman who'd talked Delores into setting her up for a date with Martin. "That's a lovely pin."

"Thank you. Shirley gave it to me for Christmas two years ago and I just love it." Babs reached up to touch the gold wreath pin she wore at the neck of her dark red silk blouse. "I suppose you've heard the news?"

"Just this morning." Hannah let it go at that and turned to Shirley. "You look great tonight, Shirley. That's a gorgeous suit, and you've cut your hair, haven't you?"

Shirley beamed, happy that Hannah had noticed. "I had it done when I went to Chicago last week. I got a promotion, you know. Del and Benton Woodley decided that DelRay should be represented at all the big trade shows, and that's my job."

"Sounds like fun."

"It is. I found out I'm a better salesman than I thought I was. They were so pleased when I came back from Chicago with two new contracts, they decided to give me a clothing allowance. Can you believe *that*? And since Babs agreed to take care of the boys for me while I'm traveling, I don't have to worry about a thing."

"Are the boys here?" Hannah asked, realizing that Shirley and Martin's young sons were nowhere in sight.

"No, they're with my mother. Babs and I thought it was

best, since"—Shirley faltered slightly—"since Martin plans to be here with *her.*"

"Oh. That's probably wise. I mean, the boys might not understand . . ." Hannah's voice trailed off as she spotted Martin Dubinski and his new wife entering the banquet room. For a new groom, Martin didn't look very happy, and Hannah briefly wondered why. But that thought left her mind completely when she caught sight of the woman on Martin's arm.

"Good heavens!" Hannah joined in the collective gasp that emanated from the throat of almost every person in the room.

Brandi Wyen Dubinski deserved a gasp and then some. She was drop-dead gorgeous. The auburn-haired beauty's skin was flawless, her eyes were a delightful shade of sea green, her lashes were long, her hair was lustrous, and her figure was so remarkable, there was complete silence in the crowded banquet room. Martin's new wife was tall, and she was obviously comfortable with her height, because she was wearing silver high-heeled boots that clung to her calves like plastic wrap.

"Wow!" Hannah breathed, blinking hard. The vision was almost too perfect to be true. Brandi was poured into a gleaming silver satin dress with a low neckline, and it was so snug it must have been tailored to hug her every curve. The smile Martin's new wife gave to the assembled multitude showed incredibly white and even teeth. She was glamour personified, theatrical and stunning. Lake Eden had never set eyes on anyone of her magnitude before.

Hannah sneaked a quick glance at Shirley. Martin's ex-wife was staring at her replacement with a slack jaw and a glazed look in her eyes. As Hannah watched, Babs nudged Shirley and whispered in her ear. Whatever Babs said, it worked. Shirley closed her mouth, sat up a little straighter, and pretended she was fascinated by the Christmas tree that sat in the middle of the room, and not in the least bit interested in the new Mrs. Martin Dubinski.

"Uh-oh," Hannah said, under her breath, wondering what she could do to defuse the situation. The tension grew as Martin spotted his mother and started to bring Brandi over to her table. Then he noticed that Shirley was there and reconsidered. It was an awkward situation, with Martin and Brandi eyeing Babs and Shirley warily; mother and ex-wife seated at the table, and husband and new wife standing only a few feet away.

There was no way Hannah was about to let the tension grow any thicker. She looked around for Andrea, caught her eye, and motioned toward Martin and Brandi. Andrea, the quintessential politician's wife now that Bill had won the race for Winnetka County sheriff, caught on immediately and headed over to greet Martin and Brandi and show them to a table as far away from Babs and Shirley's as the architecture of the banquet room would allow.

"Oh, there's Mother," Hannah said, spotting Delores as she came down the stairs. "You two enjoy the dinner. I've got to go say hello."

Hannah hurried to the bottom of the stairs and greeted her mother. And then she stared up expectantly. "Where's Winthrop?"

"Parking the car in the lot. He dropped me off right by the door. He's just so considerate that way." Delores Swensen waltzed into the room, looking for all the world like a grand duchess. "Would you take my coat, dear? I see a spot at that table over there that would be just perfect for us. Winthrop's *gauche,* you know."

"Gauche?"

"In the true sense of the word."

"You mean . . . left-handed?"

"That's right. He needs to sit at the end of the table on my left. Most people don't realize what a true handicap that is. Practically everything is designed for right-handed people."

"No doubt," Hannah said, accepting what she suspected was a new dress coat from her mother.

"Do free yourself up soon and come over to meet Winthrop, dear. He's been asking about you. And remember, we added the orange juice concentrate as a modern innovation to dear Lady Hermoine's Chocolate Sunshine Cake."

Hannah greeted a few more people, and then she spotted what could only be described as a dapper gentleman coming down the stairs. It had to be Winthrop. Hannah eyed him suspiciously as he walked toward her mother's table, smiling a greeting.

Delores caught Hannah's eye and waved. It was an order for a command appearance. Not one to dare resist such a summary summons, Hannah turned on her heel, squelched the urge to salute, and headed straight for her mother's table.

"You must be Hannah," her mother's companion stated, shooting to his feet as Hannah approached them. "So nice to meet you, my dear. Delores told me you were the beauty in the family."

Hannah resisted the urge to accuse Winthrop of being a bald-faced social liar and gave a polite little laugh. "She must have gotten me mixed up with my sisters. But anyway, we meet at last. Mother's told me a lot about you."

"All good, I hope?" Winthrop asked, exuding confidence that his question would be answered in the positive.

"Naturally." Hannah smiled, taking in her mother's significant other at a glance. Winthrop Harrington II matched Hannah's mental picture of a Regency romance heartthrob, and that meant he was right up her mother's alley. He was suave, sophisticated, handsome in a quietly understated way, and from the way his clothing fit, it had been tailored just for him. Winthrop exuded an air of quality, and he looked as if he wasn't hurting for cash, or what her mother would refer to as *blunt* if she were in Regency mode. Still, Hannah wasn't convinced Winthrop was all he claimed to be, and she eyed him the way a wary rabbit might regard a snake.

"Is the antique cake knife here, dear?" Delores asked, reacting to her daughter's silence and seeming to sense that Hannah was contemplating the wisdom of asking Winthrop some embarrassing questions.

"Yes, it's right next to the cake on the dessert table. Norman wanted us to bring out some of the prettiest desserts early so that he could take photos. Kurt Howe was really impressed when he saw your knife. He told me to tell you that it's gorgeous."

"I think so, too. And Luanne is a real genius for finding it. I tell you, she goes through all those estate sale flyers with a fine-toothed comb. This one just said, 'old silver cake knife.' When Luanne told me she had a hunch it might be something good, I sent her down to St. Paul for the auction. And the rest is . . . history!"

"How droll, my dear," Winthrop said, chuckling appreciatively and patting Delores's hand. Hannah knew she had to excuse herself soon or she'd say something she'd later regret.

Perhaps it was one of those unspoken mother-daughter communications, but Delores seemed to sense that her eldest daughter had reached the end of her patience, and she stepped in quickly. "I hate to speed the departing guest, but I know you're busy, dear. I just wanted you to meet Winthrop. You'll get to know each other much better over the holidays."

"Right," Hannah said, trying not to react to the hint that Winthrop would be taking part in their family celebrations. "See you later, Mother. Winthrop? Charmed, I'm sure."

My daughter, the humorist, Hannah imagined her mother saying, as she walked away. She resisted the urge to go back and really quiz Winthrop about his intentions, and she settled for catching Andrea's eye. Her sister was sitting with Martin and Brandi, looking about as comfortable as an overdue pregnant woman suffering from terminal boredom could look. Hannah gave her a high sign that meant she'd relieve her in a few minutes and they'd compare notes about Winthrop. Andrea nodded, catching Hannah's drift perfectly. They'd always been able to communicate without words, perhaps the result of living with a mother who always had to have the last word on everything.

Hannah glanced toward the kitchen doorway to see Edna gesturing for her. It was time to set out the food. She hurried into the kitchen, and moments later she was carrying out dishes according to Edna's instructions. Once the appetizer table was ready and Norman had photographed it, Mayor Bascomb told everyone that they were welcome to dig in. The crowd converged and Hannah rejoiced in the oohs and ahhs of the admiring diners as they sampled Spinach Rollups, Busy Day Pâté, Fiesta Dip Platter, and Caviar Pie. There were dozens of appetizers on the groaning board, including Baked Brie, Bill Jessup's Misdemeanor Mushrooms, Mrs. Knudson's Herring Appetizer, and Seafood Bread Dip, one of the appetizer recipes Carrie Rhodes had submitted for the cookbook.

Hannah took a thin sliver of her Spinach Quiche. Since they had plenty of entrées, Edna had cut it into as many thin slices as possible and arranged them on a platter as an appetizer. Then she walked over to join her sister, who had gone up to the appetizer table with Martin and Brandi and was still sitting with them.

After the introductions had been made and Hannah had congratulated the newlyweds, she leaned forward to attempt polite conversation with Brandi. "Your dress is beautiful."

"I know. Martin said I could have anything I wanted, but I'm pretty sure he didn't expect it to go to four figures."

Hannah did her best to keep the friendly smile on her

face. She knew four figures meant a thousand dollars at the least. She also knew that Martin's small business didn't make a fortune and he had two children to support. "I guess Lake Eden must be quite a change from Las Vegas."

"You can say *that* again."

Hannah had the urge to do just that. At least it would give her something else to say. What she really wanted to know was why Brandi had married Martin in the first place, but it would be rude to ask.

"So . . . you married?" Brandi asked, glancing down at Hannah's bare fingers.

"No, I'm not." Hannah felt the urge to babble just to fill the silence, and she gave in to it. "I haven't found the right man yet, I guess."

"You won't, not here. These small towns are death for single women, especially when they get to be your age. But don't get me wrong . . . you're not bad looking and some men like that natural, untouched look. I bet I could have lined you up with somebody really hot in Vegas."

Hannah frowned. She didn't even want to think about the type of man Brandi might have picked out for her and she quickly changed the subject. "Have you met Martin's sons yet?"

"No. I'm not big on kids, but at least they're boys. I get along a lot better with boys."

I'll bet you do! Hannah thought, but of course she didn't say it. Making conversation with Brandi was like trying to drive a truck out of a mud hole. Every time she managed to crawl forward a few feet, she slipped right back in the muck.

"Who's that?" Brandi gestured toward a table at the front of the room.

"Who's who?"

"That guy with that awful Christmas tie. He looks familiar."

"That's our mayor, Richard Bascomb."

"He looks like somebody I met a while back, but the name's not familiar."

Hannah nodded, but her mind was racing. Mayor Bascomb had flown to Las Vegas for a convention a couple of months ago. If he'd hooked up with Brandi and wanted to maintain his anonymity, he might not have used his own name.

"Excuse me a second, will you? I have to talk to Marty."

Hannah breathed a sigh of relief as Brandi huddled with Martin. Now she was free to talk to Andrea. "So where's Bill? I thought he'd be here by now."

"He just called me. The Tri-County Sheriff's Coalition meeting is running late, and he might not be here for hours."

Brandi turned to tap Andrea on the arm. "I never thought to ask you when Marty said your husband was the sheriff, but is there a problem with crime in this area?"

"Not at all," Andrea assured her, and Hannah almost choked on her bite of quiche. It was clear that her sister wasn't about to mention the murder cases they'd helped Bill and Mike solve.

"Oh, good! Then maybe I'll put my new fur coat in the cloakroom after dinner." Brandi reached out to stroke the coat that she wore draped over her shoulders. "Since it was so expensive, I didn't want to leave it unattended, but Marty said it was perfectly safe. I was just hoping that he was right . . . about *that,* at least."

Hannah stifled a groan at the last four words of Brandi's sentence. It sounded to her like trouble in paradise, and they'd been married for less than a week.

"Martin's right," Andrea said, smiling at Brandi. "Theft has never been a problem in Lake Eden. Some people don't even lock their doors. Did you happen to notice the silver cake knife on the platter next to the chocolate cake?"

"I saw it when we were standing in line for the appetizers.

It's really pretty. I like all those colored stones on the Christmas tree."

"They're gemstones. The big one on the top is a star-cut diamond and the smaller ones are sapphires, rubies, and emeralds. The knife is a solid silver antique worth thousands."

"But . . . it's just sitting there in plain sight and no one's even keeping an eye on it."

"I know," Andrea zeroed in to prove her point, "and that just goes to prove that you don't have to be worried about somebody stealing your fur coat in Lake Eden. People here are as honest as the day is long."

When Brandi had returned to her conversation with Martin, Hannah tapped Andrea on the shoulder. "If Bill gets hung up, I'm sure Mike will give you and Tracey a ride home."

"In his Hummer?" Andrea looked delighted when Hannah nodded. "That's just great! Tracey said it was bumpy, and it might work as well as Lisa's mother's horseback ride!"

Chapter Seven

Hannah stood up as Edna motioned to her from the kitchen door. It was time to set out the salad, soup, and bread course. "Nice to meet you, Brandi. Sorry I can't stay, but I have to help set out the next course. Andrea?"

"Yes?"

"You wanted to check on that Jell-O salad, didn't you?"

"Jell-O . . ." Andrea looked blank for a split second and then realization dawned. "Yes! Thanks for reminding me." She turned to Martin and Brandi. "It was nice chatting with you, Brandi. And congratulations, Martin. I wish you two all the best."

Hannah heard her sister give a relieved sigh as they stepped away from the table. She'd been sitting with the newlyweds for over thirty minutes, and that was above and beyond. She turned to say thank you for helping out, but that thought vanished when she noticed the shocked expression on Andrea's face.

"What's the matter?"

"Hot Stuff. And that's got to be Silver Fox."

"What?" Hannah grabbed her sister's arm. Did pregnant women start spouting nonsense when they went into labor? She really should have read one of the pamphlets Andrea had given her about childbirth.

"Hot Stuff." Andrea pointed toward an older couple at one of the long tables. "That's Vera Olsen's screen name. Don't you remember the e-mail she was answering when we were searching her attic apartment?"

"Right." Hannah felt a wave of relief sluice down from the top of her head to her toes. Andrea wasn't in labor and she wasn't crazy. She was talking about Vera's on-line romance with a man who called himself Silver Fox.

"Vera looks fabulous. She's lost weight and had her hair streaked. I think she might have had a lift, too."

Hannah glanced over at Vera. Andrea was always right when it came to noticing appearance enhancements and she could spot a facelift or a new hairstyle from a block away. "You're right. Vera looks a lot younger."

"Do you think he's Silver Fox?"

"I think so." Hannah tried to recall the photo she'd seen on the computer screen. If she remembered correctly, the handsome older man sitting beside Vera bore a close resemblance to the picture of Silver Fox standing at the helm of his boat.

"He's certainly dressed well. That's a cashmere vest and an Armani suit. And his hair's been styled by someone really good. Not only that, his manicure is perfect."

"Silver Fox has a *manicure?*" Hannah squinted, but there was no way she could match her sister's eagle eye for spotting nuances of personal grooming.

"Manicures aren't just for women, you know. Big executives make appointments for manicurists to come to their offices. I bet that's what he is."

"A manicurist?" Hannah asked, knowing that wasn't what her sister meant, but unable to resist teasing her a bit.

"Of course he's not a manicurist! He's got to be someone with a big, important . . ." Andrea stopped in mid-thought and made a strangled sound.

Hannah tightened her grip on her sister's arm. "Is there something wrong? Do you want to sit down? Is it the baby?"

"None of the above. And stop holding my arm in that death grip. I'm going to bruise."

"Sorry." Hannah dropped Andrea's arm, but she kept her hand at the ready, just in case. "Why did you make that sound?"

"Just take a look at Vera's finger and you'll understand."

Hannah took a look and made an identical strangled sound as she spotted the glittering diamond ring on Vera's third finger left hand. It was easy to see, perhaps because Vera was using her left hand to wave to everyone she knew. "Does that mean Vera's engaged?"

"I think so. I'm going to try to find out."

The sisters parted ways at the food tables. Andrea headed for the section where Vera and the man they'd tentatively identified as Silver Fox were sitting, and Hannah headed for the kitchen. She found Edna standing at the counter, surveying the platters, bowls, and the army of Crock-Pots that stood at the ready. "Where do you want the soup bowls, Edna? At the end of the table?"

"Good idea. I'll take them out and you can bring the soups."

"Do we have enough ladles?"

"Thanks to your sister we do. Put Vera's Gazpacho first, since her boyfriend flew in special for the holidays. She told me she paid a fortune for hothouse tomatoes so she could make it for him."

"He looks nice," Hannah commented, fishing for information as she picked up the large tureen Vera had brought in and followed Edna to the serving table.

"He seems all right, but you can never tell about a man until you've known him for a while . . . unless you meet him in church."

Hannah bit back a startled laugh as she thought of some notable exceptions to Edna's caveat, and headed back to the kitchen to get the four other soups. There was Sally's Radish

Soup, the one she served at the Lake Eden Inn, with its delicate pink color and surprising depth. Hannah let Edna float a few thinly sliced radishes over the top while she went back for Bridget Murphy's Quick Irish Chili.

"I've got the toppings for the chili," Edna called out following on Hannah's heels with a platter containing dishes of diced onions, sour cream, chopped black olives, and lightly sautéed celery slices. "You get the Corn Chowder, and I'll bring my Cream of Cheat Mushroom Soup."

Once the soups were set out with regular bowls and a multitude of tiny cups for those who wanted to taste all four, Hannah and Edna went back to the kitchen.

"I'll take care of the Jell-O molds," Edna said, gesturing toward the breads she'd already set out in baskets, on plates, and on breadboards. "You can put those breads out now, and come back for the Jell-O."

It took Hannah several minutes to set out the breads. Most of the local ladies had their favorites, and there was Sally's Banana Bread, Gina's Strawberry Bread, Cranberry Muffins, and Aunt Grace's Breakfast Muffins. Once those were in place, opposite the soups, she went back for Cheryl Coombs's Can Bread, which Edna had pre-sliced and arranged on a platter. She'd also cut Bridget Murphy's Soda Bread into pie-shaped wedges and reassembled them in a round on a breadboard. There was a basket of Cheesy, Spicy Corn Muffins, and a big round wicker bowl of oyster crackers that Edna had provided for Mayor Bascomb, who categorically refused to eat soup without them.

When Hannah returned to the kitchen again, she saw that Edna was ready with two of the four Jell-O molds.

"Put the Pretty Coleslaw first," Edna instructed, "and then the Waldorf Salad. I've got to tell you, Hannah, I'm having second thoughts about this Ginger Ale Jell-O mold."

"Didn't it set up right?"

"That's not it. It's nice and firm, and it looks really good.

But since it's got fruit in it, I'm wondering if it should go on the dessert table."

Hannah thought about that for a moment and then she shrugged. "That's up to you, but we've got a lot of desserts already."

"That settles it then. It's a salad. You can take it out now. I'm still trying to unmold your sister's Holiday Jell-O."

By the time Hannah got back to the kitchen, Edna had resorted to using the dunk method to get the last mold on its platter. She'd half-filled a bowl with hot water and she was immersing the mold in the bowl to within an inch of the rim. "That should do it," she said, lifting the mold and drying the bottom with a kitchen towel. "Hand me that platter, will you, Hannah?"

Hannah handed over the platter, and Edna centered it over the top of the mold. Then she held the assembled mold and platter with both hands and inverted it by twisting her wrists.

"Perfect," Hannah said as the Jell-O plopped cooperatively onto its platter. "There's one more salad, isn't there?"

"Just a big bowl of greens tossed with Claire's French Dressing. I'm going to put a couple of Ellie's Dilly Onion Rings on the top and leave the rest in a bowl for those that want them."

"How about Reverend Knudson's Quick Pickle Salad?"

Edna thumped her forehead with the heel of her head. "Bless you, Hannah. The Reverend's too nice to say anything, but not the rest of the congregation. I'd never hear the end of it if I forgot to put that out!"

"Okay, Norman." Hannah gave him the high sign as she placed the last dish on the table.

"It looks great, Hannah. Kurt wants to know when you're going to get a chance to eat."

"Soon, I hope." Hannah glanced over at the table where

Kurt was sitting and saw that he had a fully laden plate. "I see he's sampling some of the dishes."

"He's had a bite of everything so far, I think." Norman moved into a better position for a shot of Andrea's Jell-O molds. "Just let me get a couple of overviews of the table, and then you can cue in Mayor Bascomb."

Once Norman had taken his last few shots and stepped back from the table, Hannah waved at the mayor, who wasted no time inviting people to sample the next course. The diners converged, and within a few seconds people were filling their plates and soup bowls. Hannah noticed that Norman was taking shots of the line that had formed, and when he'd finished that, he moved to the tables and took shots of the Lake Eden citizens, who were clearly enjoying the dinner.

Hannah held her breath as Norman approached Martin and Brandi's table. She hoped he'd brought plenty of film, because there was no way a photographer could resist snapping multiple shots of a woman who was that photogenic. Come to think about it, any man, with or without a camera, would have lingered as long as humanly possible to bask in the light of a beauty like Brandi.

But Norman only snapped one picture and moved on, surprising Hannah so much, she gasped out loud.

"Are you all right?"

"Fine," Hannah said, whirling around as she heard a familiar voice behind her. "Michelle!"

A smile spread over Hannah's face and she stepped forward to hug her baby sister. A sophomore at Macalester College in St. Paul, Michelle wasn't exactly a baby anymore, but she *was* Hannah's youngest sister. "What are you doing here?"

"I just came for the food," Michelle quipped, hugging Hannah right back. "Don't worry, Big Sis, I didn't cut any classes. I hopped a bus this afternoon and Lonnie picked me up at the Quick Stop."

Hannah glanced around and spotted Lonnie Murphy talking to his brother and sister-in-law several tables away. Even though the youngest sheriff's deputy was carrying on a conversation, he kept glancing over at Michelle.

"Is that *him?*" Michelle asked.

"Is who what?" Hannah asked, not caring that they'd just broken at least two cardinal rules of grammar.

"Winthrop Harrington II. Over there with Mother."

"That's Winthrop."

"He looks pretty buff for a guy in his sixties."

"Late forties. He's younger than Mother."

"She didn't mention that." Michelle frowned slightly at this news. "Have you met him yet?"

"Just a few minutes ago. When you get a second, go over and introduce yourself. I want to get your take on him."

"Will do. I've got to meet the man who's responsible for Mother's shoes."

"Mother's shoes?"

"I just noticed them. They're really sexy sandals with thin little straps and high heels, the kind that just kill your feet. Only a woman on the make wears shoes like that."

"On the make?" Hannah asked, feeling a little like a parrot as she repeated Michelle's words again.

"You know . . . a woman who's trying to attract a guy. It's pretty obvious Mother's trying to attract Winthrop. And from where I'm sitting, it seems to be working."

While Hannah tried to catch a glimpse of her mother's shoes, Michelle glanced around the room, waving at a few people she knew. When she spotted the new Mrs. Martin Dubinski, she nudged Hannah. "Who's *that?*"

"Brandi Wyen Dubinski. She's a dancer from Vegas, and she married Martin a couple of days ago."

"Martin married a stripper?"

"Michelle! You don't know that!"

Michelle giggled. "Maybe not, but I bet you thought the same thing when you heard her name."

"Me? Of course I would never jump to . . ." Hannah stopped in the act of denying it and laughed instead. "Okay. I'll admit it. I did. But it's possible that Brandi was a legitimate showgirl."

"Sure it is. And it's also possible that she had parents who thought it was funny to give her a really terrible name. I'll go meet Winthrop and then I want to talk to Martin and Brandi."

"To find out about her name?"

"Not unless it comes up. I'm trying out for the part of a Vegas showgirl in the spring play, and I want to ask her some things about routines and dancing. Not only that, I'm dying to find out if they really use bubble gum to keep those skimpy tops up."

Hannah was chuckling as Michelle walked away. Her baby sister could always make her laugh. She watched Michelle shake Winthrop's hand and seized the opportunity to look at her mother's shoes as Delores got to her feet to hug Michelle.

"I'll be!" Hannah breathed, shaking her head slightly. Delores was wearing the sexy new shoes she'd bought on sale last year, the same shoes she said she was going to throw away because they hurt her feet. If Michelle was right and only a woman on the make would wear sexy but uncomfortable shoes, Mother was definitely after Winthrop.

That gave Hannah an idea, and she glanced around for Martin's ex-wife. Shirley was just coming back to her table, and Hannah had a clear view of her shoes. For a practical, no-nonsense person, Shirley had broken all the rules tonight. She was wearing cream-colored suede high-heeled ankle boots with fur around the tops. Since they were totally unsuitable for a Minnesota winter, and taking into account Michelle's sexy footwear theory, Hannah could only conclude that Shirley was on the make for someone, probably Martin.

"What a mess," Hannah sighed, her eyes roving the room again until she located Laura Jorgensen, standing at the food table. Laura was wearing red backless slings with high narrow heels, and she looked as if her feet hurt. She was definitely on the make . . . also for Martin?

Hannah had one more pair of shoes to check out, and she zeroed in on them. It was easy, because her baby sister was sitting with her back to Hannah and she had one leg crossed over the other. Along with Michelle's completely acceptable tan slacks and bright red sweater, she was wearing tan boots with flat rubber soles that looked as if they'd seen better days.

Hannah breathed a sigh of relief. According to Michelle's own theory, her youngest sister was *not* on the make. And if Hannah wanted to carry things further and look at her own feet, she wasn't on the make, either. Hannah's moccasin boots were designed for comfort, not allure. She'd worn them because she'd known from day one that she'd be helping Edna carry food to the serving tables.

And how about the sexy shoes you brought along in your tote bag? The ones that are hanging from a hook in the cloakroom? Hannah's conscience spoke up. *You're going to put those on when the dancing starts, aren't you?*

Hannah didn't like it, but her conscience was right. She'd planned to switch to the Italian ankle-strapped high heels right after she was through helping Edna, because they made her legs look so good.

Before Hannah could peruse any other shoes, or think about the advisability of trying to get rid of her conscience, she saw Edna waving at her from the kitchen. It was time to set out the main dishes and sides for the crowd that was already beginning to say that this was the best Christmas potluck dinner yet.

Chapter Eight

Hannah surveyed the entrée table with a frown. She'd carried out Edna's Not So Swedish Meatballs, her mother's Hawaiian Pot Roast, E-Z Lasagna, Rose's Restaurant Turkey, Luanne's Festive Baked Sandwich, Laura's Smothered Chicken, Chicken Paprikash, Hunter's Stew, Esther's Meatloaf, and Irish Roast Beast. There was also Trudi's Hot German Potato Salad with Bratwurst, Country Ham Casserole, Sauerbraten, Baked Fish, Barbecued Anything, and something no Lake Eden potluck dinner could be without, Minnesota Hotdish. Hannah stood there holding a crock of Scandinavian Red Cabbage that was growing heavier each passing moment. Every inch of space was filled. There simply wasn't enough room for the sides.

"What's the matter?" Norman came up behind her, prepared to take photos of the table.

"We ran out of room, and we still have at least ten sides in the kitchen on the counter."

"Sides?"

"Noodles, potatoes, rice, and veggies. Sides are all the things you put on your plate with the main course. We really need them on the same table, but it's just not possible."

"Sure, it is." Norman patted her on the back. "Go set that down in the kitchen and see if you can rustle up another tablecloth. I've got an idea that'll work just fine to almost double your table space."

By the time Hannah got back with the tablecloth, Kurt and Norman had combined the leftovers from the first two serving tables and appropriated the second empty table. They'd placed it at right angles so that it butted up to the center of the entrée table. The new T-shape was perfect for the sides, since it was smack dab in the center of the entrées, and Hannah wasted no time covering the table with the fresh cloth and helping Edna carry things out. By the time they were finished, Party Potatoes, Apple 'n Onion Dressing Balls, Holiday Rice, Sweet Potato Casserole, and Make-Ahead Mashed Potatoes were arranged on one side of the table, while Silly Carrots, Spinach Souffle, Corn Pudding, Green Bean Classic with a Twist, Oodles of Noodles, and the red cabbage Hannah had been carrying earlier had been placed on the other side.

"That looks good enough to eat," Norman said, earning a volley of chuckles from Edna, who'd never been known to laugh while managing a dinner party. Before she could protest, he snapped a picture of her smiling face and promised that he wouldn't give anyone a copy if she didn't like it.

When Norman finished photographing the main courses and sides, Mayor Bascomb called everyone to the serving tables. Instead of standing in line with the other diners, Hannah got a cup of strong black coffee and headed in the opposite direction to collapse in a chair at the empty table where Norman and Kurt had been sitting. There was only one more course to go, and that should be a snap, since they'd already set out some of the desserts for the early photographs Kurt had directed.

Hannah glanced around the banquet room, and she wasn't disappointed by people's reactions. There wasn't much conversation because everyone was busy eating. "The sound of great food is silence," Hannah murmured, remembering what her Great-grandmother Elsa had told her.

Curious about how the new Mrs. Dubinski would react to a Midwestern potluck dinner, Hannah glanced over at Brandi and Martin's table. Their chairs were vacant, and a quick examination of the food line told Hannah that they weren't filling their plates. So where were they? And come to think of it, where was Michelle? Hannah had seen her leave Mother and Winthrop and head toward Brandi and Martin, but now their whole table was vacant.

It didn't take long to spot Martin. He was standing at his mother's side. Brandi and Michelle must have gone to the restroom, and Martin had taken this opportunity to mend fences with his mother and ex-wife.

"You look tired," Kurt said, putting his plate on the table, pulling out the chair next to hers, and sitting down.

"I am, but it's worth it. What do you think of the food?"

"Everything I've had is phenomenal." Kurt tasted the ribs and groaned. "I wish I'd saved more room. These are the best ribs I ever tasted."

"They're Norman's recipe. He calls it Barbecued Anything. Make sure you tell him you like it."

"I will. Why don't you get yourself some food, Hannah? You look like a strong wind could blow you over."

Hannah laughed. "It would take a typhoon, or at least a major squall. But getting some food is a good idea. I want to have some Chicken Paprikash. It's a favorite of mine."

"I put my helping over Edna's Make-Ahead Mashed Potatoes. It's great that way."

"But those are meatballs, not chicken," Hannah corrected him, pointing to the relevant section of his plate.

"I know that. I ate the part with the chicken while I was walking back to the table. Go ahead, Hannah. I want to dig into this E-Z Lasagna of your mother's. It looks fantastic, and I just know Marcia's going to want the recipe."

"How is Marcia?" Hannah asked, knowing that Kurt had

married his publisher's daughter despite the wishes of her family.

"She's just fine. And we just found out last month that we're pregnant."

"That's wonderful," Hannah said, wishing she could pick a bone with the women who insisted on that terminology. It was inaccurate. Men didn't get pregnant; women did. Of course men were equally responsible for the pregnancy, but the phrase, *we're pregnant,* set off klaxons in Hannah's logical mind. Sharing the experience of pregnancy was one thing; blatant disregard for the accuracy of the English language was another.

"Is there something wrong?" Kurt asked, picking up on Hannah's silence.

"Oh, no! Nothing!" Hannah quickly assured him.

"Would you bring me back one of those cranberry muffins?" Kurt asked, popping the last bite of soda bread into his mouth.

"Sure. I'll be right back," Hannah promised, heading off to the food table and wondering whether she really had turned into the pedantic curmudgeon Andrea had often accused her of being.

"I'm back!" Mike declared, catching Hannah just as she'd finished filling her plate.

Hannah reveled in the feel of his arm around her shoulder for a brief moment, and then she smiled up at him. "That was fast. Did you get Shawna Lee to the airport okay?"

"Of course, but it started coming down pretty heavy on the way back. It's a good thing I took my Hummer and not the squad car."

"Right," Hannah said, biting back a smile as Mike pulled out her chair and held it as she sat down. Mike was a guy's guy, and he had the biggest, most powerful vehicle around.

His Jeep hadn't been a wimpy vehicle, but Mike had wasted no time in trading it in on a Hummer last month. It wasn't the most comfortable ride for passengers, something Shawna Lee had undoubtedly discovered for herself, but it was powerful enough to get through almost anything a Minnesota winter could throw at a motorist.

"Thanks, Hannah," Kurt said, as Hannah handed him his muffin. He put it on his plate and turned to Mike, who'd just sat down next to him. "Did I hear you say it was coming down hard out there?"

"Yeah. Visibility isn't good at all."

"Do you think the roads are still passable? I have to get back to the Cities tonight."

Mike thought about it for a moment. "I think you'll be all right if you leave right now. The storm's blowing in from the north and you should be able to keep ahead of the worst of it. What type of car do you have?"

"A mid-size SUV."

"Four-wheel drive?"

"All-wheel drive with anti-lock brakes."

"High profile?"

"Not that high, but it has good clearance."

"You should be fine, then. I'll go out to the parking lot with you and help you shovel out. When I drove past, I noticed there's a big snowdrift at the exit."

"Thanks, but I'm not in the lot. I came in early and there was still parking on the street."

After Kurt had tendered his apologies for cutting the evening short, Mike walked him out to make sure he got on his way safely. Hannah noticed that on Mike's way back in, he stopped at her mother's table to say hello, and it was clear Delores introduced Winthrop, because the two men shook hands. Hannah had already marshaled the questions she wanted to ask Mike about his impression of her mother's date when Mike came back to take Kurt's vacant chair.

"That's the guy you and Andrea are so worried about?" Mike got in the first question, despite Hannah's resolve to quiz him.

"What did you think of him?"

"He seemed all right to me. Have you met him yet?"

"Yes, tonight. He was perfectly polite to me, but he's just so . . ." Hannah paused to struggle for the word that most correctly described her feelings, an unusual predicament for someone who'd come within a thesis of getting her doctorate in English Literature.

"Slick?"

"That's it exactly! There's nothing glaringly wrong with him, and I can see why Mother's so attracted to him. But I don't feel comfortable around him, and I still have my suspicions."

Mike gave her shoulder a supporting squeeze. "No problem. Did you know that Bill ran him this morning?"

"I had no idea. Did Andrea ask him to?"

"I don't think so. Anyway, absolutely nothing turned up. The guy's so squeaky clean, he's never even had a speeding ticket. You girls can stop worrying. Your mother's not going out with an axe murderer."

"I know *that!* But I can't seem to get rid of my reservations. I mean, he's younger than she is, for Pete's sakes! And he picked up on her at dance class when they were learning the tango, or the mambo, or whatever it was."

Mike was silent for a moment and then he leaned closer. "So maybe you have reservations because you don't want to see your mother with anyone other than your dad?"

"That's not it!" Hannah said, reacting immediately. But then, after she thought about it for a moment, she backtracked. "You could be right, but I'm not willing to admit that quite yet. Why don't you go get some food before it's all gone? I'll save your place for you."

After Mike had gone off to the food tables, Hannah thought

about what he'd said. Her dad had been dead for almost four years now, and maybe it was time for her mother to look for someone new. The problem was that whenever Hannah thought about another man in her mother's life, it seemed disloyal to her father's memory. She realized that her attitude wasn't fair, or perhaps not even rational, but that didn't change the way she felt about it.

Rather than dwell on this unhappy problem for any longer, Hannah gazed around the room while she waited for Mike to come back. Norman was off snapping pictures, the students from the Jordan High Jazz Ensemble were setting up their music stands and chairs for an interlude of music during dessert, and Brandi's chair was still vacant. Hannah glanced over at Babs and Shirley's table. Babs wasn't in her chair and neither was Shirley. The whole Dubinski family seemed to be missing.

Lonnie Murphy caught Hannah's eye and waved. As Hannah waved back, she noticed that Lonnie was sitting next to an empty chair. Was Michelle still in the ladies' room with Brandi, asking her about her showgirl career, while Martin was off somewhere talking to his mother? Or was Babs in the ladies' room with Brandi, grilling her about how she came to marry Martin, while the man in question was off with Shirley, trying to explain how he had spent so much money on Brandi? There were just too many possibilities, and Hannah gave up. The only thing she could be sure of was that Martin wasn't in the ladies' room. If he'd followed Michelle, his ex-wife, his mother, or his new wife in there, Hannah would be hearing one heck of a commotion.

"Great job on the pâté," Mike said, sliding into his chair. "You made it just the way my sister does."

Hannah was about to say that there was no way anyone could mess up such a simple recipe, but this time she remembered her mother's warning. "Thank you," she said, smiling up at him. Then she turned to glance at Delores to see if her mother–daughter radar was working and she somehow knew her eldest daughter had taken her advice. But Delores seemed oblivious to anything anyone else was doing or saying, because she was too busy smiling up at Winthrop.

Was it a sign of neurosis when a grown woman felt the urge to mother her mother? Hannah pondered that for a moment as she watched her mother put her hand on Winthrop's arm and give him a little pat. What did that mean? Was Delores being casually affectionate, or was Hannah's mother actually falling for the lure of tailored clothes, a title, and a country manor with hedgerows and primroses an ocean away from home?

"Hannah?" Mike, nudged her.

"Yes?"

"I think Edna wants you for something. She's signaling with her arms and pointing in our direction."

"You're right," Hannah said, recognizing the *I-need-you* expression on Edna's face. She gave Edna a wave to acknowledge that her message had been received, and pushed back her chair. "Save my place. I'll be back."

"You'd better be," Mike growled, giving her his best fierce look. "We've got a date, remember?"

"Then you'd rather I wouldn't set out the desserts?"

Mike pondered that for a moment and then he grinned. "I didn't say that. I just don't want you to forget you're going home with me."

"Right." Hannah answered his grin with one of her own and headed for the kitchen. Then she realized what Mike had said and came dangerously close to stopping in her tracks. Going home with him? That hadn't been discussed or decided. It hadn't even been mentioned before this! Of course it could have been a figure of speech that meant Hannah shouldn't forget that they were leaving the community center together.

"Oh, boy!" Hannah breathed, startling a teenager who was

carrying a trombone case toward the alcove by the cloak-room.

"Excuse me, Miss Swensen?" he said, phrasing it as a question.

Hannah smiled, more amused than embarrassed. "Just talking to myself. It's something people do when they get old."

"But you're not old!"

"Thank you," Hannah said, rewarding him with a smile. She'd have to ask Kirby the trombone player's name. Not only was he cute with his curly blond hair and runner's physique, he had the gift of saying the right thing at the right time, something Bridget Murphy would call blarney. This boy could go far.

Several people stopped Hannah on her way and she ended up answering questions about such diverse things as what next Friday's pie was going to be, to who she thought should play Santa at the Lake Eden Children's Christmas Party. She was just passing the alcove where the jazz ensemble had set up, when one of the students called her name.

"Miss Swensen?" It was Beth Halvorsen, the flute player they'd so sorely missed at the Fourth of July parade.

"Hi, Beth." Hannah reacted to the worried expression on Beth's face. "What's wrong?"

"Mr. Welles isn't here yet, and it's almost time for us to start playing. Do you know where he is?"

"Sorry, Beth. I haven't seen him. Can't you just start playing without him?"

"No way, Miss Swensen. Mr. Welles is filling in for our regular drummer, and we'd sound awful without percussion."

Hannah caught movement out of the corner of her eye and she turned to see Kirby Welles rushing up.

"Sorry, I got held up," the bandleader apologized to his ensemble. "Are you ready to play?"

Everyone nodded, including the trombone player Hannah had found so personable. She gave them a wave and headed off to the kitchen as the strains of "We Wish You a Merry Christmas" followed her. The music was perfectly audible, but not too loud to impede conversation. In other words, it was perfect for a dinner party. Hannah resolved to tell Ken Purvis, Jordan High's principal, that Kirby's jazz ensemble was perfect for the occasion.

"Took you long enough," Edna grumbled when Hannah came through the kitchen doorway. "We've got a crisis here."

"What?" Hannah asked, feeling her heart rate gear up to what she thought was crisis mode.

"It's not on the table!"

"What's not on the table?"

"Your mother's cake knife!" Edna wailed, reaching out to grab Hannah's arm. "It's missing, and I can't find it anywhere!"

Chapter Nine

Hannah groaned as Edna's words sank in. "Mother's cake knife is missing?"

"That's what I said."

"And you looked on the dessert table?"

"That's what I said, too!"

"All right. Don't panic. It's got to be here somewhere."

"Where? I looked everywhere!"

"Take a deep breath and let it out slowly," Hannah advised, taking a moment to do exactly that. "When is the last time you saw it?"

Edna did exactly what Hannah said, inhaling and exhaling slowly. It was proof of how upset she was, since Edna rarely took anyone's advice about anything. "It was on the dessert table when I carried out the second crock of meatballs. I remember thinking how pretty it looked under the lights."

Hannah glanced at the elaborately carved wooden container on the kitchen counter. "Maybe someone put it back in the chest?"

"Nope. I checked that right off. That box is as empty as Redeemer Lutheran on the Sunday after Jordan High's homecoming game."

Hannah bit back a laugh at Edna's description. It was true that most people celebrated a bit too much on homecoming weekend and not that many had the urge to get up early on Sunday morning and make it to church.

"I'm sure you're right, but . . . I just have to check for myself." Hannah walked over to the box and raised the lid. It was empty, just as Edna had said. "Sorry, Edna."

"That's all right. I checked it twice myself."

Both women leaned up against the counter to think about the seemingly insurmountable problem at hand. They were so quiet Hannah could hear the kitchen clock ticking as the minute hand moved up a notch.

"Do you think someone could have used it for something else?" Hannah finally asked, after another notch had clicked off. "I mean, picture this . . . someone in the buffet line needs another knife for the turkey, or whatever. They're about to go back to the kitchen to get one when they notice Mother's knife on the dessert table. So they take it and use it and . . ."

"And they leave it on the entrée table!" Edna interrupted, somehow managing to look doubtful and hopeful at the same time.

"Exactly right. It could have happened that way."

"That means we'd better check the other buffet tables. I don't want your mother to know it's missing until we know for sure. Will you do it . . . um . . . you know . . ."

"Surreptitiously?" Hannah supplied the word she thought Edna was trying to say.

"That's exactly what I mean. I'm so upset, I couldn't think of the polite word for sneaky."

A cake knife the size and commanding presence of her mother's antique silver heirloom couldn't hide for long on any of the other tables. Just to be sure, Hannah lifted platters and checked under bowls and centerpieces, but she really hadn't expected to find it, and she wasn't surprised when it didn't turn up.

"You didn't find it," Edna said, reading Hannah's expression when she returned to the kitchen.

"I'm afraid I didn't."

"Your mother's going to kill me. You know that, don't you? We've just got to find it before she realizes that it's missing." Edna sat down on a kitchen stool, thought for a moment, and raised her head to look at Hannah. "Do you think someone stole it?"

"In Lake Eden?"

"You're right. Nobody here would do something like that."

"Chances are it's just misplaced, and that means it has to be around here somewhere. Why don't you take a look to see if anything on the tables needs replenishing? I'll stay in here and go through every cupboard and drawer in this kitchen."

"Good idea," Edna said, taking the top from a huge Tupperware container shaped like a dress box. "While I was out there looking for the cake knife, I noticed that some of your Christmas cookies were gone. Can't say as I blame the folks that took 'em early. Your cookies are prettier than the ones they show in the magazines."

"The pretty part is Lisa's doing. She decorated them. All I did was bake them."

"They're tasty, too. Sweet and crunchy, with the taste of butter in every bite."

"You ate one?" Hannah was surprised. When Edna managed a potluck dinner, she waited to eat until they'd carried the food back into the kitchen. And unlike Hannah, who sometimes couldn't resist sampling something yummy, Edna wasn't the type of person to eat dessert first.

"It was a Santa with one leg broken off. If I'd put it on the platter that way, sure and shootin' some child would have had nightmares about it." Edna headed for the door, but she turned back for a final comment. "I've got a bad feeling about this, but I'm going to keep my fingers crossed."

Once Edna had left to restock the cookie platter, Hannah searched systematically, determined to go through every cupboard and drawer. Edna buzzed in and out, putting out more food where it was needed. Then she began to get out the rest of the desserts and prepare them for presentation.

Hannah met Edna's eyes several times while the older woman was cutting cakes and pies in even slices and arranging platters of cookies and cookie bars. Each time Edna's eyebrows elevated in a question, Hannah shook her head. The missing cake knife was still missing, and Hannah's hope that she'd find it stuck away in a drawer or mixed in with other serving implements was dwindling faster than an ice cube in a mug of steaming hot coffee.

It took awhile, but at last Hannah knew she'd left no metaphorical stone unturned. She'd been so thorough, she would have sworn on a stack of Bibles that her mother's cake knife was not in the Lake Eden Community Center kitchen. Hannah headed for a stool at one of the center work islands. She had to tell Delores the bad news before she discovered it for herself. There was no way Hannah would shirk that duty, but she did need time to think of a way to phrase the message that wouldn't immediately result in the death of the messenger.

Delivering bad news had never been one of her skills. Hannah tended to blurt things out, a bit like jerking a bandage from a wound rather than inching the tape off. She didn't think she was quite as outspoken as Edna, but people weren't that far wrong when they accused her of having no tact.

The pantry door was open slightly and Hannah noticed that the light was on. She hadn't bothered to check the pantry, because she'd assumed that no one had used it. Since it was a potluck dinner, everyone had brought in fully cooked dishes. Edna and her helpers had simply kept things warm or chilled, depending on the dish, until it was time to serve.

Hannah's mind spun, imagining a possible scenario. Someone who'd brought in a dessert suddenly realized they'd forgotten powdered sugar to sprinkle over the top. Rather than rush home to get it, the frantic cook stepped into the community center pantry hoping to borrow some. Had that person also picked up the antique cake knife, intending to use it to slice her dessert? It was certainly possible . . . perhaps unlikely, but still possible.

Rising quickly, Hannah hurried to the pantry and opened the door. A quick scan of the neatly stocked shelves disproved the theory that had seemed plausible only moments ago. The cake knife was nowhere in sight. Hannah was about to turn off the light and step back out into the kitchen when she noticed that the dead bolt on the door to the parking lot wasn't locked.

Hannah opened the door and took a step outside. Through the blowing snow, she could see the icy hulks of parked cars. This was the delivery entrance and since it opened onto the parking lot, it would be a perfect escape route for a thief. If someone really had stolen her mother's antique knife and ducked out to the parking lot through this door, they'd be long gone by now.

A blast of cold wind carrying icy needles of snow made her shiver. Hannah was about to step back into the warmth of the pantry when she noticed something bulky on the ground between two of the parked cars. It looked furry, like some sort of animal, but it was too small for a bear, and too large for a dog.

Curiosity trickled, gathered force, and grew into a mighty waterfall. There was no way Hannah could turn around and go back inside without finding out what kind of animal was in the parking lot. She headed out at a trot, glad that she was wearing her all-purpose footwear, the moosehide moccasin boots that were so politically incorrect with people who'd never even seen a moose . . . or smelled one, for that matter.

Hannah's sweater was dusted with flakes of snow by the time she got close enough to see. She bent over to examine the large lump of fur, and reached out to steady herself on the nearest car. The animal she thought she'd seen had been made into an expensive fur coat that Martin's new wife was wearing. The only other animal in sight was the reindeer sugar cookie that was broken near Brandi's feet, along with the pieces of a Christmas tree cookie, and a bell decorated in red and green icing. Brandi must have taken several cookies from the dessert table and come out here to eat them. The big question was, did she also take the antique cake knife?

Hoping that she'd just slipped and fallen, Hannah reached down to tap Brandi on the shoulder. "Brandi? Do you need help getting up?"

There was no answer and Hannah began to frown. This didn't look good. "Brandi?" she called out again, shaking her a little harder and wondering if she should go for help. The former dancer wasn't moving, but she could be faking it. If Hannah left her alone and Brandi had the cake knife, she might make a run for it with the valuable antique.

Hannah knew that it was dangerous to move someone who had undetermined injuries. Accident victims had died from the ministrations of well-meaning bystanders who had tried to move them without backboards and stabilizing collars. Hannah certainly wouldn't risk moving Brandi, but she'd taken a first aid class in college and she knew there was a pulse point just under the jawbone on the side of a person's neck.

The collar of Brandi's coat was in the way and Hannah pushed it back. This caused the coat to fall open and Hannah gave a strangled gulp as she caught sight of Brandi's chest.

Hannah felt for a pulse, even though her rational mind told her it was useless. No one could live with a wound that deep. She'd just straightened up, dizzy and slightly sick to her stomach at the sight of the blood that had been soaked up by the expensive fur, when the pantry door banged open and she heard Edna's voice.

"Hannah? Are you out there?"

"I'm here."

"Did you find the knife?"

Hannah glanced down at her mother's valuable antique knife, buried to the hilt in Brandi's too-perfectly-proportioned-to-be-natural chest. "I found it."

"Thank the Lord," Edna shouted out gratefully. "Bring it here before your mother realizes it's missing."

Hannah considered that for a moment. The urge to jerk the knife out of Brandi's chest and head for the kitchen at a run was strong. But equally strong was the awareness of her civic duty. Brandi didn't stab herself, and that meant murder. And disturbing a crime scene by removing the murder weapon was a big no-no. "Sorry, Edna . . . I can't bring it in."

"Why not?"

"Because Brandi's got it." And with that said, Hannah turned and headed back to the kitchen to explain.

Chapter Ten

Once she'd told Edna what had happened and sworn her to secrecy, Hannah went back into the banquet room and tapped Mike on the shoulder.

"Hi, Hannah," Mike said, smiling up at her. "How are the desserts coming?"

"The desserts are fine. The dessert knife isn't. You need to come with me. There's something you have to know."

"Now?" Mike asked, looking down longingly at his helping of Sauerbraten.

"Right now," Hannah said, practically dragging him from his chair. "I'll have Edna save your plate for you. Take your jacket."

"We're going outside?"

"Just smile, Mike. I don't want anyone to think there's something wrong."

"But there *is* something wrong?"

"Oh, yes," Hannah confirmed it, leading him into the kitchen and handing his plate to Edna. "Will you save this for Mike? And can I borrow your parka?"

" 'Course," Edna said, slipping Mike's plate into the microwave and gesturing toward the stool that held her parka.

"Another murder in the pantry?" Mike asked, as Hannah opened the pantry door.

"No."

"Good! For a second there, I thought history was repeating itself. So there's no dead body this time?"

"I didn't say that." Hannah opened the delivery door and grabbed Mike's arm. "There's a dead body, but this time it's in the parking lot."

Things moved fast once Mike took charge of the crime scene. He used Hannah as an errand girl, sending her in for Doc Knight, who was just finishing a double helping of Esther's Meatloaf.

Doc took his time examining the body, and then he looked up at Mike. "Okay. I'm through for now."

"Time of death?" Mike asked, flipping open his notebook.

"I'd say no longer than thirty minutes ago, give or take ten."

"Is it murder?" Hannah asked, moving slightly closer. She'd been standing as far away as she could while Doc examined Brandi's body.

Doc looked over at her and raised his eyebrows. "Well, it's certainly not a suicide."

"Why's that?"

"A woman who intends to kill herself doesn't usually choose to do it with an antique cake knife on the coldest night of the year in a parking lot."

"Too bad it's snowing," Mike said, staring down at the drift that was beginning to pile up around Brandi's body. "Any tracks the killer left are long gone by now. At least we know one thing for certain."

"What's that?" Doc Knight asked.

"The killer went back inside after he stabbed Brandi."

Hannah's jaw dropped open for a second and then she closed it with an audible clack. "How do you know *that?*"

"There's no way anybody drove over that snowdrift at the

exit. It's just too deep. And if they'd tried to walk over it, they would have sunk down to their eyeballs. I'm almost positive that nobody has come or gone from this lot since I got back."

"But how do you know for certain that Brandi was alive when you got back here?" Hannah posed the important question.

"I was looking around for you and I noticed her."

Hannah wasn't sure whether she should be flattered, or angry. Mike had just admitted he'd been looking for her, but he'd noticed Brandi. Was that a plus or a minus in the grand scheme of things?

"Uh-oh," Doc Knight said, reaching for the cell phone in his pocket. "They weren't supposed to call me unless it was an emergency."

Hannah and Mike stood there trying to pretend they weren't listening as Doc Knight took the call. Of course they couldn't help but hear what he said. Other than the occasional whoosh as the wind picked up and blew snow against the parked cars, nothing else was happening out here in the parking lot.

"Appendectomy," Doc said, returning his phone to his pocket. "I've got to go. Do you want me to send my paramedics for the body?"

"Yes," Mike said. "We'll preserve the crime scene until they get here."

"I'll send them just as soon as I get back to the hospital. I don't want her to freeze before the autopsy."

Hannah shuddered and it wasn't from the cold. Even though she knew that Brandi was dead, she'd prefer not to think about her freezing.

"Thanks, Doc," Mike reached out to clap him on the shoulder. "You're not parked back here, are you?"

"I double-parked in front. I figured that if I had to get out, it would be a medical emergency. And it is. Gonna give me a ticket?"

"No way," Mike said, deferring to the Winnetka County coroner. "You've got a county exempt placard on your dash. That entitles you to park wherever you want."

"But I don't park illegally unless I really need to. That would be misusing the power of the office. I take it you want me to keep mum about what happened out here?"

"That would be best until I get it sorted out. Do you want me to come with you to make sure your car starts? Hannah can stay here with the body."

Hannah bit her tongue so she wouldn't say anything. There was no way she wanted to stay here with the body, but it was pretty clear she didn't get a vote.

"No, that's all right. My truck can get through just about anything, and I've got my cell phone if I run into trouble. Earl Flensburg's on call with his tow truck, and he'll come right out to get me."

Hannah waited until Doc Knight had left, and then she turned to Mike. "Would you really have made me stay out here with . . . with her? All by myself?"

"Why not?" Mike asked, clearly puzzled. "You were out here with her before. And you were by yourself."

"I know, but I didn't know she was dead then. It's different when you know they're dead."

"I'll take your word for it," Mike said, but he put his arm around her shoulders and gave her a little squeeze. "Sorry, Hannah. Sometimes I forget you're not one of the guys."

The arm around the shoulders was nice, and the squeeze was nice. But forgetting she was a woman wasn't nice at all. Still, two out of three wasn't that horrible, and Hannah snuggled a little closer. "Is there anything I can do to help you?"

"You bet. Could you go back inside and tell Rick Murphy to come out here?"

"Sure." Hannah shoved her hands in Edna's parka pockets. The wind was starting to blow harder and her fingers felt numb. "Anything else?"

"Find Lonnie and put him in charge of securing the perimeter, one guard for every outside door. No one leaves, not without running it past me."

"Got it," Hannah said, resisting the urge to salute.

"Actually . . . nobody should leave anyway."

"Why not?"

"The wind's picking up. This could turn into a real blizzard and it's just not safe. Some of these folks have a long ways to go on country roads."

"You're right," Hannah said. Strong winds whipping up snow from flat stretches of landscape could make the roads impassible in the space of a few minutes. The snow could swirl so fiercely, a driver could lose sight of the road. Sense of direction was the next thing to go, and that was when people ended up in the ditch. "I'll tell Lonnie not to let anyone leave. Anything else?"

"I want only the essential people to know that Brandi's dead. If the killer doesn't know that her body's been found, he may do or say something to give himself away."

"You mean . . . you really think the killer's still here, sitting around waiting for dessert?!"

"I'm almost positive he is."

"But how do you know he wasn't parked in front? He could have waltzed back inside, made some excuse about having to leave early, and gone out through the front door as big as you please."

"Maybe, but when I came back in after seeing Kurt on his way, I noticed that Lisa and Herb were sitting at a table in the lobby eating their dinner. They would have seen anyone who left."

"Do you want me to ask them?"

"Yes."

"Okay. How about Bill? Are you going to try to contact him?"

"Of course. I'll call dispatch and they'll find him." Mike

took his arm from Hannah's shoulder and turned her to face him. "Now do you want to go inside and take care of all those things for me? Or have you changed your mind and do you want to stay here with . . ."

"I'm going, I'm going," Hannah said, heading for the kitchen door at a pace that would have done a runner proud.

"Excuse me, Lonnie." Hannah tapped him on the shoulder. "Could I speak to you for a minute? You too, Rick."

Once she'd pulled the Murphy deputies to the side and delivered Mike's messages, Rick headed out to the parking lot to relieve his superior, and Lonnie quickly found enough personnel to man the exits. Since Lonnie had decided to take the front door himself, Hannah headed up the stairs with him to quiz Herb and Lisa about anyone who'd gone out or come in.

"Just Mike and Kurt Howe," Lisa responded to Hannah's question. "Kurt drove away, Mike took his parking spot, and then he came back in."

"And Doc Knight," Herb reminded her. "He left about ten minutes ago. What's going on, Hannah? Lonnie's trying to be discreet about it, but I can tell he's guarding the front door."

Hannah thought about it for a moment and came to a decision. Mike had said to tell only the essential people and as far as Hannah was concerned, Lisa and Herb were essential. Besides, Herb was a sworn law enforcement officer. It didn't matter that it was only parking enforcement. Herb could still help in a situation like this.

"It's murder," Hannah said, motioning them closer so that she could tell them all about it.

* * *

Less than ten minutes later, everything was under control. All of the exits were staffed with deputies, Herb had gone to find Mike to see if there was anything he could do to help, and Hannah and Lisa had helped Edna carry out the last few desserts. Norman had taken pictures and Hannah was about to give Mayor Bascomb the okay to invite people for dessert, when she saw Mike make a beeline for the mayor.

Mike and Mayor Bascomb conferred for long moments. Then the mayor walked over to Kirby Welles and the jazz ensemble stopped playing abruptly, right in the middle of "The First Noel."

"Ladies and gentlemen," Mayor Bascomb sounded very serious as he took the mike and addressed the crowd. "I've got some news you're not going to like."

Lisa looked surprised as she nudged Hannah. "I thought you said Mike didn't want to tell anyone."

"That's what he said, but maybe he changed his mind."

Mayor Bascomb looked around the room, and a grin spread over his face. "I know how tough this is going to be, but I'm afraid we're stuck here for at least a couple more hours, maybe longer, with all this good food and music."

There were several hoots of laughter from various tables and the mayor acknowledged them with a smile. "It's a good thing we're having fun in here, because it's not fun outside. The national weather service is predicting a blizzard and I believe they're right, for once. I was just outside, and the wind nearly knocked a big guy like me off his feet."

Laughter rang out from several tables again. It was no wonder that Mayor Bascomb was serving his fourth term. He really knew how to talk to a crowd.

"Anyway, you're a lot safer here than you would be out on the roads, and the community center can accommodate everyone until the winds die down and it's safe to go home. If you absolutely must leave, tell me or one of the sheriff's deputies

I've stationed at the doors, and we'll arrange for a snowplow escort to get you wherever you need to go. Barring an emergency, I want everyone to sit tight. I value each and every person here, and a winter storm as bad as this one isn't anything to fool with."

Many heads nodded at the mayor's last statement. Minnesotans who'd survived other blizzards weren't about to take the chance of getting caught alone and exposed to the elements.

"While we're waiting for the weather to clear, Janice Cox is going to open Kiddie Korner for the little ones. She's got games, books, and toys. She's even got blankets and cots, if this ends up being a long night. I think we've got some high school student aides here tonight, don't we?"

There was a cheer from a table near the back where a crowd of Lake Eden teenagers were sitting together.

"I thought so! Well, this is your big chance to get some more on-the-job training. If some of you want to help Janice entertain the kids, she says she'd appreciate it."

Hannah wasn't surprised when the table emptied and a dozen teenagers headed over to the stairs where Janice was waiting. Many Lake Eden kids grew up taking care of younger siblings, and they enjoyed helping.

"Herb Beeseman checked and the cable's out, but if some of you older kids want to watch a movie, there's a whole shelf of them up in the senior center. And down here, we'll have dancing and"—Mayor Bascomb paused and let the tension build until everyone was leaning forward, just waiting for the word—"dessert! And speaking of dessert, Edna wants me to read you this list. It says, Candied Pecans, Christmas Date Cake, Poppy Seed Cake, Chocolate Fruitcake, Lady Hermoine's Chocolate Sunshine Cake, Coconut Green Pie, Pumpkin Pie for a Thanksgiving Crowd, Pecan Pie for a Holiday Crowd . . . . Do I need to go on?"

"No!" several people shouted in unison, and laughter filled the air.

"Well, I *could* go on. I haven't even started in on the cookies, and we've got at least a half-dozen different kinds. And for those who want to be healthy, there's a whole box of oranges that were shipped here from California with a cluster of kumquats on top. You know what a kumquat is?"

The no's outnumbered the yes's and Hannah could understand that. A kumquat was rather exotic, and not many were seen in Minnesota.

"Hannah? Tell them what it is!"

Hannah wanted to tell the mayor to buzz off, but all eyes were on her and she had to answer. "It's a small citrus fruit that's not worth the trouble of peeling. But you should try one and make up your own mind."

Laughter erupted at Hannah's answer, and Mayor Bascomb looked pleased. "Edna says to tell you that the dessert table's all ready. There's enough to feed an army so you can get right up and help yourselves."

"He did a wonderful job!" Lisa breathed, staring at Mayor Bascomb with a mixture of shock and admiration. "I guess I never realized that he was so . . . so . . ."

"Political?"

"Maybe, but what do you mean by that?"

"I mean, he told people that they were locked in and they couldn't go home. And they love him for it."

"I guess that *is* political. But how does he pull that off?"

"Years of practice," Hannah said, and she didn't add, *lying to his wife*. "Come on, Lisa. We need to find Mike and tell him that nobody left while you and Herb were upstairs."

"Hannah!" Delores called out, swooping down on her eldest daughter.

"Hello, Mother. Where's Winthrop?"

"In the *necessary*, dear. Need I say more to someone who's familiar with Regency England?"

It took a moment for the memory banks to attain warp speed, but then Hannah remembered that a *necessary* in

Regency England was a men's room in today's terms. "Okay, Mother. I understand."

"Did you use the knife to cut your cake, dear?"

"I certainly did," Hannah said truthfully, not mentioning that it had also been used to cut certain parts of Brandi's anatomy. "Norman took pictures and Kurt wants to use one in the cookbook."

"Wonderful! Winthrop will be so proud."

Hannah's mind did a quick backstep. "You mean Winthrop's family has something to do with the cake knife?"

"No, it's just that it's old English, and Winthrop reveres things that are old English."

"Right," Hannah said, wondering why, if that were true, Winthrop wasn't involved with the duchess of someplace-or-other, rather than her mother.

"So do you think we could leave soon, dear? I know what Ricky Ticky said," Delores used the nickname she'd given Mayor Bascomb the summer she'd been his babysitter, "but it's not really that serious, is it?"

"It's that serious."

"You mean . . . they won't even let us go home?"

Hannah shook her head. And all the while she was asking herself, *Where's home? Would that be Mother's place? Or Winthrop's?* "You can't leave, Mother. I'd really worry if you did."

"You would?" Delores looked pleased.

"Oh, yes," Hannah gave her heartfelt response. Of course she'd worry, but not about the blizzard. She'd be worrying about Winthrop.

"Well . . . I guess we'll just stay then. Winthrop said he wanted to taste Lady Hermoine's cake. And perhaps we can get Kirby to play something a little more upbeat for dancing."

Lisa waited until Delores was far enough away and then she turned to Hannah. "So . . . ? Should I tell Herb to start heating up the tar? And do you want me to start plucking birds for feathers?"

"Not quite yet. I'm tempted, but he could be exactly what he says he is, an English lord on vacation."

"But you don't think he is."

"No. But I'm naturally protective when it comes to my mother. And I'm naturally paranoid by nature. So . . . Winthrop could be okay, but I'll bet the farm that he isn't."

Chapter
Eleven

"Just a second, Hannah!"

Hannah turned to see Martin Dubinski rushing up to her. She started to smile politely, but then thought better of it. If Mike had informed him of Brandi's death, it wouldn't be appropriate to smile. On the other hand, if Mike hadn't told him, Hannah didn't want to alert Martin that anything was wrong. Hannah settled for what she hoped was a pleasant and totally inexpressive expression, the same one worn by the teddy bear she'd lugged around as a child.

"I'm so glad I found you," Martin said, smiling broadly. "I didn't want to say anything in front of Brandi, but thank you for putting Shirley's cake in the cookbook. It was her mother's favorite recipe, and she passed it on to Shirley."

"It's a good cake," Hannah said, taking note of Martin's smile. If he was smiling, Mike hadn't gotten to him yet, and it was appropriate for her to smile back.

"Have you seen Brandi?"

The smile Hannah had just decided to wear slipped alarmingly before she could stop it. Of course she'd seen Brandi, but she'd rather not remember that. And she didn't want to admit that anything was wrong until Mike had spoken with the husband of the dearly departed.

"I'm really worried about her. She went to the ladies' room

an hour ago, and I haven't seen her since. I even asked Kate Maschler to go in and see if she was okay, but Brandi wasn't there."

Hannah sighed, accepting the inevitable. Since she'd stumbled into the middle of this mess, she was caught between lying and telling Martin that his new wife was dead. Neither option pleased her, so she'd just have to settle for taking Martin to the room that Mike was using as an office and letting the long arm of the law take charge.

"Have you seen her, Hannah?" Martin asked again.

"I've seen her. Come with me, Martin. I want you to talk to Mike Kingston. He knows exactly where Brandi is now."

Thankfully, the room that Mike was using for his office was only a few steps from the top of the stairs and Hannah was able to successfully dodge questions as she walked Martin down the hall and knocked on the door. Once she'd delivered her lamb to the slaughter, Hannah went in search of Andrea, to see how her heavily pregnant sister was reacting to Bill's absence and the blizzard warnings that were blanketing the state.

"Hi, Hannah," Andrea greeted her. She was sitting on a chair near the cloakroom, eating a piece of Chocolate Fruitcake. "This cake is absolutely delicious. I think it's my very favorite dessert."

"Glad to hear it. You're feeling all right, aren't you?"

"Just fine."

"And you're not nervous about Bill and the blizzard?"

"Why should I be? He's got a cell phone, a car phone, and a radio to connect him to dispatch. If he goes in the ditch on the way here, he'll have plenty of help getting out."

"You're right, and I'm glad you're not worried. Since Doc Knight took you off restriction, do you feel like doing a little investigating?"

"Investigating?" Andrea's eyes widened. "You mean there was a murder?"

"Yes."

"Right here at the party?"

"Yes."

"Who got killed?"

"Brandi."

"Where? How?"

Hannah knew her answer would sound as if they were playing a game of *Clue,* but she gave it anyway. "In the parking lot with Mother's antique cake knife."

"Good thing I'm eating chocolate." Andrea looked a little sick, but that didn't stop her from popping the last bite into her mouth. "I have a feeling I'm going to need all the energy I can get. Have you told Mother?"

"No."

"Are you going to?"

"Not just now. Mike wants only the essential people to know that Brandi's dead."

"I'm essential?" Andrea looked pleased when Hannah nodded. "Okay, you can count on me to do whatever you need."

"Your napkin."

"What?"

"I need something to write on."

"Oh. Sure."

Hannah took the paper napkin that Andrea offered and flipped it open to write on the inside, where it was free of cherubic angels with halos floating in a star-studded sky. She retrieved the pen she'd found in the kitchen and stuck behind her ear, and used the wall as a desk. "Okay. The first thing we need to figure out is who might want to kill Brandi, and why."

"You mean besides Shirley? And Laura Jorgensen, because they're both jealous?"

"Yes." Hannah jotted down their names.

"Okay, there's Martin's mother. From what I heard, Babs didn't approve of Brandi, but I'm not sure that's a strong enough motive for murder."

"I'll put her on the list anyway. Let's try to think of something less obvious. This could be the work of someone from Brandi's past, or some Lake Eden person she knew that we don't know she knew."

"Huh?" Andrea looked mystified.

"Maybe someone from Lake Eden went to Vegas and met her there. And maybe they didn't like the fact she married Martin," Hannah suggested, thinking of Mayor Bascomb.

"Got it. It's jealousy again."

"A very powerful motive," Hannah reminded her. "Other than the fact every woman here wanted to kill Brandi for looking so gorgeous, there have to be other motives. You talked to Brandi and Martin for at least a half hour before I came over to their table. Did you learn anything important about her?"

"I certainly did! Brandi's mink coat wasn't just any old mink. It was a Blackglama ranch mink stroller."

"Stroller?"

"That's a coat that comes to the knees. It's what Mother used to call a car coat. And the price tag was twenty-two point five, not just twenty-two. Do you think someone killed her for her coat?"

"If they did, something scared them off before they could take it. Brandi was still wearing it when I found her and that's why I didn't see blood in the snow. The lining of the coat soaked it up."

Andrea's face turned pale and Hannah reached out to steady her. "Are you all right?"

"I think so. I'm just sick about it, that's all."

"I'm sorry I was so descriptive. I shouldn't have mentioned that part about the lining."

"It's not that. I was just thinking about what a waste it is. Martin probably couldn't afford that coat in the first place and now he can't even sell it back to the furrier." Andrea stopped and looked thoughtful. "I wonder if a really good dry cleaner could get out Brandi's blood."

"Maybe. Forget about the coat. When you were talking to Brandi and Martin, did you learn anything personal about her?"

Andrea thought about that for a moment and then she shook her head. "Not really. All she could talk about was how she'd given up her career to marry Martin."

"Did she mention where she worked?"

"No, I was listening for that. She didn't really give me any information at all, not even how old she was. It was like she didn't want anybody to know anything about her."

"That's interesting."

"That's what I thought. It was almost like she was in the witness protection program, or something like that. She just didn't say anything about her background. She did tell me all about their wedding, though. An Elvis look-alike performed the ceremony, and they did it at three in the morning at some wedding chapel on the Strip."

"Do you remember the name of the chapel?"

"I don't think she mentioned it. She just talked about how good the minister's Southern accent was and how much he sounded like the real Elvis when he got out his guitar and sang *Love Me Tender* in honor of their marriage."

"The theme song from *Titanic* would have been more appropriate," Hannah muttered, and immediately felt mean for saying it. Brandi might have been an opportunistic stripper who'd latched onto Martin for what she could get, but she certainly hadn't deserved to die.

"So what do you want me to do first?"

Andrea's question brought Hannah back to the here and now. "Will you try to find Shirley Dubinski? I really need to talk to her. Just give me the high sign when you do and I'll come over to you."

"You don't want me to tell her about Brandi, do you?"

"Absolutely not. Mike said to keep it under wraps. He's hoping that the killer will say or do something incriminating."

The color fled from Andrea's cheeks. "You mean . . . Mike thinks the killer's still here?"

"Yes. That's why it's so important to be on our toes."

"I will be . . . at least metaphorically," Andrea said, levering herself out of the chair.

"You mean figuratively."

"Whatever. I'll go look for Shirley, but first I'm going to get another helping of dessert. I have a feeling I'm going to need all the chocolate I can get."

With Andrea off locating Shirley, Hannah looked around for Michelle. She found her youngest sister sitting at the table that Lonnie had recently vacated.

Michelle stood up to greet her and whispered in Hannah's ear, "Murder?"

"How do *you* know?"

"Lonnie's upstairs guarding the front entrance, Mike's talking to people in the room down the hall with the door closed, and every time I look around for you, you're either deep in conversation with Andrea, or you're running around like a chicken with your head cut off."

"It's true I was talking to Andrea, but I'm not running around like a chicken with its head cut off."

"Yes, you are."

"No, I'm . . . well, maybe I am," Hannah conceded. "Do you want to help us investigate?"

"Of course I do. Who got killed?"

"Brandi. Did you get to talk to her?"

"Right after I left Mother and Winthrop. And we need to talk about him later. Anyway, I got over to Martin and Brandi's table just as she was excusing herself to go to the ladies' room."

"And you went along?"

"Of course. You know how that goes here in Minnesota . . . you can't go alone."

"I know," Hannah frowned slightly. She'd never understood why women had to go into the ladies' room in pairs, but that's the way it was in the Midwest.

"Brandi was talkative once we got away from Martin and the other people at the table."

"What did she say?"

"A lot. She married Martin only five hours after she met him, and she grew up not very far from here."

Hannah appropriated someone's fairly clean napkin, turned it wrong side out so she didn't have to write around the garlands of holly, and grabbed the pen she'd stuck behind her ear. "Did Brandi say where?"

"No, but she remembered the Quick Stop when it was still a bar and she said she wished the Tri-County Mall had been built when she was living here."

"Anything else?"

"Yes. Brandi's real name is Mary."

"Mary what?"

"She didn't say. All she told me was that she ran away from home when she was sixteen, hitched a ride to Vegas with a trucker who was driving straight through, and ended up living with an older guy who ran a tattoo parlor until she landed her job dancing."

"Anything else?" Hannah asked. It seemed that Michelle had inherited the family trait of being able to get information from a stone.

"She told me a lot. Do you want to know what Brandi's first roommate talked her into piercing?"

"I don't think so," Hannah answered quickly. "I think I could live a very long time without that particular information."

"That's probably best. But Brandi was very forthcoming—even showed me her tattoos—probably because I complimented her on her dress."

"That was smart," Hannah said, giving her sister a smile.

"It was just that she seemed to want to talk and I was non-threatening. She said she'd forgotten what small towns were like, how boring it was because there wasn't anything to do at night, and how everybody knew everybody else's business."

"That's all true. What else did she say?"

"She was upset because she had a fight with Martin on the way to the community center."

Hannah readied her pen. This could be pay dirt. "Do you know what the fight was about?"

"Yes. Brandi wanted to wear her engagement ring tonight to show it off, and Martin said she shouldn't."

Hannah thought back to when she'd joined Brandi and Martin at the table. Try as she could, she couldn't remember anything about Brandi's engagement ring. "Did you see the ring?"

"You bet, and it was beautiful!"

"Could you be a little more descriptive?" Hannah asked, her pen hovering over the napkin.

Michelle sighed, shrugging slightly. "I'm sorry, Hannah. I really don't know that much about gemstones."

"Just describe it the best you can."

"There was a big green stone in the center and it had what looked to me like diamonds around it." Michelle looked up, meeting Hannah's eyes. "Do you want to know why Martin didn't want Brandi to wear it?"

"Of course I do."

"Well . . . Martin was afraid that people would think she was showing off if they saw Brandi in her fur coat *and* an expensive engagement ring."

Hannah thought about that for a moment and then she refolded the napkin, stuck it in her sweater pocket, and perched the pen behind her ear. "Okay. I think you ought to go upstairs and tell Mike what you learned from Brandi."

"Are you kidding?" Michelle looked shocked. "What's

going on, Hannah? I thought you liked to keep the results of your questioning to yourself."

"I do . . . usually. But it's different tonight. Mike's really short-handed and I want to help him."

"Okay, if you say so." Michelle didn't look convinced, but she let Hannah lead her up the stairs and down the hall to the room that Mike had commandeered. "Should I tell him everything?"

"Everything," Hannah said, feeling generous. Shawna Lee was gone, perhaps never to return, and Mike was all hers if she wanted him. She thought she did, at least partially. And unless Mike got high-handed and told her to back off on his investigation, she'd help him all that she could.

Chapter
Twelve

Hannah chatted with a few people while she was waiting for Andrea to find Shirley. She was on a fishing expedition for reactions to Martin's new wife without letting anyone know that Brandi was dead. Most women thought it was a shame that Martin had brought his younger, more glamorous wife to the party, since it was bound to upset Shirley. Most men just shrugged and claimed they really didn't have an opinion, but Hannah saw the gleam in their eyes, and she knew that Brandi had made an impression even if they wouldn't admit it in front of their wives.

"I'm sorry, but I have to run. Andrea's waving at me," Hannah said, spotting Andrea and Shirley behind the dessert table and excusing herself from a conversation with Immelda Giese, Father Coultas's housekeeper. A devout Catholic, Immelda had just told Hannah that despite the tenets of Christian charity, she thought Shirley should scratch Brandi's eyes out.

Hannah arrived at her sister's side slightly winded. People were still hovering in front of the dessert table, and she'd had to excuse herself more times than she could count. She turned to Shirley and smiled. "I'm glad Andrea found you. We really need to talk."

"What about?" Shirley asked.

"Martin. And Brandi."

"Oh," Shirley said, drawing a deep breath and looking a lot like Moishe the last time he'd tipped over his litter box.

"Where were you for the past hour?"

"Do you really need to know?"

"Yes, I do." Hannah put on the most no-nonsense expression she had, the same one she'd used when she'd told Moishe never to tip over his litter box again. It hadn't worked with him, but she hoped it might work with Shirley.

"Well . . ." Shirley clasped her hands together and gave a deep sigh. "I guess I'd better confess."

Andrea gasped, and Hannah gave her a warning glance. "Confess to what, Shirley?"

"I still love Martin and he still loves me. That's why we were together for the past hour. When Brandi went to the ladies' room, he came over to our table and talked to us for a few minutes. Then he said he needed to talk to me in private, and we went to that space under the stairs where they store all the tables and chairs."

"What happened once you got there?" Hannah asked, hoping she wasn't about to hear something risqué.

"Martin said he had a real problem on his hands, that he'd made an awful mistake."

"His marriage?" Andrea asked.

"That's right. He said he was a fool not to realize how much he still loved me. And then he said that just as soon as he could get rid of Brandi, he wanted to marry me again."

"He said he was going to get rid of Brandi?" Hannah repeated, picking up on that ominous phrase.

"Yes, right away. And I said I'd help him any way I could."

"Oh, boy!" Hannah sighed, glancing over at her sister who looked equally distressed. "Did you tell anybody else about the conversation you had with Martin?"

"Of course I didn't. It was private, just between Martin and me. And I knew that if I repeated it, Brandi would be embarrassed. You girls have known me for a long time now. I'm not the sort of person to embarrass anyone in public."

"Actually . . . you couldn't embarrass Brandi if you tried," Hannah said, deciding it was time to cue Shirley in.

"Why not?"

"Because Brandi's dead. She was killed out in the parking lot."

"What?" Shirley gasped, swaying slightly on the heels of her boots and looking completely dumbfounded. She just stared at Hannah for a long moment and then she asked, "Was she in an accident?"

Hannah gestured to Andrea who grabbed Shirley's arm to steady her for the next bout of bad, or good news, depending on your perspective. "It wasn't an accident. Brandi was murdered."

"That's . . . that's horrible! You must have thought I was awful when I was talking about getting rid of her. I meant that Martin was going to divorce her, that's all."

"We were sure that was all you meant," Andrea comforted her.

"Murder," Shirley repeated, her voice quivering slightly as she looked up at Hannah. "When did it happen?"

"Almost an hour ago."

"At least no one can blame Martin! I was with him the whole time except for the past twenty minutes or so."

"Then you alibi each other," Andrea pointed out. "Nobody can suspect you, either."

"Thank goodness for that! Does Martin know yet?"

"I'm sure he does, by now," Hannah said. "I took him up to see Mike about ten minutes ago and he's probably still there. It's that little conference room right next to the library. Why don't you run upstairs and confirm Martin's alibi?"

"I'll do that right now."

"Good. And don't mention it to anyone else on your way

up there. Mike's trying to keep everything under wraps for now."

"I won't, I promise."

Hannah watched Shirley as she threaded through the crowds of people and reached the stairs. True to her word, Shirley hadn't stopped to talk to anyone.

"I guess you can cross her off," Andrea said, "and Martin, too. Who's left?"

Hannah reached into her pocket and pulled out the crumpled napkins she'd been using for notes, instead of her steno pad. "Babs, and Laura Jorgensen. Let's get Babs first."

Babs Dubinski was easy to find. She was still sitting at the same table, drinking coffee and eating a piece of Andrea's Jell-O Cake. "Hello, girls. This is a wonderful cake. It's moist, and it's pretty, too."

"Thank you. It's my recipe." Andrea gave her a big smile, and it was clear she was pleased. "Did you have some of Hannah and Lisa's Christmas Sugar Cookies? I think they're my favorites."

Babs gestured toward a red and green dessert plate with a few cookie crumbs on it. "I had a star. It was delicious."

"I need to ask you some questions," Hannah spoke up before the discussion of desserts could continue.

"You look serious, Hannah. Is there something wrong?"

"I'm afraid so. Can you tell me where you've been for the past hour?"

"Me? Well . . . right here, mostly. Martin came over and talked to us for a while. And then, after he left with Shirley, I went back for some of Kitty's Salmon Loaf. On the way back, I stopped to talk to a couple of people, and then after Mayor Bascomb made his announcement, I got in line at the dessert table. I went to the ladies' room, too. I almost forgot about that. And . . . I really can't account for every minute, Hannah. Is it important?"

"Very important." Hannah took a deep breath and prepared to deliver the news. "Brandi was killed in the parking lot."

"You mean . . . Martin's Brandi?" Babs looked astonished when Hannah confirmed the news. "Was Martin with her? Is he hurt?"

"Martin's fine. He's upstairs talking to Mike Kingston right now, and Shirley's with him. And no, he wasn't with Brandi."

"Thank goodness for that! So what happened?"

"Someone stabbed her with my mother's cake knife."

"Saints preserve us!" Babs fanned herself with her paper napkin. "You mean she was *murdered?*"

"That's what it looks like. Mike's investigating it as a homicide until the results of Doc Knight's tests are in."

Babs fanned a bit faster. "I hope no one thinks that Martin did it!"

"No one does. Martin was talking to Shirley at the time, and that provides them both with an alibi."

Babs looked relieved for a moment, but then she stared hard at Hannah. "So that's why you were asking me all those questions about where I was! You think I did it!"

"We couldn't ignore that possibility," Andrea stepped in, giving Babs her sweetest smile. "Of course, we didn't really believe you could do anything like that, but we couldn't let our fondness for you get in the way of a murder investigation."

Hannah didn't say a word, but her mind was busy forming compliments for her sister. *Good going, Andrea. I wish I could learn to be that smooth. Obviously, the smooth gene passed me by, because I would have grilled her to within an inch of her life.*

"I can understand why you suspected me," Babs said. "It's no secret that I was upset over Martin's marriage."

"Of course you were!" Andrea glanced over at Hannah to let her know she'd taken over the questioning. "What a disappointment that must have been for you! I know how much you like Shirley, and you must have hoped that they'd put aside their differences and get back together for the sake of the boys."

"I did hope that," Babs admitted.

"It must have been terribly painful for you when Martin came back from Las Vegas and announced that he was married."

"It was, especially since I had no warning. He just brought Brandi over to the house and introduced her as his new wife."

"What did you think of her?"

"I tried *not* to think," Babs said candidly. "I was polite to her, of course, but I couldn't help feeling that Martin had made a terrible mistake by marrying her. But they *were* married. And there wasn't anything I could do about that except grit my teeth and make the best of it."

Andrea smiled and shook her head. "I'm not sure I would have been so forgiving in your place. Then you were ready to welcome Brandi into the family?"

"I wouldn't go that far. But I love my son and there's no way I wanted to alienate him. I didn't have to like Brandi, but I did have to get along with her."

Andrea glanced at Hannah, who shook her head. There was nothing more to ask Babs. Andrea expressed their condolences and made the appropriate parting comments. Hannah cautioned Babs not to tell anyone else that Brandi had been killed, and then the two sisters headed their separate ways. Andrea went up to check on Tracey at Kiddie Korner, and Hannah walked over to the Jordan High Jazz Ensemble to give them some well-deserved kudos.

"Nice job," Hannah said to Kirby Welles, who was just getting ready to step off the riser the ensemble was using as a stage.

"Thanks, Hannah. The kids are going to take a break for

dessert. Edna said she'd save some goodies for them in the kitchen."

"Great. I'd hate to think they missed out. I just came over to compliment you on the music and warn you that it could be a long night."

"I know. The blizzard. It's okay, Hannah. We've got a big repertoire."

"I hope it's gigantic." Hannah considered it for a moment and then she decided that Kirby would have to be one of the essential people she told about Brandi's murder. She hopped up on the riser, took his arm, and walked him a couple of steps toward the back of the stage. "I have to talk to you, Kirby."

"Not right now, Hannah. I've got something really important I have to do."

"This is more important. I need you to keep this under your hat, but it's not just the blizzard that's keeping people from leaving. Martin Dubinski's new wife was murdered in the parking lot and Mike thinks the killer's still here."

Kirby's face paled and he reached out to steady himself on a music stand. "You mean . . . Brandi?"

"That's right." Hannah watched as Kirby's hands started to shake. She was no doctor, but Jordan High's music teacher looked as if he were about to collapse. "Are you okay?"

"Shock," Kirby forced the word out between bloodless lips.

"Come on. You'd better sit down." Hannah guided Kirby to a chair and took one for herself. Kirby still looked as if a puff of air from a hair dryer could blow him over. Was he this squeamish at the mere mention of murder? Or did he have a personal reason for being so upset?

"I'm sorry I just blurted it out like that," Hannah apologized, deciding to go for a fake pass and an end run. "I didn't realize that you knew Brandi."

Kirby blinked and a little color began to come back to his face. "I didn't. Not really. Martin introduced us tonight. How was . . ." Kirby gulped and cleared his throat. "How was she killed?"

"She was stabbed with my mother's antique cake knife."

Kirby groaned as if he couldn't help himself, and Hannah went on full alert. His reaction was certainly overboard for someone who claimed he'd met Brandi only an hour or so ago. Rather than trying to couch her question in polite terms, as Andrea or her mother would have done, Hannah just came out with it.

"So . . ." she said, staring at Kirby closely. "Don't you think you overreacted if you just met Brandi tonight?"

Kirby nodded, looking a little embarrassed. "I know I did. It's just that murder is so horrible, especially when it's violent. And she was alive just minutes ago. It made me think of how short life can be, and it scared me silly."

"I understand," Hannah said, even though she wouldn't have bought Kirby's excuse at a fire sale. It was true that most people would be disturbed if someone they'd just met was killed. And some of those people might think about life and how transient it was. But Kirby had come close to fainting before she'd pushed in him down in the chair. No one was that sensitive just *hearing* about the death of someone they barely knew.

"Kirby?" Hannah roused him. It was time to get down to business and pursue his strange reaction later.

"Yes?"

"Can your group play for a couple more hours? Mike needs to keep people distracted while he investigates."

"Of course we can," Kirby said, looking a little calmer now that Hannah had given him a task to do. "Are they going to make an announcement about . . . you know?"

"No. No one except a few select people know about it. That's why we need you to keep this completely under wraps and play for as long as you can. We want people to think that everything is completely normal, except for the weather."

"Got it," Kirby said, nodding sharply. "Don't worry about us, Hannah. I brought extra sheet music just in case. We can play all night, if that's what it takes."

Chapter
Thirteen

Hannah was about to go trolling through the crowded room for her sister when Andrea came up carrying another dessert plate. "This pecan pie of yours is just wonderful! Remember when I was afraid I'd have the baby at Thanksgiving and I wouldn't get to have your pie?"

"I remember."

"Well, I had your pie at Thanksgiving, and now I'm having it again. And I *still* haven't had the baby!"

"No one can hurry nature," Hannah intoned, realizing how pompous that sounded, but unable to take it back.

"Sure they can. If there was a horse here right now, I'd take Lisa's mother's suggestion and ride him around the room until something happened."

"And I'd probably boost you up in the saddle," Hannah said, picturing the scene that would make and exploding in laughter. A scant second later, Andrea began to laugh, too. It was one of those wonderful moments when sisters who were very different happened to be on the same wavelength. When she was able to speak again without sputtering, Hannah said, "While we're waiting for that horse, I've got a question for you. I need to know about Brandi's engagement ring. Michelle saw it, but she couldn't describe it except to say that she thought it looked expensive. Did you notice it?"

"Of course I did! It was gorgeous, and it looked like a really valuable antique."

Hannah grabbed Andrea's napkin, turned it inside out so she could write on a spot that wasn't covered by Santa and his reindeer, and held her pen at the ready. "Okay. Describe it for me."

"It was a square-cut emerald, at least two carats, surrounded by a frame of Tiffany-cut diamonds."

Hannah gave a low whistle. Even though she knew next to nothing about jewelry, the ring Andrea was describing sounded expensive.

"The diamonds were blue-white, a really excellent color, and they had to be at least a half-carat apiece. And the setting was platinum. That's more expensive than gold or silver."

"Okay," Hannah jotted it all down. "Do you have any idea how much a ring like that would cost?"

"Not really, but I'd guess it was worth a lot more than her fur coat. And Brandi and Martin were fighting about it."

"Fighting?" Hannah asked, leaning forward.

"She wanted to wear it and he told her to take it off. They stared each other down for a minute and then she took it off her finger and dropped it in her purse. Is that all you need? I want to go back to the dessert table for some Candied Pecans."

"Hold on, Little Piggy," Hannah said, smiling to show her sister that it was a term of endearment. "Do you have your cell phone with you?"

"Of course I do! I'm a real estate professional."

"Could you help me out and call all the wedding chapels in Las Vegas to find out where Brandi and Martin got married? There's something I need to know."

"Sure. It shouldn't be that hard, especially since I know an Elvis impersonator married them. Once I find the right chapel, what do you want me to ask?"

"Try to get them to tell you what name Brandi used on

the marriage license. Michelle found out that her real first name was Mary, and Brandi let it slip that she grew up not too far from here."

"I knew that had to be a stage name," Andrea gave a little snort. "It was just too cutesy to be real. Brandi Wyen. I mean . . . really! I'll go up to the lobby to call. The reception's better up there."

"Okay, just stick close to Lonnie. Don't forget that there could be a killer in the building."

"I won't forget," Andrea said, looking very serious as she headed up the stairs.

As Hannah approached the dessert table, she noticed that the Candied Pecans were almost gone. Since Andrea was doing her a favor and might miss out on the dessert she wanted, Hannah got in line, grabbed one of the little paper cups Edna had set out, and took some.

"Hey, Hannah?"

Hannah turned around to see Earl Flensburg, the county snowplow and tow truck driver, standing there in his boots and jacket. "Hi, Earl. Since you're here, why don't you get something to eat?"

"That's what Edna said. She's fixing me a plate in the kitchen. But before I can eat, I need to find Mike."

"He's upstairs in the little conference room right next to the library. He's using it as a temporary office."

"Okay. I need to get a paper signed for the paramedics. I plowed out that drift in the parking lot so they could get their rig in, but they can't take . . . you know, what they came to get . . ." Earl's voice faltered, and he cleared his throat noisily. "Heck of a world, huh Hannah? Anyways, they need Mike to sign this release paper."

"I understand." Hannah patted Earl on the back. For a gruff guy who bragged that he'd shot more game than anyone else in the county, he could be surprisingly sensitive when it came to human death.

Earl had just walked up the stairs when Andrea came down. There was a huge smile on her face and Hannah assumed she'd been successful in talking to whoever was on duty at the wedding chapel.

"That was fast!" Hannah met her sister at the bottom of the stairs.

"Of course it was. I just called one of the casinos, spoke to the woman at the desk, and got the number of the wedding chapel with the Elvis impersonator."

"And the person at the chapel told you Brandi's real name?"

Andrea gave Hannah an impudent grin. "Of course. But I'm not going to tell you until you hand over those pecans."

"No problem. They were running low, and I figured I'd better snag some for you."

"Thanks, Hannah. Now all I need is a fresh cup of coffee and a couple of those new cookies you brought."

"Which new cookies? Lisa's Pieces, or Heavenly Tea Cookies?"

Andrea looked surprised. "I didn't know you had two new cookies! This changes everything."

"I'm sure it does. You want one of each?"

"That would be perfect. Could you hurry, Hannah? These nuts won't last me for long. This has got to have something to do with the baby."

"What?"

"The way I've been eating tonight. I'm craving sweets with a vengeance. I've eaten more dessert than I've ever eaten before in my life, but I still want more."

It didn't take Hannah long to fetch the coffee and cookies. "Here you go," she said, putting them down on the table in front of her sister.

"Are these Lisa's Pieces?" Andrea asked, picking up one of the cookies and raising it to her mouth.

"Yes. You promised to tell me. Now, give."

"Minglemurber."

"What?"

"Minglemurber." Andrea shook her head, swallowed twice, and took a sip of coffee. "Sorry about that. That cookie was delicious, by the way. Brandi's real name was Mary Kay Hinklemeyer."

Hannah jotted it down on the inside of the snowflake napkin she'd taken from the dessert table. She held it up so her sister could see. "Spelled like this?"

"That's right. She was twenty-six years old when she married Martin, and her place of birth was . . ."

"Was where?" Hannah asked when Andrea stopped speaking and gave her an impish grin. "Cut it out, Andrea! If you say you want more cookies before you'll tell me, I'll have Mike lock you up for extortion."

Andrea laughed. "I was going to tell you . . . really. I just wanted to draw it out a little and build up the surprise. Mary Kay Hinklemeyer was born in Browerville, Minnesota!"

"Browerville?" Hannah asked, hardly daring to believe her ears. "Now we're getting somewhere! There's got to be someone here who used to live in Browerville, or someone who has relatives in Browerville. They would have known Mary Kay when she was growing up, and they'd probably know the family."

"I'm back!" Michelle announced, rushing up to their table. "I talked to Mike and told him everything that Brandi told me."

"Great. I hoped he appreciated it."

Michelle shrugged. "I don't think so. I was just getting to the part about the ring when he got a call and he told me he'd talk to me later."

Hannah thought about that for a moment. The ring could be important, but Mike didn't seem all that interested. Perhaps he was just snowed under by too much information coming at him at once. She could help. She could go upstairs and tell him that the ring appeared to be a bone of contention between Martin and Brandi, and it could be important. She could also describe it, thanks to Andrea.

"Ready to go back to work?" Hannah asked, noticing that Andrea had eaten both cookies.

"Sure," Andrea said, taking a last gulp of coffee. "That Tea Cookie was great! What do you want us to do?"

"Canvass the room and see if you can find anyone who knew Brandi when she lived in Browerville."

"Browerville?" Michelle looked excited when Hannah nodded. "I know a couple kids who come from there. I can ask. Do we know her last name?"

"Yes, thanks to Andrea. It's Mary Kay Hinklemeyer. Just take the names of everyone who knows the family and we'll question them later."

"Okay," Andrea levered herself to her feet. "What are you going to do?"

"I'm going to beard the lion in his den and tell him that Brandi's engagement ring might be important."

"Yes?"

The voice that barked out when Hannah knocked on the door Mike was using as an office caused her to step back in pure reflex. Mike didn't sound very friendly. "I'm sorry if I'm interrupting, but I need to talk to you."

"Come."

That response wasn't very friendly either, but Hannah shrugged and opened the door. "It's about Brandi's engagement ring. Was it on her body?"

"You don't need to know that."

"Fine. But then you don't need to know what kind of ring it was and what it was worth. And you also don't need to know that Martin and Brandi were fighting about whether she should wear it in public, or not."

"Okay . . . sorry, Hannah." Mike gestured for Hannah to

come in and shut the door. "I shouldn't have yelled at you. I apologize."

"That's okay. I know you're under a lot of pressure." Hannah sat down in the chair in front of the desk. "What do you want to know first?"

"Describe the ring. I'll take notes."

Hannah emptied her pocket of crumpled napkins and found the correct one. "Emerald in the center, at least two carats, perhaps larger. Surrounded by Tiffany-cut diamonds of approximately a half-carat apiece. The setting was platinum. That's very expensive."

"And the total estimated cost?" Mike asked, looking up to meet Hannah's eyes.

"Uh . . ." Hannah took a deep breath and tried to keep her stomach from doing aerial gymnastics. Mike looked tired and haggard, and sexier than any other man on earth. "Andrea saw it, and she estimates close to fifty thousand. Do you think Brandi was killed for her ring?"

"It's possible."

"Then it wasn't on her finger?"

"I didn't say that."

"You didn't have to," Hannah said, giving him a smile. Perhaps it wasn't fair when he was so tired, but she always felt good when she could outwit Mike. "I'll let you know if I hear anything else. And just send someone to get me if you need me for anything."

"I always need you, Hannah." Mike bent over the desktop to touch his lips to hers. "Don't ever think I don't. Now go back and amuse yourself. I've got work to do here."

Hannah headed out the door not sure whether she should be pleased or angry. Mike had said he always needed her, a compliment if she ever heard one. But he'd also told her to go amuse herself because he had work to do, a thinly veiled insult that negated his earlier compliment. Did that mean they were even?

Still debating the scorecard between them, Hannah headed back to the banquet room. As she descended the stairs, she saw Michelle at the bottom waiting for her.

"Good, you're back. I've got something. It's not exactly what you were expecting, but it's something you should know."

"Okay, what?" Hannah asked, leading Michelle over to an unoccupied corner.

"I asked Bertie Straub about the Hinklemeyer family, but Bertie didn't know them. I was about to move on, but then Bertie told me some really interesting gossip. She said Mrs. Bascomb thinks the mayor met Brandi on his last trip to Vegas. Bertie heard them arguing about it. I think it's true, Hannah. They're sitting about as far apart as two people can get at the same table."

"You didn't try to talk to them?"

"No, I thought I should wait and tell you."

"A wise decision," Hannah said. "And while you're a lot more tactful than I am, I think this is a job for Mother."

"Mother?" Michelle sounded shocked.

"Yes, Mother. She used to babysit for Mayor Bascomb, and she'll get the truth out of him."

"You're going to sic Mother on him," Michelle said, looking pleased. "I admire you for thinking of it, Hannah. That's completely diabolical."

Chapter Fourteen

Hannah approached the table with reluctance. She really wasn't looking forward to dealing with Winthrop again, but perhaps she could spirit her mother away for a private talk. "Mother?"

"Why, hello!" Delores called out, greeting Hannah and then reaching out to take Winthrop's hand. "This is quite an experience for Winthrop. He's never been stuck in a blizzard before."

"Right, dear girl." Winthrop patted her hand and then pulled his away. Either he'd read the disapproval in Hannah's eyes, or he was of the opinion that holding hands in public was tacky.

Hannah resisted the urge to tell him that the only way to experience a blizzard was to get out there alone and walk a couple of blocks, and she turned to her mother instead. "Could I see you for a moment, Mother?"

"Of course. Sit down, dear."

"No. I mean . . . I need to see you privately."

Delores frowned slightly. "Whatever it is, you can talk about it in front of Winthrop. We have no secrets from each other."

"Maybe you don't have any secrets from Winthrop, but *I* do."

"That's only as it should be," Winthrop said, and then he turned to Delores. "Go have a little *coze* with your daughter, dear girl. I'll be perfectly fine here."

"Coze?" Hannah repeated, as her mother got up and followed her to an unpopulated spot near the Christmas tree that Andrea had decorated.

"Comfy coze. I know they used the term in Regency England, and I assume it's still in use today. It means an intimate chat. Oh, dear!"

Hannah glanced in the direction her mother was gazing and had all she could do to keep from grinning. The moment Delores had left the table with Hannah, three women had converged on Winthrop. Carrie Rhodes was now seated on one side of him, Bertie Straub was on the other, and Florence Evans had taken the chair directly across from the British lord.

"Sharks in a feeding frenzy," Delores muttered. And then she turned to frown at Hannah as her eldest daughter gave a startled laugh. "Well, they are."

"You could be right." Hannah saw Carrie give Winthrop her sweetest smile, and she pulled her mother around to the other side of the Christmas tree where she wouldn't be distracted.

"What's so important?" Delores asked a bit sharply.

"Murder, Mother."

"Murder?" Delores whirled to face Hannah instead of attempting to see Winthrop and the three women through the branches. "Here?"

"Yes."

Delores rolled her eyes toward the angel at the top of the tree. "Don't tell me you found the body!"

"Shhh!" Hannah cautioned, putting her finger to her lips. "Mike doesn't want anybody to know about it yet."

"You have *got* to stop finding dead people, Hannah! Winthrop's going to get the wrong impression of you."

"Right," Hannah said, biting back several additional comments that would have assured her mother's immediate defection.

"Well, who was it this time?"

"Martin Dubinski's new wife. She was stabbed in the parking lot." Hannah knew that discretion was the better part of valor and she decided not to mention that her mother's antique cake knife was the murder weapon.

"Good heavens! Do they know who did it?"

"Not yet. That's the other reason nobody can leave."

Delores was nothing if not perceptive. Her eyes narrowed and she bent forward to stare at her daughter. "You mean . . . the killer could still be here?"

"That's what Mike thinks. Anyway, I need your help with the mayor. Bertie overheard them fighting. She told Michelle that Mrs. Bascomb was accusing her husband of knowing Brandi in Vegas."

"Knowing? As in the Biblical sense?"

"I think so. And that could be the reason Mrs. Bascomb was so upset."

"Poor Stephanie," Delores said with a sigh. "With his track record, she's probably right. And you want me to ask him if it's true?"

"Yes. I know you two go way back, and I think he's still a little afraid of you."

"He should be. Fear was the only thing that kept him in line the summer I worked for his mother. I'll do this one on one. It'll work better that way. You wait here and keep an eye on Winthrop. If he looks desperate, go rescue him."

Fat chance, Hannah thought, taking a peek through the branches. Winthrop looked as happy as a clam to have three women doting on him. "Okay, Mother. Good luck."

"Luck has nothing to do with it. Intimidation is an art form, and don't you dare forget it!"

* * *

Hannah was just thinking about going over to spill some coffee on Carrie, who was definitely poaching in her mother's absence, when Delores came up smiling broadly.

"You found out?" Hannah guessed.

"Of course I did! I had him completely on the defensive from the very start. Ricky-Ticky was all set to spend a few intimate hours with Brandi when he went to Vegas last October, but he had a few too many and passed out in his hotel room before he could meet her in the bar for their date."

"Date? That's a polite way of putting it."

"That's exactly what I said. And then I asked him if he had to pay her anyway."

"Mother!"

"I was curious."

"So am I. Well? Did he pay her?"

"Only half. That was the up-front part. He was supposed to pay the other half later."

"Do you think he was telling the truth?"

Delores nodded. "I'm almost positive he was. It would have been less embarrassing if he'd lied and said he'd been with her."

"You're right. Good work, Mother. It's too bad Mrs. Bascomb doesn't know she has nothing to worry about on the Brandi front."

"I'd tell her, but Ricky-Ticky deserves a rough time for his past flirtations."

"Nicely put, Mother."

"Yes, wasn't it? And speaking of flirtations, I think I'd better get back to Winthrop before my partner and the woman I hope might be your future mother-in-law does something I can't forgive."

* * *

Hannah ducked into the kitchen to see if she could find an empty spot to gather her thoughts. Earl Flensburg had obviously finished eating and left, because the circular booth the builder had put in to accommodate the kitchen workers was empty. Hannah carried Earl's plate to the sink, rinsed it off, and slipped it into the hot soapy water that Edna had left for dishes that came in after the load in the industrial dishwasher had been started. Then she grabbed a mug of coffee from the kitchen pot, slid into the booth, and pulled her stash of crumpled napkins out of her sweater pockets.

Once she'd straightened out all the napkins and placed them in order, Hannah surveyed the results of the investigation so far. They'd eliminated two suspects, Martin and Shirley, and although Babs didn't have an alibi, her motive was weak. Babs had been prepared to get along with Brandi for her son's sake. She might have hoped that Brandi would leave Martin, but it was unlikely that Babs would have killed her new daughter-in-law just to get her out of the way.

Mayor Bascomb's name was under Babs Dubinski's. Hannah had written it down when Michelle had told her that Lake Eden's first couple was fighting about Brandi. But Delores had found out that nothing happened between the mayor and the stripper-turned-bride. Hannah picked up her pen and drew a line through Mayor Bascomb's name. If nothing had happened between them, the mayor had no reason to kill Brandi.

Way down at the bottom of the napkin was a name that appeared on every suspect list that Hannah had ever written. *Someone Unknown* was the name, and *Reasons Unknown* was the motive. And in order to figure out who *Someone Unknown* was, Hannah needed to know more about Brandi's life.

Hannah was sure there were people in Las Vegas that she could interview, but they were there and she was here at the

Lake Eden Christmas party in the middle of a blizzard. Perhaps she couldn't learn anything about Brandi's recent past, but she could certainly find out more about Brandi's school days at Browerville High.

The moment Hannah thought of it, she was on the move, stuffing the napkins back into her sweater pockets and heading out to talk to Marge Beeseman. The *Lake Eden Journal* had reported that the community library, run by Marge, had been designated as the tri-county repository for school documents.

Marge was sitting at a table with Lisa and her dad. Hannah greeted them all and then she turned to Lisa. "Where's Herb?"

"He's helping Mike with something or other." Lisa leaned closer and spoke in a barely audible voice, "They don't know."

Hannah turned to Marge. "Congratulations about the tri-county repository designation."

"Thank you. It's a lot of work going through all the documents, but we get a very generous stipend for storing the material."

"That's great. I was just wondering if that school material included high school yearbooks."

"Yes, it does. I just finished shelving them yesterday."

Hannah smiled. Her hunch had paid off. "I know this is an imposition, but do you think you could open the library for me so I could take a look at some of them?"

"Of course I can. I was about to go up there anyway to show Lisa and Jack the new magazine racks that the Jordan High shop class built for me."

Once Hannah, Lisa, Marge, and Jack had climbed the stairs and gone down the hall to the library, Marge unlocked the door and flicked on the lights. "The yearbooks are against the back wall in the center sections. There's a stepstool there if you can't reach the top ones. What are you looking for, Hannah?"

"Um . . . it's nothing, really. I just wanted to see if someone I know has changed a lot since high school."

Hannah crooked her finger at Lisa, and her partner followed along. They found the proper section and Lisa asked, "What are we really looking for?"

"A picture of Mary Kay Hinklemeyer in one of the Browerville High yearbooks. It would have been about ten years ago, because she left home at sixteen."

"And Mary Kay Hinklemeyer is . . . Brandi's real name?"

"You got it."

"And she's from Browerville?"

"You got that, too."

Lisa took down one of the Browerville yearbooks and flipped to the back. "This is going to be easy. Each book has an index listing names and photos."

With both of them sitting at a library table, looking through the yearbooks, it didn't take long to locate a photo of Mary Kay Hinklemeyer. There was one picture of her as a junior varsity cheerleader jumping up, legs spread, arms akimbo, with the other cheerleaders at a basketball game. Lisa stared at the photo for a long moment without speaking, and then she passed it to Hannah for a similar silent perusal.

"Do you think that's Brandi?" Lisa asked.

"I think so."

"Okay, but you couldn't prove it by me. She really changed a lot since she was in school."

"That she did," Hannah commented, biting back a quip about the wonders of nose jobs, hair coloring, and other surgical enhancements. "Let's go through the whole yearbook together and see if we recognize anyone else."

They turned the pages in silence for a few moments until they came to a photo of a pep rally in the school gym. Brandi and the other cheerleaders were in front of the crowd and the band was seated behind them.

"Is that who I think it is?" Lisa asked, pointing to a boy with dark-rimmed glasses who was holding a trumpet.

"Kirby Welles?" Hannah guessed, flipping back to the index. "Here's his name. I didn't know he went to Browerville High."

"Neither did I."

Lisa started paging through the yearbook again, looking for anyone else she might recognize. Hannah was silent, barely looking at the pages. She was too busy going over the conversation she'd had with Kirby. He'd claimed he had just met Brandi tonight and that was clearly a lie. He'd known Brandi since she was Mary Kay Hinklemeyer, junior varsity cheerleader. And that explained why Kirby had been so upset to hear that she was dead.

"Thanks for your help, Lisa," Hannah said, pushing back her chair.

"You're welcome. You're going to see Kirby Welles?"

"Oh, yes," Hannah said, heading out of the library at a fast clip. By virtue of his lie, Jordan High's bandleader had just become her prime suspect.

Chapter Fifteen

While Hannah was upstairs, the banquet room had undergone a transformation, thanks to the Jordan High athletic department, whose members had volunteered to move tables and chairs for the party. Except for two long rectangular tables near the kitchen, the dining tables had been folded and returned to the storage area under the stairs. In their place, dozens of round, four-person tables had been arranged near the giant Christmas tree, leaving a good-sized circular area, with the tree in the center, for a dance floor.

The lights had been dimmed, the coffee had been replenished, and Hannah noticed that quite a few adults were availing themselves of the punchbowl full of English Eggnog that Rod Metcalf was manning. A second punchbowl, almost identical but lacking the rum that flavored the first, was available for those who didn't want to consume, or weren't old enough to legally consume, the alcoholic version.

Kirby Welles and the jazz ensemble had gone through their Christmas music, and now they were playing a medley of jazz standards. A half-dozen couples were dancing to "Strangers in the Night," and Hannah watched them without any real interest until she caught sight of Laura Jorgensen dancing cheek-to-cheek with a tall, dark-haired man. The couple turned and Hannah recognized Drew Vavra, a member of her graduating class at Jordan High and a graduate of the University of Minnesota. Just this September, Drew had been hired to replace Boyd Watson, and he was the new history teacher and head coach of the Lake Eden Gulls.

Hannah glanced down at Laura's feet again. Drew was a nice guy, steady and reliable, and not bad to look at, either. Hannah hoped that Laura was wearing the special shoes for him. Since she would have been hard-pressed to slip a sheet advertising the cookie specials of the day at The Cookie Jar between them, it was a safe bet that Laura and Drew were a lot more than casual acquaintances.

The medley ended and Hannah headed straight for Drew and Laura. She caught them before they could even leave the dance floor. She greeted them both and was trying to think of a way to spirit Laura off to ask her where she'd been at the time of Brandi's murder, when Laura solved the problem for her.

"Would you get me a cup of that wonderful eggnog, Drew?" Laura waited until Drew had left for the table with the punchbowl and then she turned back to Hannah. "I want you to be the first to know, since you were Drew's classmate and he told me that you were the only reason he got through algebra. We just got engaged!"

"Congratulations!" Hannah exclaimed, giving Laura a little hug. "And I think I just blew it. I'm supposed to say that to Drew, not you. But I really am happy for both of you. And if Drew ever needs to solve a quadratic equation, you know where I live."

Laura laughed and she looked happier than Hannah had ever seen her. "We've only been dating for three weeks, but we've spent almost every minute together. I just couldn't believe it when we started to dance, and he slipped the ring on my finger and asked me to marry him."

"That's so romantic," Hannah said, and she meant it. "And your ring is beautiful."

"I know. And to think I've been pining over Martin for two years! I was so wrong, but it took meeting Drew to make me realize it."

"Well . . . I'm really glad you did!" Hannah said, glancing up at the stage. The jazz ensemble was breaking up, some students heading toward the kitchen and whatever food was left, and others rushing for the coolers of soft drinks that sat on a table next to the punchbowls. "Please tell Drew I'm delighted for both of you. I'd love to stay and tell him myself, but I've got to talk to Kirby before he takes his break."

Hannah headed off toward the makeshift stage, mentally crossing Laura off her list. There was no way Laura was jealous enough to kill Brandi, not when she was head over heels with Drew.

"Kirby?" Hannah called out, catching the bandleader in the act of stepping off the riser. "We need to talk."

"Couldn't it wait. . . ?"

"Now," Hannah interrupted him, climbing up to grab his arm. "Why didn't you tell me you knew Brandi when you were in high school and she was Mary Kay Hinklemeyer?"

"I . . . she didn't want me to say anything. And I only knew her when we were kids, before she ran away from home."

"What was she like?"

"Um . . . kind of wild, but she was a fantastic dancer and we used to enter dance contests as a couple. We always won when we danced together and we . . . uh . . . we dated occasionally."

"Does *dated* mean what I think it means?"

Kirby turned a dull shade of red. "Yeah."

"So did you tell Martin that you already knew Brandi when Martin introduced her to you?"

"No. I was about to say something about going to high school with her, but Mary Kay gave me a warning look. I'm pretty sure that Martin didn't know she was from right around here."

Hannah got down to business. "Did you get a chance to talk to Brandi privately before she was killed?"

"Um . . . well . . . actually . . ." Kirby turned a little pale. "I did. She stopped by the stage and asked me to meet her in the cloakroom."

"And you did?"

"It was nothing out of the way, or anything like that. We just talked about old times and what happened to the other kids we'd gone to school with."

Something about this conversation was bothering her, and it took Hannah a moment to figure out what it was. There was something Kirby wasn't telling her. It was in the way he failed to meet her eyes, and his stance, which was as defensive as that of a cornered 'possum. It was time to probe for the truth.

"So what did you think about Brandi's marriage to Martin?" Hannah asked, watching closely for Kirby's reaction.

"I thought it was a big mistake. And actually, so did Mary Kay. She said Martin was no fun at all and . . . and she was going to dump him. And then . . ." Kirby faltered and raised stricken eyes to Hannah's face. "Do you really need to know this?"

"I do. You need to tell me everything if we're going to catch Brandi's killer."

"Okay. But please call her Mary Kay. That's the way I want to remember her. She . . . she asked me to leave Lake Eden with her."

Hannah blinked hard. "You mean, Bran . . . I mean, *Mary Kay* was going to dump Martin for you?"

"No! It wasn't like that, Hannah, really. Mary Kay was dumping him anyway. And she wasn't interested in marrying me, or anything permanent like that. She just didn't like being alone, and she wanted me to come along with her for company."

"I see," Hannah said, even though she didn't. "Did . . . um . . . Mary Kay tell you when she was planning to go?"

"Tonight. She was going to wait until Martin was busy talking to somebody, and then she was going to take off with his car and leave it at the airport in Minneapolis."

"She was flying back to Las Vegas?"

"Not Vegas. She was going to the Bahamas, and she offered to buy my ticket if I'd come along. She said she could get at least fifty thousand for her coat and the ring Martin gave her, and if that wasn't enough, she had an antique knife that was worth a bundle. She told me that we could live high on the hog in the Bahamas."

"So what did you say?"

"I told her I couldn't go, that I liked my job in Lake Eden. At first, she thought I was kidding, but when she realized I was serious, she called me a . . ." Kirby stopped, clearly embarrassed. "You don't really have to know, do you?"

"No, I don't. How about the antique knife she mentioned? Did she show it to you?"

"No. I had no idea she was talking about stealing your mother's antique cake knife until you told me that it was the murder weapon."

Hannah thought about what Kirby had said for a moment. She was almost sure that he was telling her the truth. "Why didn't you tell me all this the first time we talked?"

"I couldn't! I figured if you knew about the history Mary Kay and I had between us, you might think *I* killed her!"

"Did you?"

Kirby stared at Hannah in absolute shock. "Of course I didn't kill her. I loved Mary Kay. She was my first real girlfriend. I kept thinking about that when the group was playing and remembering how much fun we used to have. You know how you caught me that first time just as I was about to leave on break? And I didn't want to talk to you because I had some-thing important to do?"

"I remember. What was so important?"

"I was going to find Mary Kay and tell her I'd go with her after all!"

Hannah found Andrea at a table with Claire, Reverend Knudson, and his grandmother Priscilla. She chatted for a few moments and then she turned to Andrea. "Will you meet me in the lobby upstairs in five minutes?"

"Sure," Andrea said, and there was a question in her eyes.

"I'm going to find Michelle and ask her to meet us, too." Hannah ignored the question Andrea was dying to ask and excused herself to Claire and the Knudsons.

Hannah's youngest sister was sitting with Luanne Hanks and Danielle Watson. "Hi," Hannah said, plunking herself down in a chair. "How's the dance business, Danielle?"

"It's great. I was just asking Luanne if she knew anyone who might like to handle one of my senior ballroom dancing classes. I've got three going now and my waiting list is large enough to start another."

"That's just wonderful." Hannah admired the transforma-tion her friend had undergone. Danielle had been a timid and abused wife when she'd first come to Lake Eden, but now she was a successful businesswoman with plenty of self-confidence. "You're not trying to recruit Luanne, are you?"

Danielle shook her head. "Are you kidding? Your mother and Carrie would kill me if I tried to hire Luanne out from under their noses."

"You've got that right," Luanne said with a laugh. "And starting next week I'm going to be even more valuable to them."

"What happens next week?" Hannah asked.

"Mom, Suzie, and I move into the other half of Nettie's

duplex. That means I can work later in the winter because I won't have to match my hours to the county snowplow schedule."

"Good for you!" Hannah said with a smile. She was glad that Luanne was leaving the isolation of her family home at the end of Old Bailey Road and moving to town. And she was doubly glad that Nettie Grant would be able to spend time with Suzie. After the losses the former sheriff's wife had suffered in the past three years, it was bound to lift her spirits to be around a sunny little girl like Suzie.

"Michelle?" Hannah turned to her youngest sister. "Will you meet me in the upstairs lobby in five minutes?"

Michelle nodded, and as Hannah watched, she assumed the identical expression that her next-older sibling had worn. It was obvious that Andrea wasn't the only Swensen sister who was dying of curiosity.

" 'Bye, ladies. See you later, Michelle." Hannah headed up the stairs to wait for her sisters. She waved at Lonnie, who was manning the outside door, and walked over to the grouping of chairs around the miniature Christmas village.

There was a large gilt-framed mirror on the wall behind the village and Hannah frowned as she caught sight of her hair. Her unruly red curls had been tousled by the wind and snow in the parking lot, and they looked as if they hadn't seen the tender ministrations of a hairbrush in months. Hannah smoothed them down as best she could, and paused to admire the new sweater Norman had given her. It fell gracefully from her shoulders and came to just the right length in back to minimize that I-wish-it-were-smaller part of her anatomy.

"Gorgeous," Hannah said, turning a bit so that her skirt swirled against her legs. But what was that bulge at her hips? She looked like an anatomically incorrect chipmunk with his cheeks lower than his waist.

Hannah reached in her pocket and drew out dozens of

paper napkins, far too many for the lines of the sweater. Even though she'd folded them neatly and divided them between the two pockets, the piles had grown, and now her sweater pockets were ballooning with a plethora of paper Santas, reindeer, snowflakes, Christmas trees, angels, and snowmen. It was definitely time to scare up a steno pad, and she knew just the place to find one.

A few moments later, Hannah was standing at Janice's desk in Kiddie Corner, begging office supplies. The younger kids were crowded around the Christmas tree in the corner, listening to one of the high school girls read a story, and the older children, like Tracey, had gone off to the library to watch a Disney movie with several high school seniors as chaperones.

"How about this?" Janice asked, pulling a neon-pink steno pad from her center desk drawer. "I know you like the green ones, but it's all I have at the moment. Here's the pen that goes with it. The Velcro attaches to the cover, see?"

"It's just perfect," Hannah said gratefully, even though she would have preferred something less conspicuous. It was exactly as Delores had taught her; beggars couldn't be choosers.

"I'm glad you're here, Hannah. I've got something I want to show you." Janice opened a drawer and took out a stack of letters. "I had the older kids write letters to Santa, and the high school girls helped them with the spelling. Linda Nelson came up to tell me that Tracey had asked her to spell some very strange words for a letter to Santa."

"Like what?"

"Like *blizzard*. Linda didn't think that was so odd, because we're in the middle of one, but the next word Tracey wanted was *detective*. And then she asked Beth if *body* had two *d*'s or one."

"Uh-oh."

"Exactly. I looked it over, and I thought you should read

it, too. I'm crazy about Tracey, but that girl is too smart for
her own good!"

Hannah took the letter Janice handed her and sat down in
one of the little chairs by the blackboard. The chair was so
low that her knees almost touched her chin, but she barely
noticed how uncomfortable she was once she started to read.

Dear Santa,

*How are you? I am fine. I sure hope you remember
me, what with all the kids who write to you this time of
year. My name is Tracey Todd and I live in Lake Eden,
Minnesota. My daddy's the new sheriff of Winnetka
County and my mommy's a real estate professional. I
asked you for a dollhouse last year and you gave it to
me. It's real nice.*

*I'm writing this to help my Aunt Hannah. You prob-
ably remember her. Those were her cookies that we left
out under the tree for you. We're all stuck here at the
community center after the big recipe-testing Christmas
party dinner. The food was great and it was fun, but we
can't go home. It's supposed to be because of the big
blizzard, but that's not the real reason. Right after Edna
Ferguson finished cutting the cakes, I saw Aunt Hannah
come in from the parking lot and she had that look on
her face. Then she pulled Uncle Mike (he's Daddy's
most important detective) off in a corner so they could
talk. They looked real worried, and that's why I think
Aunt Hannah found another body. She does that a lot.
Anyways, they want all of us kids to stay busy writing
letters to Santa, and watching movies, and things like
that. I bet they figure that way nobody will guess
what's really wrong.*

*I better start writing my Christmas wish list now so
you know what to bring me.*

The first thing I want is for Mommy to have the new

baby. She's awful big, so could you please let her have it right away? I can tell Daddy's worried about her and they'll both be happy after the baby's born. Mommy says he's a boy and his name is Billy. That's nice, but if you can still do it, could you please make Billy a girl? I'd much rather have a little sister.

The next thing I want is for Rose from Hal and Rose's Café to give my Aunt Hannah her famous coconut cake recipe for the cookbook. Poor Aunt Hannah's asked for it a bunch of times, but Rose won't give it to her. Could you get it, please? Tonight was supposed to be the last chance to test recipes for the cookbook, but Aunt Hannah's editor is very nice, and I bet he'll let her put it in.

This next thing is a big favor I need. I know this is your busy season, but if you have time, please talk to Uncle Mike. Tell him that Aunt Hannah would make a perfect wife and he should ask her. And then please talk to Uncle Norman. I want him to ask Aunt Hannah, too. That way she can make up her mind which one she likes best and I'll get to be in another wedding. I'm already going to be in Lisa and Herb's wedding. It was supposed to be on New Year's Eve, but Lisa and Herb didn't have time to do everything, so Lisa asked Mommy to help her. Now it's on Valentine's Day, and Mommy says I get to wear a beautiful red velvet dress and carry white roses with the thorns cut off.

There's another thing I want, Santa. Mommy and Aunt Hannah are all worried about Grandma and Winthrop. They think he's a crook. If he is, please make him leave Grandma alone. If he's not, I guess it's okay, even though I don't like him very much.

I don't really want anything else for Christmas ex-

cept maybe a puppy. I think I'm going to get that anyway, but not right away.

Love,
Tracey

P.S. If it's not a secret, will you tell me how you got my dollhouse inside our living room last Christmas? I know it's too big to fit down the chimney. I measured.

Chapter Sixteen

"Sorry about that," Hannah said, hurrying to the group of chairs where her sisters were sitting. "I got hung up at Kiddie Korner borrowing this steno pad."

"Did you see Tracey?" Andrea asked.

"No, she was at the library watching a Disney movie with her friends." Hannah opened her mouth to tell Andrea about the Santa letter, but she thought better of it and clamped her lips shut again. Andrea would only worry if she knew that Tracey had guessed about the murder. "Did you find anyone who knew Mary Kay Hinklemeyer?"

"Not a single person," Andrea said, sounding very frustrated. "The closest I came was Joe Dietz. He said he served with a guy named Sam Hinkelmeyer when he was in the army, but he was pretty sure Sam came from Idaho."

"Same here, except I didn't find anybody who knew any Hinklemeyers at all," Michelle reported.

"Okay. Since we're not going to get anywhere with that, let's regroup." Hannah reached into both of her sweater pockets and drew out the stacks of folded napkins. "The first thing to do is transfer these notes to the steno pad Janice gave me."

Andrea picked up one of the napkins and attempted to read it. "Is this a blot from your pen, or food?"

"I don't know. You take notes and I'll read the napkins,"

Hannah delegated, handing the pink notebook to Andrea. "You listen, Michelle, and if you think of something I missed, sing out."

"Right." Michelle got up to fetch the wastebasket that stood near the front door, pausing to give Lonnie a little pat on the arm before she returned. "Here, Hannah. After you read them, toss them in here."

Hannah picked up the first napkin and squinted at it. Andrea was right. The ink had run, and the area where it had met a grease spot looked a lot like the first Rorschach card. "It looks like . . ." Hannah resisted the urge to say *a vase*, or *a mirror image of a person in profile*. Instead she concentrated on making out the letters. "Kirby. It's Kirby Welles. As far as I know, he was the last person to talk to Brandi before she was killed. Kirby told me he met Brandi in the cloakroom shortly after seven-thirty."

"That was right after she went to the ladies' room with me," Michelle pointed out. "Better write that down, too."

Andrea looked a bit exasperated. "I've got it. Actually, I've got it in two places. I'm making a timeline here. What time did you go to the ladies' room, Michelle?"

"A quarter after seven. I looked at my watch."

"Okay, Brandi was at the table with Martin until seven-fifteen. Then she went to the ladies' room with Michelle. You talked to her until seven-thirty, Michelle?"

"That's right. I was asking her questions about her life in Vegas."

"And you learned what?"

"Hold on!" Hannah complained, "I'm looking for a toy soldier here."

"You're *what?*" both younger sisters asked in perfect unison.

"A toy soldier. I used a napkin with a toy soldier on it to write down what Michelle told me. Here it is!" Hannah held her disreputable prize aloft and waved it like a flag.

"It's falling apart," Andrea commented.

Michelle agreed. "And somebody spilled frosting on it and it's all stuck together in one corner."

"I can still read it," Hannah insisted, spreading it out with the care of someone who was performing open-heart surgery on an ant. "It says, *ring, green stone, diamond surround, M. afraid plus coat show-off.*"

"You saw the ring," Michelle said to Andrea, "so you can give a better description than mine. And that other part is Hannah's shorthand telling us that Martin didn't want Brandi to wear the ring. He told her it was because she had the fur coat and he thought two expensive items like that might make people resentful."

"People like Shirley," Hannah pointed out, "who admitted that she told Martin she'd do anything she could to help him get rid of Brandi so that they could get remarried."

"Motive!" Michelle cried out.

"Alibi," Hannah countered. "Shirley was with Martin in that little room under the stairs at the time that Brandi was killed. The fact that they were together means that both of them are in the clear."

"I've got all that," Andrea said, putting down her pen and massaging her fingers. "Let's get back to the timeline. Do you know what time Brandi was killed?"

"I found her at eight-fifteen, and Doc Knight didn't think she'd been out there for more than thirty minutes. That puts the time of death anywhere from a quarter to eight to when I found her."

"Seven forty-five to eight-fifteen," Andrea repeated, her pen racing across the page, whose color had certainly been modeled after the inside of a Pepto-Bismol bottle. "That really narrows it down. How about Kirby? Why did he talk to Brandi in the cloakroom?"

"She asked him to meet her there."

"So *that's* why she kept looking at her watch!" Michelle

spoke up, and Hannah couldn't help thinking that if her youngest sister were a cartoon character, a light bulb would have gone off in the little balloon over her head. "I thought she was worried about getting back to Martin, but she must have told Kirby what time to meet her."

"Makes sense," Hannah said.

"What did they talk about?" Andrea asked, her pen at the ready.

"Old friends they knew in high school and . . ."

"Kirby went to high school with Brandi?" Andrea asked, coming very close to dropping her pen.

"Yes, with Mary Kay Hinklemeyer. She was Kirby's first girlfriend."

"I'll be!" Michelle breathed. "Do you think he killed her because she married Martin instead of him?"

Hannah shook her head. "It's not feasible. For one thing, I'm almost sure that the jazz ensemble was playing the entire time, and I already know that they wouldn't have sounded good without Kirby. And for another thing, Kirby wasn't jealous."

"Are you sure?" Andrea asked.

"I'm positive. You see, Brandi told Kirby she was leaving Martin. She was going to take his car out of the parking lot and drive it to the Minneapolis airport. From there she was going to fly to the Bahamas, and she asked Kirby to go with her."

"That's . . . romantic," Michelle breathed.

"It's also money-grubbing, illegal, and immoral," Hannah reminded her. "Brandi told Kirby they could live like kings if she sold her ring and mink coat. And . . . her antique knife."

"What antique . . ." Andrea started to ask, but she stopped, and this time the light bulb could have gone on over *her* head. "You mean Mother's antique cake knife?"

"One and the same."

"So Brandi stole it?" Michelle asked, frowning slightly.

"That's a likely scenario."

"And the killer managed to take it away from Brandi and stab her?" Andrea asked, paling slightly at the thought.

"That's part of the same scenario. Hold on a second and let me find the caroling penguins. That's where I wrote the list of suspects."

Hannah paged through the remaining paper napkins, reading off several notes to Andrea. There was their conversation with Shirley, her meeting with Martin, and their mother's grilling of Mayor Bascomb and how he admitted that he'd seen Brandi's strip show and hired her for a "date" he was too drunk to keep.

"And I really thought she was a showgirl," Michelle said with a sigh. "I feel really awful about all those questions I asked her."

Hannah slipped a comforting arm around her youngest sister's shoulder. "I'm sorry she disappointed you, Michelle."

"Oh, she didn't disappoint me, not exactly. But if she'd admitted that she was a stripper who partied on the side, I would have asked her a whole different set of questions and tried out for an entirely different part in the play!"

Ten minutes later, they had reached an impasse. Hannah had found the caroling penguins, but every single suspect except the unknown suspect with an unknown motive had been eliminated.

"What now?" Hannah asked, throwing out the question and hoping that one of her sisters would have an answer.

"I don't know," Michelle said, shaking her head. "It beats me."

"Me, too," Andrea sighed. "It just makes me wish we had some outtakes to watch this time around."

"Outtakes?" Hannah asked, thoroughly puzzled.

"You know, like we did when we were investigating Boyd

Watson's murder. We went through all those tapes of the Hartland Flour Bakeoff."

"But we didn't find anything," Hannah reminded her.

"I know, but we could have. I'm just sorry somebody wasn't videotaping tonight. There might have been something in the footage we could use."

"Hold on," Michelle said, an excited expression crossing her face. "Norman's been taking photos of everyone all night long. What if he caught someone following Brandi when she filched the knife and ran off to the parking lot with it?"

Andrea shook her head. "If Norman saw something like that, he would have raised the alarm."

"But maybe he doesn't know he saw it. Just imagine this for a second . . . Norman's concentrating on taking a picture of someone getting a second helping of something or other and the dessert table is in the background. He snaps pictures of his main subject, but he also gets a picture of Brandi in the background stealing the knife. Norman might have something we could use, and not even know he's got it."

"That makes sense," Hannah said, catching some of her sister's enthusiasm. "We'd better find Norman right away and ask him to develop his photos. Even if he goes straight home to the darkroom, that'll take him a couple of hours."

"I don't think so, Hannah. We might just get instant results."

"How?"

"I saw Norman's camera earlier, and it looked like a digital to me."

Finding Norman was no easy trick, but Hannah managed to locate him in the kitchen, where Edna had set him up with a platter of leftovers that would have fed the Lake Eden Gulls football squad. "Hi, Norman," Hannah said, sliding into the kitchen booth to face him.

"Hi, Hannah. The Christmas party's a huge success. I heard a lot of people saying that the food was the best ever."

"Good to hear." Hannah berated herself for not telling Norman about Brandi's murder sooner. She should have found him right away, but circumstances had intervened. She took a deep breath and prepared to give him the shocking news. "I need you, Norman."

"I figured you would."

That took Hannah back a pace or two. "But . . . you don't know *why* I need you."

"Does it matter?"

"I don't know," Hannah said, thinking about that for a moment. "I guess it doesn't, not really."

"I didn't think so. It's enough that you do. Well, who do you like?"

"Like?"

"For Brandi's murder. That's cop talk. Mike told me that's what they say in the squad room."

"You know about the murder?"

"Of course I do. The police photographer couldn't get here, and Mike had me take the crime scene photos. It's definitely an art. I couldn't have done it without his instructions."

Hannah had a sobering thought as she looked into Norman's face. What if Mike had already gone over all of Norman's photos? What if there was nothing that Norman had captured on film, or disk, or whatever it was called in digital photography? But was it digital photography? That should be her first question. "Are you using a digital camera tonight?"

"Yes. The technology's great, and I've got to say the results are as good or better than the traditional method. It's amazing, Hannah."

"Instant gratification?"

"Precisely. You shoot it and you view it. Then you keep it, or you ditch it, all in one fell swoop. And it's not at all expensive, considering all the money a photographer's got to put into a darkroom."

Hannah felt herself getting impatient. "Okay. Wonderful. Come with me. Andrea, Michelle, and I need you upstairs with your camera and whatever it is that holds those photos you took tonight."

"Not quite yet," Norman said, shoving his coffee cup across the table. "Drink this. And eat this chocolate-dipped pear. You're getting cranky."

"I am not!" Hannah said, and then she had the grace to laugh at the crabby tone in her voice.

"That's better." Norman looked amused as she took a sip of coffee and a bite of the pear. "Do you want to take some chocolate upstairs? Your sisters might need a pick-me-up too."

"Good idea," Hannah said sweetly and it wasn't an act. She really was feeling much better, but she wasn't sure if it was due to the chocolate, or Norman. "I have a feeling we could have a long night ahead of us."

Chapter Seventeen

"**D**id you get it?" Andrea called out. She was sitting in the first row of three dozen seats in the community center's mini-auditorium, the only Swensen sister who was too large to slip behind the big-screen television to hold tools for Norman while he hooked up his camera.

"We got it!" Michelle emerged, smiling broadly. "All we had to do was unhook the cable and attach the camera's feed."

Hannah came out right behind Michelle. She dusted off her hands and frowned slightly. "I don't think anyone ever cleans behind there."

"Probably not." Andrea handed Hannah one of the napkins Norman had thought to bring with the plate of fruit. "This television is Mayor Bascomb's baby. Bill told me that he watches every Vikings game in here and he holds his own tailgate party."

"Tailgate? Like in the parking lot?" Michelle wanted to know.

"No, right here in the auditorium. It's not really a *tailgate* party, but there's food and drinks, and all the mayor's friends come to watch the games with him. For the really important events like the Super Bowl, he sends out printed invitations. Bill thinks he'll get one, now that he's sheriff."

"If he does, will you go?" Hannah asked. Andrea was probably the most disinterested sports fan in town. She memorized the scores and took note of the big plays so that she could mention them to her real estate clients, but often she just settled for the old, tried-and-true *How about those Vikings, huh?*

"I can't go. It's a guy thing, with no wives allowed. I think that's because it gets a little rowdy."

"You're probably right," Hannah said, but she wondered if the mayor invited any women who weren't in the spouse or helpmate category. She doubted it. If there were any non-wifely females present, Stephanie Bascomb and her friends would hear about it on the Lake Eden gossip hotline and the Super Bowl parties at the community center would soon be ancient history.

"Turn it on, will you?" a voice floated out from the rear of the television, and Hannah hurried to turn on the set. A few seconds later, she saw the image of Edna standing by the Christmas tree.

"You got it," Hannah called out to Norman, walking closer to examine the image that was almost the size of the real Edna.

"For a second there, I didn't think it was going to work." Norman came out breathing a deep sigh of relief. "At the last minute, I noticed that I had the input in the output."

Hannah decided she wouldn't touch that comment since she had no idea what Norman was talking about. "It's a great photo, Norman, but how are we going to tell when you . . ."

"Hold on and I'll turn on the date–time feature," Norman interrupted her.

"Perfect," Hannah said, taking a seat next to Andrea and watching as the numbers appeared at the bottom of the screen. "Can you page forward to those shots you took of the knife?"

"Sure, but it's not *page* forward."

"I realize that, but you know what I mean." Hannah kept her eyes on the screen as Norman began to advance the photos, giving them a quick peek of each.

"Six-twenty," Michelle called out when the first shot of the cake knife came on the screen. There were several more shots, one with Hannah holding the knife, and then Norman had moved on to the kitchen, where Edna and her helpers were setting out the appetizers.

"So we know that the knife was still there at six twenty-three." Andrea flipped open the pink notebook, jotted down the time, and turned to Hannah. "What do we look for next?"

"Any shots Norman took after Brandi met with Kirby Welles. That was at seven-thirty, wasn't it?"

Andrea flipped to the page with the timeline. "That's right."

"We should watch for any shots with the dessert table in the background, or Brandi walking toward the kitchen door. If we're lucky, Norman got a shot of someone following her."

"The killer," Michelle breathed.

"Right."

Norman advanced his camera until the time code read seven twenty-nine. "Okay . . . let's start watching."

Their eyes were glued to the screen for several minutes and then Hannah called out. "There's the dessert table! But it's so far away, I can't tell if the knife is missing."

"Hold on. I'll fix that," Norman said.

Hannah gasped as the shot began to zoom in. "I didn't know you could do that!"

"It's the beauty of digital photography."

There was a brief moment of silence and then all four of them gasped.

"Look!" Michelle was the first to speak. "Norman caught a hand reaching for the knife!"

"Is it Brandi's hand?" Hannah asked, turning to Andrea. "You notice manicures and things like that."

"I think so," Andrea said, but she didn't look convinced. "It looks like she's wearing Pearl Blush nail polish, and that's what Brandi was wearing, but it's a really popular color right now. And she's got her hand tipped, so I can't see if she's wearing her ring."

"Michelle?" Hannah turned to her youngest sister.

"I think it's her, but I couldn't swear to it."

Hannah sighed. "Unfortunately, that doesn't cut it in a murder investigation. The only thing we know for sure is that a woman wearing pink nail polish picked up the knife."

"But she could have put it back down again," Andrea said.

"That's right. She might have picked it up to have a closer look. Let's see the next shot, Norman. Maybe that'll tell us more."

Norman put the next photo up on the screen. It was a second shot very similar to the first, but the time code read two seconds later. He zoomed in and let out a holler. "The knife's gone, and there's nobody else even remotely close to the dessert table. Whoever that woman was, she took it."

"What's this?" Hannah asked, getting to her feet and pointing at the screen. "Is that her leg, walking away?"

"I don't know what else it could be."

"Brandi was wearing silver boots," Hannah reminded them. "Can you pan down to her calf, Norman?"

"Sorry, no. The lower half of her leg is hidden behind that plant in the foreground. I can zoom in a little more on what I've got, but that's it."

"There's a spot on her leg," Andrea commented, staring intently at the zoom of what they assumed was Brandi's thigh.

"Let me see if I can enhance it a little more," Norman offered, fine-tuning some controls on his camera. "How's that?"

"It's Brandi!" Michelle shouted, getting so excited she hopped up and down in her seat.

"How do you know that?" Hannah asked. "You have to be certain, Michelle."

"I *am* certain. Remember when I told you that I saw her tattoos? Well, that's the first one she ever got. It's a tiny little brandy snifter."

"She's right. Somebody gave us a set of four just like that for a wedding present, and it's a distinctive shape." Andrea turned to Hannah. "Do you want me to write down that Brandi stole the knife at seven forty-two and walked off with it?"

"Absolutely. Let's see what you've got next, Norman. And let's keep a sharp eye out for Brandi going into the kitchen."

"This could do it," Norman said, as he put up the next shot. "It's a shot of Edna and her workers by the Christmas tree, but someone's going through the kitchen door in the background."

Hannah held her breath as Norman zoomed in and she let it out in a whoop. "It's Brandi, all right! Now all we need to do is find a shot of someone following her."

The next few shots yielded nothing, but three minutes later, in the background of a shot Norman had taken of a table of diners, the kitchen door was partially open.

"Hold on . . . I'll zoom in," Norman said, and then he sighed. "It's a woman, but she's almost completely blocked by the foreground. The only thing I can tell for sure is that she's wearing a black skirt."

Andrea gave a little gasp of excitement. "But that's enough! We solved another one, Hannah! All we have to do is look for a woman wearing a black skirt and we'll have Brandi's killer!"

"Not necessarily. The woman in the black skirt could have some perfectly reasonable reason for going into the kitchen. For all we know, she went in, washed her hands, and came right back out again."

"So it all depends on how long she was gone," Michelle said, looking thoughtful. "How long does it take to kill someone?"

Hannah shrugged. "She'd have to walk through the kitchen, go through the pantry, open the outside door, and follow Brandi all the way out to Martin's car. That would take a couple of minutes. And then it would take another couple of minutes to stab her. This is just a ballpark figure, but I'd say that if she's gone for more than five minutes, she's definitely a suspect."

"She's definitely a suspect," Norman said, and all three Swensen sisters turned to look at him. "While you were speculating, I've been running through the photos on the internal camera screen. It's a lot faster that way. I've gone through five minutes and she hasn't come out of the kitchen yet. Unfortunately, I don't have anything after five minutes."

"Why not?" Hannah asked.

"I moved on to take pictures of the jazz ensemble. And then I took a couple of the Plotniks in front of the Christmas tree. After that, I moved upstairs to do some photos of the miniature Christmas village. I'm really sorry, Hannah, but I don't have anything in that area again until after you found Brandi's body."

"There's no need to feel sorry. You gave us the only lead we've got." Hannah turned to smile at him. "You're a great photographer, Norman."

"Thanks. So what do we do next?"

"We look at it logically. Either the woman in the black skirt is the killer, or she's a material witness. If she didn't stab Brandi, she knows who did because the killer must have passed right by her in the kitchen. The upshot is, we need to talk to her. And the caution is, we have to be careful because we don't know if she's Brandi's killer, or not."

"Makes sense," Michelle said, nodding quickly. "What do you want us to do?"

"Just observe for right now. We need to canvass the whole community center and make a list of every woman who's wearing a black skirt or dress."

"That shouldn't take long if we split up," Norman said, pulling a notebook from his camera bag. "I've got a couple of extra pens, if anyone needs them. They're leftover Rhodes Dental Clinic giveaways from last Christmas."

Michelle raised her hand. "I need one. My roommate gave me five dollars for the last one you gave me. She said she'd never seen a pen shaped like a toothbrush before and she just had to have it."

"Maybe I should give up dentistry and manufacture pens for a living," Norman quipped. "Where do you want me to start, Hannah?"

"Will you take the south end of the banquet room and work your way to the center? That way Michelle can start on the north end and meet you halfway."

Andrea began to frown. "How about me? You want me to help, don't you?"

"Of course I do. I need someone to check every room up here and that'll give you a chance to see Tracey. And don't forget the high school kids who came up here to watch movies in the library and the Senior Center. Let's just make lists for now. We won't ask anybody any questions quite yet. We can meet in the lobby in twenty minutes to compare notes."

"What are you going to do, Hannah?" Michelle asked.

"I'll canvass the kitchen, the ladies' room, the cloakroom, and the dance floor. But first, I'm going to talk to Mike and tell him about the lady in the black skirt. It's only fair. And I'll let him know that we're just doing the legwork and we'll leave the actual questioning up to him."

"And you really think he'll believe you?" Norman did his best to maintain a straight face and failed.

"Of course he'll believe me. It's the truth. It's just as I told Michelle and Andrea earlier. It's a different situation, this time around. Mike's shorthanded, and I'm going to give him all the help I can."

The door to the room Mike was using as a temporary office was closed, and Hannah stood there, frowning. She didn't want to interrupt, but the information she had could lead to the capture of Brandi's killer. Mike might be angry at the interruption, but he'd be grateful just as soon as she told him why she needed to talk to him.

Hannah knocked and put a welcoming smile on her face. Mike would be startled to see her, but he was bound to be pleased once she'd had her say. She shifted from foot to foot, waiting for the sound of the latch clicking open, but the door remained closed.

"Come on, Mike," Hannah muttered, knocking again, a little harder this time. Again, she waited, her smile in place, but no one answered the door.

It was possible Mike had left. He could be in another part of the community center, checking up on a lead. Perhaps she should open the door. If Mike wasn't there, she'd leave him a note telling him she had urgent information for him.

Hannah turned the knob and eased open the door. Mike was there, and he was in the middle of an interview. If the scowl on his face was any indication, he wasn't at all happy about being interrupted.

"I'm busy here, Hannah," Mike said, waving her away.

"I can see that. I'm really sorry to interrupt, but I have to talk to you right away. So if you could just step outside in the hall, it'll only take a second or two."

"No."

"No, it'll take longer than a second or two? Or no, you won't come out in the hall?"

"No to both. I'm in the middle of an interview here. I'll talk to you, later, Hannah."

"But you don't understand. I came here to help you. This is really important, Mike!"

"I said later, Hannah. Please don't interfere. I'm trying to run an official investigation, and I don't have time to talk to you now. Just shut the door and let me get on with my job, okay?"

Hannah shut the door, perhaps just a wee bit harder than was necessary. She'd given Mike his chance, and she thought she'd been extremely polite about it. And now she didn't have to feel the least bit guilty when she caught Brandi's killer and did his job for him.

Chapter
Eighteen

Hannah was still fuming as she went down the stairs. As always in times of great stress, she headed straight for the kitchen. Not only would it make her feel better to be in the room at the community center she liked best, but she could check out the ladies who were helping in the kitchen at the same time.

Edna's after-dinner helpers were working to clean up the kitchen, wash the serving bowls, and store the leftover food until it could be taken to Reverend Strandberg's soup kitchen in the basement of the Bible Church and the Lake Eden Convalescent Home. All it took was one glance to see that no one was wearing black.

The dance floor was next. Hannah found a table near the edge of the area that had been set aside for dancing and sat there watching the couples as they danced. The light was fairly dim and she had a few anxious moments when she spotted Cheryl Coombs in what she thought was a black skirt, but before she could even begin to wonder what possible motive Cheryl could have for killing Martin's new wife, Cheryl's partner danced her closer and Hannah realized that her skirt was dark green.

The cloakroom was next. Hannah went into the long, narrow room and flicked on the overhead light. There was a startled gasp and she turned to see the high school couple she'd interrupted. The girl blushed as she smoothed her hair and the boy gulped. "Sorry, Miss Swensen. We were just . . . uh . . ."

"It's okay. I don't want to know," Hannah said, interrupting his effort to put a spin on what had obviously been a romantic moment. "Shouldn't you be dancing, or something?"

"That's a great idea. 'Bye, Miss Swensen," the girl said, grabbing her boyfriend's hand and pulling him out of the cloakroom before things could get even more awkward.

Hannah grinned as she watched them hurry out the door. The girl was wearing blue, and they'd obviously been the only ones here. She was about to leave to check the ladies' room when she spotted a small puddle of water on the floor next to a tote bag, the kind women used to carry their shoes when they were wearing their boots.

Her curiosity aroused, Hannah unzipped the bag and examined the shoes. They were a pair of standard black pumps with a small heel, the kind many women wore for dress. There was nothing unusual about the shoes themselves, except for the fact that they were soaked. Hannah picked up a pair of boots placed under a coat on the next hook. They were dry. She checked another pair and her suspicions were confirmed. The woman who'd worn the wet shoes had been outside recently. But why would someone go outside in dress shoes when they had their boots with them? Hannah figured that the lady in question must have been in too much of a hurry to switch to her boots.

It was a second bit of information, and Hannah intended to take full advantage of it. All she had to do was look for a woman in a black skirt, or dress, who was wearing boots. There couldn't be that many of them.

Hannah headed off to the ladies' room to do some uncharacteristic primping while she checked out the other women who were there. Unfortunately, since her brush was in her purse, and her purse was in a drawer in the kitchen, her primping was limited to running her fingers through her hair. She couldn't even freshen her makeup, since all she was wearing was lipstick, and the Pretty Girl lipstick that Luanne had sold her before she'd gone to work at Granny's Attic was still sitting on Hannah's dresser at home.

Luckily, it didn't take long to check out the occupants of the ladies' room. Hannah said hello to Charlotte Roscoe and Sally Laughlin, in red and light blue respectively. Then Carrie, wearing winter white, came in and Hannah greeted her, too. She was about to leave when she noticed a pair of feet wearing boots in one of the stalls.

"I just wanted to tell you that Norman's doing a great job with the photographs," Hannah said to Carrie, wishing that she had inherited the gift of making polite chitchat.

"Of course he is. Norman's wonderful at whatever he does."

"True," Hannah was quick to agree. "Anyway, the reason I mentioned it is that if Savory Press uses any of Norman's photos in the book, he'll get credit as a photographer."

"I'm sure he'll like that," Carrie said, pulling Hannah over to a corner. "What's the matter? Why are you staring at that stall?"

Hannah sighed. She'd obviously been obvious. "I need to know if that lady's wearing a black skirt."

"Why?"

"A man sent me in to check on his date. I don't know her, but he said she was wearing a black skirt."

"Your mother's right. You don't have a deceitful bone in your body."

"What?"

"Tell the truth, Hannah. You made up that whole story about a man and his date, didn't you?"

"Oh. Well . . ."

"Never mind. I'm sure you have a good reason for wanting to know. Hold on for a minute and I'll find out for you."

Hannah held on. What else could she do? And a minute or two later, Carrie was back.

"Striped skirt, silver and blue," Carrie announced in a sibilant whisper. "Is that all you wanted to know?"

"That's it. Thanks, Carrie." Hannah turned and headed for the door.

"I've got a question for you, Hannah."

Hannah prepared herself mentally to lie again if it was necessary. "What is it?"

"I want to know what you think of Winthrop."

"Oh. Well . . . I only met him briefly . . ." Hannah stalled while she tried to think of something innocuous to say ". . . but I did think he made a very strong first impression."

That seemed to satisfy Carrie, and Hannah managed to escape. As she entered the banquet room again, she glanced at her watch. She had five minutes before she could meet her sisters and Norman in the lobby and give them the new information she'd learned. That was just time enough for a fresh cup of coffee.

As Hannah headed for the kitchen, she noticed that Babs Dubinski was sitting alone. Babs looked glum, and Hannah certainly couldn't blame her. This whole week had been a series of shocks for her. First there was Martin's unexpected marriage. And then there was his choice of wife, a Las Vegas dancer. There was the money Martin had spent on Brandi, money that should have gone to his sons. Now Brandi was dead, and that was another big shock, even though Babs hadn't liked her.

Hannah gave a little wave as she neared the table where Babs was sitting. "Hi, Babs. I'm just going to get some fresh coffee. Do you want me to bring you some?"

"That would be nice." Babs reached out to hand Hannah her empty cup. "No sense dirtying another."

Hannah took the cup, and that's when she noticed that Babs had teamed her dark red silk blouse with a black skirt.

She was so startled, she almost dropped the cup and that gave her an excellent idea.

"Uh-oh!" Hannah said, and she dropped the cup deliberately. "Good thing it was empty. Hold on a second. I'll trash it and get you a new one."

Hannah moved to retrieve the cup, hoping that Babs wouldn't guess it had been an excuse to bend over to check her footwear. She glanced at Babs's feet and barely managed to stifle a gasp. Boots! Babs was wearing boots with her black skirt!

If you see someone in a black skirt, just write down the name and don't ask any questions, Hannah's own advice floated through her mind. *Be really careful. We don't know if we're dealing with a material witness or with Brandi's killer.*

Hannah straightened up to stare at Babs for a minute, and then she plunked down in a chair, all set to ignore her own advice. She couldn't imagine Babs as a killer, but the circumstantial evidence was mounting up. There was no way Hannah could wait to talk to her sisters and Norman. She had to strike while the iron was hot.

"What's the matter, Hannah?" Babs looked concerned.

"This is serious, Babs. I want you to tell me exactly what happened in the parking lot with Brandi."

"With Brandi? What do you . . ." Babs broke off in the middle of what was sure to be a denial and gave a shuddering sigh. "All right. I can't stand to keep this to myself any longer. I'm the one who killed Brandi, but it was an accident. You've got to believe me, Hannah!"

Hannah grabbed a clean napkin with a poinsettia on the front. Andrea could translate it later. "Just tell me the truth, Babs, and I'll believe you."

"Part of the reason I didn't like Brandi was that I didn't trust her. The first time Martin brought her to the house, I think she took my watch."

"You *think* she took it? Aren't you sure?"

"I wasn't sure enough to accuse her. The band pinches a

little, so I only wore it when I went out. I usually kept it by my chair in the living room, or in a dish on my dresser, or in the kitchen on the windowsill. Well, after Martin and Brandi left, I couldn't find my watch. I tore the place upside down and backwards looking for it, but I couldn't swear for certain that I hadn't misplaced it myself."

"I understand."

"That's the reason I had my eye on Brandi tonight. I wanted to make sure she didn't steal anything and give Martin a bad name around town."

"Did she steal anything?" Hannah asked, although she already knew the answer.

"She stole your mother's antique knife. I watched her do it, Hannah. She draped her mink over her arm and sidled up to the dessert table as pretty as you please and pretended to be looking at the platter of cookies you and Lisa made. She picked up a couple, I watched her, and then she moved on down the table to look at the cake. She was so fast, I almost didn't see her, but she grabbed the knife, hid it in her coat, and headed for the kitchen door."

"And you followed her?"

Babs nodded. "But first I looked around for Martin. After all, she was his wife, and he could have taken care of it. Martin and Shirley were both gone, so there was only one thing for me to do. I followed Brandi into the kitchen to confront her. I was going to make her put the knife back."

"Was she in the kitchen?"

"No, it was deserted. But the pantry light was on, and when I looked inside, I noticed the door to the parking lot wasn't shut all the way. I stuck my head out and there she was, heading across the lot."

"So you went out after her."

"Yes. I thought about running back inside for my coat and boots, but I didn't want to give her time to hide the knife. I hadn't gone more than a couple of yards when I heard a car door slam and a motor start running over the sound of the wind. Brandi was in Martin's car, and there was only one reason she would have started it. She was going to leave, and I had to stop her."

Hannah reached out to pat Babs' hand. The older woman was obviously upset. "Go on."

"I ran through the snow and got to the car before she could back up. She must not have seen me coming, because she hadn't locked the driver's door, and I pulled it open. There she was, munching on one of your cookies while the car heated up. I reached right past her to turn off the key and then I grabbed her arm and tried to pull her out of the car. She fought back, but I managed to do it."

"What then?"

"That's when I noticed that she was wearing my great-grandmother Dubinski's ring, the emerald and diamond heirloom I gave to Martin and Shirley on their wedding day. I saw red and grabbed for the ring."

"And Brandi fought back?"

"Like a tiger. She punched me in the chest and I went down in the snow. I was just getting up when she reached into the car, grabbed your mother's cake knife, and slashed out at me."

"Did she cut you?"

"No, she missed. And I managed to grab her wrist. We grappled for the knife, and Brandi slipped. That made me slip, and somehow I ended up on top of Brandi in the snow."

"So when you got the upper hand, you stabbed her?"

"No! My hand was on her wrist, never the knife. I thought she was just stunned, that's all. I got to my feet, slipped the ring off her finger, and looked around for the knife to take it back inside. I searched around in the snow for a minute, and then I saw that it was stuck in her chest."

"What did you do then?"

"I reached down to feel for her pulse, but there wasn't any."

"So you didn't call for an ambulance? And you didn't come back inside to tell anyone what had happened?"

Babs shook her head. "I'm not proud of what I did next, but I was so cold and so shocked, I just brushed the snow off my blouse and skirt, and came back in the kitchen."

"No one saw you?"

"No one was there. I ran some warm water in the kitchen sink and soaked my hands until I could feel them again. There were no bloodstains. I checked for that. And then, since my shoes were soaked all the way through, I went to the cloakroom and switched to my boots."

Hannah folded the napkin and stuck it in her sweater pocket. "You know what I have to tell you to do, don't you?"

"I know. I'll go up and tell Mike, but please let me tell the kids first. I want Martin to hear it from me."

Hannah thought about that for a moment. It was highly unorthodox and definitely against police procedure, but she was no longer working with Mike and she didn't have to follow his rules. "Okay," she said. "Let's go find Martin and Shirley."

It didn't take long to locate Martin and Shirley and find a quiet corner so that Babs could tell them her story. When she was through, Martin made a strangled sound. "You killed Brandi?"

"She didn't kill Brandi," Shirley spoke up. "It was an accident. The only reason Babs went after Brandi was to recover the stolen knife."

Babs nodded. "Shirley's right. I'm really sorry, but it was an accident. She came after me with the knife and both of us slipped in the snow. I just hope Mike will believe me. I have to go tell him now."

"You can't!" Martin objected, grabbing his mother's arm. "Don't tell him, Mom. He'll arrest you for murder!"

"I don't think he will. After all it *was* an accident. And don't forget that Brandi had a weapon and I didn't."

"But he won't know that. No one else saw Brandi steal the knife, and some smart lawyer could argue that you took the knife and went out to confront Brandi to get the ring back. You could be convicted, Mom. You could go to jail!"

"Relax, Martin," Hannah said. "Norman has a photo of Brandi stealing the cake knife."

"He does? That's . . . that's great! Then you think everything is going to be all right?"

"I think it will be, especially since your mother's fingerprints won't be on the knife. She might have to spend a few hours down at the sheriff's station, and she may even have to stay there until they can corroborate her account of what happened with Doc Knight's findings, but I'm sure she'll be cleared."

"We'll go along with you, Mom," Martin said, taking his mother's arm.

Shirley took her other arm. "Absolutely. And once we get over this hurdle, Martin and I have some news for you."

"Really?" Babs gave the first smile Hannah had seen cross her face all evening. "I think I know what it is, and that's just wonderful!"

Once Hannah had escorted Babs, Martin, and Shirley to the room that Mike was using for interviews, she raced back to the lobby to meet her sisters and Norman and tell them what had happened.

"You ignored your own advice?" Norman asked, looking more amused than angry.

"That's right."

Andrea's eyes narrowed. "But you would have been madder than a wet hen if we'd ignored your advice."

"That's right, too."

"Come on, everybody," Norman said, playing the role of a peacekeeper. "Let's go see if there's any chocolate left. I'm beginning to droop a little, and we can't go home until the storm lets up."

As they trooped toward the stairs leading down to the banquet room, Hannah glanced out the large window by the front door. Norman was right. The storm was still raging. The wind was every bit as fierce as it had been before, and it was still dangerous to drive. As she stared out the glass at some of the worst weather a Minnesota winter had to offer, a snow-covered figure materialized at the end of the sidewalk leading up to the front door.

"There's somebody out there," Hannah said, squinting through the driving snow. "I think it's Bill!"

"Where?" Andrea asked, rushing back to join Hannah.

"Out there at the curb. I'd better tell Lonnie to go out and help him in. You catch Michelle and ask her to go get him a hot cup of coffee."

Lonnie wasted no time fetching Bill. Once Bill got inside, Andrea helped him out of his parka and Hannah hung it up on the coat tree by the front door. Bill looked half frozen, and he took the coffee gratefully when Michelle brought it up to him. "It's cold out there. My heater went out halfway to town."

"Oh, honey," Andrea said, snuggling up to him in an effort to warm him up. "You shouldn't have tried to make it all the way here. It's all over now."

"What's over?"

"The case," Michelle told him. "We solved it about fifteen minutes ago. Sip some coffee and warm up a little. Then we'll take you to the room Mike's using for interviews."

"What case? What interviews? What's going on?"

"Didn't the dispatcher tell you?" Hannah asked, frowning a bit. "I know Mike tried to reach you right after I found the body."

"What body?" Bill's head swiveled from Andrea, to Hannah, to Michelle, and then back again.

"Martin's new wife, Brandi Wyen Dubinski. She ended up dead in the parking lot. We'll tell you all about it right after we thaw you out," Andrea promised. "All we really need to know right away is how soon Mike can release Mother's antique cake knife. We need to get it back to her before she finds out."

"Before she finds out what?"

"That it was used as a murder weapon . . . except it really wasn't," Hannah explained, getting up to see if Norman had managed to find any chocolate. It was obvious that Bill really needed some because they were explaining things perfectly, and it was taking him forever to catch on.

Chapter Nineteen

"**Y**ou're a really good dancer," Michelle said, as Norman led her back to the table.

"I took lessons. I didn't want Hannah to turn me down when I asked her to dance."

Hannah laughed, her good mood at the beginning of the evening fully restored. It was wonderful to know that Lake Eden hadn't been the scene of another murder. Now she could relax and have fun for the rest of the evening. "I'm no Pavlova, Norman. There was a good reason why Mother didn't name me Grace."

"I'll check on that right after I dance with your other younger sister." Norman held his hand out to Andrea. "Are you up to it?"

Andrea smiled. "I love to dance, but . . . I don't think so tonight. I'm feeling extremely awkward and extremely full. I must have eaten twenty desserts."

"Close," Hannah mumbled under her breath adding up the desserts she'd seen Andrea consume. It was at least a half-dozen, and that was probably the tip of the iceberg. "You're feeling all right, aren't you?"

"I'm fine. It's just that I'm a little tired, and my feet are swelling. I'll sit here and watch you, and put my feet up on your chair."

"I'll get my down jacket and you can put your feet up on that," Michelle said. "You'll be more comfortable that way."

Norman held out his hand and Hannah took it, but she turned back for one more question before she went off to the dance floor. "You don't think anything's going to happen while we're gone, do you?"

"Oh, I think so," Andrea said. And then she laughed at the shocked expression on Hannah's face. "It's not what you're thinking. You're going to enjoy dancing with Norman, that's all I meant."

When they got to the dance floor, Kirby and the jazz ensemble were playing "Moon River," and Hannah snuggled up to Norman as they danced. For once, she didn't have the urge to lead, a residual effect of having taught Andrea to dance. Andrea hadn't wanted to get mixed up, and Hannah always had to be the "boy."

Norman was warm and steady, a perfect partner for dancing cheek to cheek. Of course cheek to cheek was also chin to shoulder, which didn't sound even remotely as romantic, and it was also chest to . . .

"Excuse me." A deep, achingly familiar voice interrupted the thoughts she probably shouldn't have been thinking anyway. Norman turned her around and pulled back slightly, and Hannah found herself face to face with Mike, except that it was her face to his chest, because he was taller.

"You want to cut in?" Norman asked, and Hannah thought he looked just a tiny bit jealous.

"No," Mike said, and then he smiled at Hannah. "Not that I wouldn't like to, but I'm still on the job. I just came over to tell Hannah that Bill and I are taking Babs Dubinski to the station."

"You're not going to charge her, are you?"

"No. We're just going to take her formal videotaped statement. We won't charge her unless the results of Doc's autopsy prove that her account of Brandi's death couldn't be accurate."

"That's good news," Norman said, squeezing Hannah's hand. "Thanks for telling us, Mike."

"No problem. You guys did all the legwork for me, and I appreciate it."

Hannah clamped her lips together so that she wouldn't blurt out what was on her mind. What was Mike talking about? They'd done a lot more than legwork. They had solved the whole case for him!

"Anyway, I just wanted to tell you that Shirley and Martin are following us in Shirley's car, and Earl Flensburg's leading the way in the county snowplow."

"You're not taking your Hummer?" Hannah was surprised.

"No. She can go through just about anything, so I want her to stay out front in case anyone needs to leave."

Hannah grinned. "You shouldn't anthropomorphize inanimate objects."

"Huh?"

"Your Hummer. She won't like it."

Mike looked blank, but Norman caught on right away. He started to chuckle, but he held it in. Since his arms were still around Hannah, she felt as if she were riding out an earthquake.

"Whatever," Mike waved her comment away. "The point is, Earl won't be back for at least an hour and you can use her if there's some kind of emergency."

Hannah couldn't believe what she was hearing. Mike's Hummer was his baby. He must trust her a lot to let her drive his powerful new toy.

"Here." Mike dropped the keys in her hand. "I'm putting her in your hands, Hannah, and I'm trusting your judgment. If someone has to leave, look around for a guy who knows how to handle her."

Hannah's blood pressure began to rise. She should find a *guy* who knew how to handle his Hummer? She was so angry, it felt as if her eyes were burning smoldering circles into his back as he strode off across the dance floor. Mike Kingston was tall, handsome, unbelievably attractive, and about as sexist as a man could get.

"What?" Norman asked, noticing Hannah's intent expression. "I thought that was a very generous thing Mike did. Everybody in town knows how he loves his Hummer."

"Sure, he loves it. And sure, it was generous. I'm sure the *guy* I choose to drive it will think so, too!"

"Oh," Norman said, leaving it at that, but Hannah knew he understood. "Let's finish our dance. I love to dance with you."

"I love to dance with you, too." Hannah smiled as Norman pulled her close into his arms and they moved smoothly across the floor. She was just starting to really enjoy herself again when someone tapped her on the shoulder.

It was Andrea, and Hannah turned to greet her sister. "Hi, Andrea. Did you change your mind about dancing?"

"No. I don't want to cut in. I just came out here to tell you it's time."

Hannah stared at her sister for a moment in absolute disbelief. Then she asked, "Do you mean what I think you mean?"

"I mean exactly what you think I mean. And I think we'd better hurry."

Chapter Twenty

Less than a minute later, they had gathered up their coats and boots and they were headed for the stairs, Norman on one side of Andrea and Hannah on the other. Luckily, Delores was dancing with Winthrop and she failed to notice the exodus of her pregnant daughter, her eldest daughter, and her dentist.

Michelle was talking to Lonnie, who was still manning the front door to discourage anyone who might be foolish enough to brave a blizzard. Hannah called out to Michelle as they helped Andrea up the final stair.

Michelle's face paled as she caught sight of Andrea. "Is it . . ."

"Yes," Hannah told her. "Norman and I are taking Andrea to the hospital in Mike's Hummer. I need you to do a few things for us here."

"Anything. What?"

"We need you to deal with Mother. She's bound to guess what's happening when she realizes that we're gone. You have to convince her to stay here and not try to get to the hospital."

"Mother would drive to the hospital in a blizzard?"

"Absolutely," Andrea gave a little grin. "She wants to be the first one to see her namesake."

Michelle looked stunned. "You mean . . . you're going to name the baby Delores?"

"I said I would if the baby was a girl. But that won't happen."

"It won't? How do you know that?"

"I had the test. And since it's a boy, I can get full credit for offering, and I don't actually have to do it."

"Nice," Michelle said. "Don't worry about a thing here. I'll make sure Mother doesn't get within fifty feet of a motor vehicle."

"There's one other thing you can do. If she's too excited to take charge of Tracey, will you do it?"

"Of course I will!" Michelle reached out to give Andrea a little hug. "This is so exciting. I get to be an aunt again!"

Hannah turned to Lonnie. "Will you help us get Andrea out to Mike's Hummer? It rides pretty high off the ground, and she might need a boost up. Michelle can guard the door until you get back."

With Lonnie helping, it didn't take long to load Andrea in the backseat of the Hummer. The moment he'd run back inside, Hannah turned to Norman and held out the keys. "Do you want to drive?"

"You do it. I'll ride in the back with Andrea."

"But don't you want to drive a Hummer?"

"Sure, but not as much as I want to see the expression on Mike's face when you tell him you drove."

Hannah could hear Andrea panting as she started the engine and pulled away from the curb into the swirling blanket of white snow that awaited them. "What are you doing back there?"

"Panting. It slows down labor. I'm just glad Norman's here with me."

"Why?"

"I know dentists take some of the same classes doctors

do. And so I was hoping that . . . do you know how to deliver a baby, Norman?"

There was a long silence from the backseat and then Norman chuckled. "I think I can handle it. It can't be all that different from a root canal."

Once she'd navigated the first few blocks, Hannah concluded that Mike's Hummer was a perfect vehicle for such horrible weather. It plowed through dense drifts that would have stopped other trucks cold, and the traction was nothing short of miraculous on the icy patches of road. Under other circumstances Hannah might have enjoyed driving Mike's prized vehicle, but not with the stakes this high.

Driving through town wasn't bad, and Hannah was just starting to feel confident when she turned onto Old Lake Road. Then things changed for the worse. The land was flat here, and there were no buildings to act as windbreaks. Visibility was only a foot or two, and it was almost impossible to distinguish the ice-packed shoulder of the road from the pavement itself. Hannah forced herself to hold the wheel steady and prayed that she was on the right track. The snow swirling and whipping in front of the headlights didn't help. It caused her to lose all sense of direction, until it was virtually impossible to tell left from right, or even up from down.

Somehow, Hannah knew she'd never be sure exactly how they'd made it, they arrived at the turnoff for Lake Eden Memorial Hospital and successfully navigated the circular driveway. Hannah stopped only inches from the emergency room door and leaned on the horn with a vengeance.

"We're here!" a burly orderly shouted out, opening up the rear door. "Lonnie Murphy called us to say you were coming."

"Hannah?"

"Yes, Andrea." Hannah turned back to watch the orderly help her sister out onto a gurney.

"I don't bake the cake."

"What cake?"

"The Jell-O Cake. I buy a pound cake at the Red Owl. I just wanted you to know that. I don't think you're supposed to go into the delivery room with a lie on your conscience."

Once Andrea had been whisked inside, Norman and Hannah spent a full minute in silence, she in the front seat and he in the back. Finally Norman broke the silence. "You want coffee?"

"Yes."

"Inside?"

"Yes. Were you nervous?"

"Of course I was. I'm a dentist, not an obstetrician."

Without another word they opened their respective doors and headed straight through the emergency room to the coffee machine in the lobby.

"Here, Hannah." Norman handed her a small fortune in change. "You get the coffee and I'll find out where they took Andrea."

Before the coffee had time to cool and turn into the tar that Hannah was sure it would, Norman was back. "Andrea's in the maternity ward. That's down at the end of the south wing. The nurse said we can go down there and wait in the expectant fathers' room."

"Okay," Hannah said, handing Norman his paper cup of coffee and following him down the hall. "I should probably find a phone and call Bill."

"I did that already. There's nothing for us to do now but wait."

"Waiting is the thing I hate to do the most," Hannah said, gazing around as they entered the waiting room. There was a small Christmas tree on the table in the corner, and someone had strung red and green paper chains across the expanse of the ceiling. "This is nice. They decorated for Christmas. I wonder how long it takes to have a baby."

Norman shrugged. "I asked the nurse that and she said, 'It depends.' She also told me that Doc Knight would come to tell us when the baby was born."

Ten minutes passed as they paged through outdated magazines and pretended interest. Another five minutes passed as they stared at the small Christmas tree. The chairs were comfortable enough, and there was a television set that was programmed to play shorts entitled, "Baby's First Bath," and "Burping Your Baby," but neither Hannah nor Norman felt like watching it.

"Restless?" Norman asked, catching her mood.

"Yes. Let's walk."

The hallway was wide and long, and Hannah wondered whether it had been designed for expectant fathers who wanted to stretch their legs. It felt good to walk off the tension, and Hannah linked arms with Norman and let him set the pace. The hallway was also decorated for Christmas with cutouts of Santas, reindeer, holly, wreaths, snowmen, and Christmas trees. Hannah counted the number of times they passed the snowman with the red muffler, and she was nearing one hundred when Mike came rushing down the corridor.

"How's it going?" he asked.

"We don't know," Hannah told him. "Norman asked the nurse and she said Doc Knight would come out and tell us once the baby's born. Is Bill here?"

"Not yet. He's still interviewing Babs, but he'll come as soon as he can. Good thing I left you the Hummer." Mike turned to Norman. "She handles great, doesn't she?"

"Like a champ. Hannah didn't have a bit of trouble."

Hannah felt like applauding as Mike's mouth dropped open. Norman certainly knew how to deliver a zinger. She gave him a little wink behind Mike's back and then she reached out to take Mike's arm. "Come walk with us. There's nothing to do here except pace the floor."

Time seemed to go a little faster with three of them pacing, or perhaps it was the conversation. Mike was just telling them about how Bill had come close to getting stuck only a few feet from the turnoff for the sheriff's station, when Earl Flensburg came running down the hall.

"Boy, am I glad to see you here!" Earl said, reaching out to pump Hannah's hand. "I went back to the community center and your little sister told me where you went. I just grabbed a cup of coffee and then I got back on the road and followed in your tracks. I figured that if you went off in the ditch, I could pull you out."

"I came close a couple of times," Hannah said, sneaking a quick glance at Mike's face. He didn't look happy, but he was wise enough not to ask if there was any damage to his Hummer. Of course, he probably *knew* there wasn't, because he'd sneaked a look before he came inside.

"Edna sent this," Earl told her, pulling a giant metal thermos from the deep back pouch in his county issue parka. She said you shouldn't be tortured with hospital coffee."

"I'll get the cups," Norman said, dashing inside the expectant fathers' waiting room and coming back with four Styrofoam cups.

When everyone had a good cup of coffee, Hannah raised hers high. "To Edna. She's a lifesaver!"

"How's your sister doing?" Earl asked once the cups were empty.

"Fine I guess, or we would have heard something. The nurse said Doc Knight will come out and tell us right after the baby's born."

Just talking about it made Hannah nervous, and she started to pace again. Mike quickly took one of her arms, and Norman took the other. Earl watched them for a moment, and then he took up a position by Mike's side and started to pace with them.

It was a good thing it was a wide hallway, because Lisa appeared next. She rushed up to Hannah and asked, "Did she have the baby yet?"

"Not yet. How did you get here?"

"Herb borrowed the biggest truck in the lot and drove us. He'll be here in a minute."

"How's Andrea doing?" Herb asked Hannah, rushing up to take Lisa's arm.

"We don't know," Hannah said, wondering if she should borrow some crayons from the children's waiting room and make a sign. "Everything must be okay, or we would have heard something. Doc Knight's going to come out and tell us right after the baby's born."

Lisa and Herb watched them pace for a moment, and then they joined in. Herb took his place next to Norman and Lisa paced next to Herb.

Hannah had just passed the snowman in the red muffler for the three hundred-and-fourteenth time when she saw Bill rushing toward them from the end of the hallway. "Here comes Bill!"

"How's Andrea?" Bill asked, panting a bit as he sprinted the last few yards.

Hannah smiled to set the expectant father at ease and chastised herself mentally for not making that sign. "She must be okay, or we would have heard something. Doc Knight's going to come out and tell us right after the baby's born."

"Great. What are you doing?"

"Pacing. We couldn't think of anything else to do."

"Sounds reasonable to me," Bill said, linking arms with Lisa and taking up the outside position on the left. Let's pick up the pace a little. I'm getting nervous."

All they needed was music and the ability to kick in unison, and they could have tried out for a cabaret. The Todd party horizontal conga line was just rounding the corner for the forty-third time since Bill had joined them, when Doc Knight appeared at the end of the hallway.

"You can stop wearing out my linoleum," he said, smiling widely. "It's a girl, and mother and baby are just fine!"

"A girl!" Bill exclaimed, grinning from ear to ear. "That's wonderful!"

"A *girl?*" Hannah asked, wondering if Doc Knight was so worn out from working long hours that he'd gotten Andrea's son mixed up with another female baby he'd delivered tonight.

As everyone crowded around Bill to offer congratulations and slap him on the back, Hannah rushed up to Doc before he could go off to do whatever doctors do after they deliver a baby.

Doc Knight turned as she grabbed his arm. "What is it, Hannah?"

"You said Andrea had a girl. Are you sure?"

"Of course I'm sure. You can't be in this business for as long as I have if you can't tell a girl baby from a boy baby."

"Right. I just thought maybe . . . well . . . she had the test, and she told me it was ninety-nine percent accurate."

"That's true, but she just happened to hit that one percent. Your sister had a baby girl, seven pounds, three ounces. I'm sorry if that disappoints you, but those are the facts."

"I'm not disappointed," Hannah did her best to explain. "It's just that Andrea promised to name a girl after Mother and Regina Todd. And the only reason she did that was because she was sure she was having a boy. Now it turns out to be a girl, and . . ."

"She's in hot water," Doc Knight finished the sentence for her. "No wonder she cried when I told her the baby was a girl."

"She cried?" Hannah asked, feeling a bit like crying herself.

"Not for long. One look at her daughter and she was

happy again. But just as soon as the new daddy goes off to celebrate with his friends, I think you sisters had better put your heads together and see if you can come up with a name that'll please both families."

"Are you okay?" Hannah asked, entering Andrea's room the second that Bill had vacated it.

"I'm fine, but Mother and Regina won't be. There's no way I'm naming my darling little daughter Delores Regina or Regina Delores!"

"I can understand that," Hannah said.

"So what am I going to do? You've got to help me!"

Tears threatened to roll down Andrea's cheeks and Hannah reached out to give her a hug. "I'll think of something. Just give me a minute. Did you promise specifically to use their *first* names?"

"No."

"That's good. That means we have at least two more names to work with. Mother's middle name is Elizabeth. Do you know what Regina's is?"

"Anatolia," Andrea said promptly. "Since they had such a common last name, Regina's mother decided to give her children distinctive names. Regina Anatolia is the Italian baby. Bill's aunt, Martinique Renée, is the French. And then there's the youngest sister, Dona Esmeralda, and she's the . . ."

"That's enough family history for now," Hannah said, holding up her hand in a gesture that meant *halt* in any language. "I think I might have come up with something that'll please everybody, you included."

"What?" Andrea asked, looking hopeful.

"Bethany."

"That's one of my favorite names! But . . . how do you get Bethany out of Regina Anatolia and Delores Elizabeth?"

Hannah grinned, feeling rather proud of herself. This had

taken some fast brainwork. *"Beth* is a nickname for Elizabeth. And *Annie* could be a nickname for Anatolia. Combine the two and you get *Beth-Annie* or *Bethany."*

"Perfect," Andrea said, reaching out to give her older sister a hug. "You did it, Hannah. Mother's going to be pleased, and so is Bill's mother. You're a miracle worker, especially if you can find me some chocolate somewhere in this hospital."

Chapter
Twenty-One

D ue to a stroke of good fortune, Hannah just happened to have her emergency stash of three Chocolate Chip Crunch cookies in plastic wrap in her coat pocket, and she turned them over to Andrea without a whimper. Then she hurried off to the nursery to have a peek at Bethany. She was about to leave in search of Mike so that she could return the keys to his Hummer, when Mike found her at the nursery window.

"Is that her?"

There was something close to reverence in Mike's tone and Hannah smiled. "That's Bethany. Andrea just named her."

"I like it. It was one of the names on our list when . . ."

Mike stopped in mid-sentence and Hannah reached out to squeeze his arm. She knew his wife had been killed by a stray bullet from a drive-by shooting when she was pregnant with their first baby. "So, do you think she's pretty?"

"She's the most beautiful baby in the nursery," Mike said with a smile. "Of course she's also the only baby in the nursery, but that doesn't count."

Mike's arm tightened around her, and Hannah did her best to switch gears. They had unfinished business. Since Shawna Lee had already landed in Georgia, they were no longer engaged in the brownie wars. She needed Mike to return the pan of Hot Brownies before he tasted them.

"You know those brownies I brought out to the sheriff's station this morning?" Hannah dived right in. "I hope you haven't tasted them yet, because I think I might have made a mistake and left out an ingredient. If you'll give them back, I'll dump them and bake you another batch."

"No way!" Mike said, staring at her with a frown.

"Why not?"

"Because I tasted them, and they're terrific. They've got jalapeños, right?"

"Uh . . . right," Hannah said, and she swallowed hard. Mike didn't look all that angry, but you could never tell about a guy who was used to hiding his emotions in an interrogation room.

"That was a stroke of genius. You're the only one I know who'd think to put diced jalapeños in brownies. Sure, they've got a little burn, but if you eat them with milk on the side, they're great. I'm going to get some vanilla ice cream tomorrow and try them à la mode."

Hannah stood there with a gaping mouth, not even noticing that little Bethany Todd wore the same puzzled expression as her aunt. "You . . . uh . . . you liked them?"

"The chilies really bring out the taste of the chocolate. You don't have to take out an ad or anything, but Shawna Lee's brownies can't hold a candle to yours!"

Hannah stared up into Mike's face. He was serious. He liked her jalapeño brownies. Should she confess that she'd baked them out of meanness, and spite, and jealousy?

Oh, sure. When pigs fly. Hannah smiled demurely, no easy task for her, and gave Mike a little hug.

"Thank you for the compliment," she said, following her mother's golden rule. "I'm so glad you liked them."

Appetizers

Baked Brie

Preheat oven to 375 degrees F., rack in
the middle position

*This is Lisa Herman's recipe, and she says to tell you
that it's the easiest appetizer she ever made in her life.*

6-inch round just ripened baby Brie *(5-inch will
   also work)*
one round, unsliced loaf of bread, 10 to 12
   inches in diameter

¼ cup chopped green onion *(clean and peel
   them first—then you can use up to two
   inches of the stem)*
¼ cup chopped shallots
¼ teaspoon white pepper
2 Tablespoons white wine *(or 1 Tablespoon
   water, 1 Tablespoon vinegar)*
½ teaspoon Season Salt *(See Priscilla
   Knudson's recipe on page 365)*

Slice the top from the bread. Keep the top—you'll
need it later. Hollow out the inside of the bread, leaving at least ¾ inch of bread in place on the sides and 1
inch on the bottom.

Slice off the top rind of the baby Brie. *(If you dip
your knife in water frequently, it won't stick as much.)*
Leave the rest of the rind in place. Place the Brie in the
bread.

In a small bowl, mix together the green onion, shallots, white pepper, white wine, and Season Salt.

Spread this mixture on top of the Brie, replace the top
slice of bread, and wrap the entire loaf in aluminum foil.

Bake at 375 degrees F. for 30 minutes.

Serve with cubed bread or crackers.

Busy Day Pâté

This recipe is from Mike Kingston (Actually, it's from his sister but she said Mike could use it.)

8-ounce package of braunschweiger *(liver sausage—I used Farmer John's)*
¼ cup horseradish sauce *(4 Tablespoons—I used Heinz)****

*** If you can't find horseradish sauce where you live, mix 1 Tablespoon of horseradish with 3 Tablespoons of mayonnaise, and it should work just fine.

Cut the braunschweiger into chunks and place it in the bottom of a microwave-safe bowl. Heat it on HIGH for 45 seconds. Stir it around a bit, and if it's still cold, heat it on HIGH for another 10 to 15 seconds, or until it's soft enough to be mashed with a fork.

Mash up the braunschweiger and add the horseradish sauce. Mix until it's blended.

Transfer the warm pâté to a bowl, cover it with plastic wrap, and refrigerate it for at least 3 hours before serving.

A half-hour before you're ready to serve, take the pâté out of the refrigerator and let it warm to spreading consistency.

Serve with a basket of assorted fancy crackers.

Caviar Pie

Carrie Rhodes got this recipe when she went to Los Angeles on vacation and stopped off at an estate sale. A lady named June Pierce kept her from spending too much money on a silver vase that wasn't really silver and gave her this recipe to boot.

8-ounce or larger jar of lumpfish caviar *(you can also use red caviar)*
1 ½ teaspoons good olive oil
4 hardboiled eggs, finely diced
⅓ cup finely diced sweet onion *(or green onions)*
½ to one cup sour cream
2 Tablespoons mayonnaise (⅛ cup)
1 teaspoon salt

Put lumpfish in a small bowl. Pour in olive oil, stir, and refrigerate while you make the rest of the recipe.

Boil the eggs. Cool them, peel them, and dice them. *(If you have a food processor, use the steel blade—if you don't have one, use a sharp knife to chop them finely.)*

Put the diced eggs in the bottom of a 9-inch glass pie plate or shallow glass dish. Press them down with a metal spatula.

Dice the onions and sprinkle them over the diced eggs. Press them down.

Mix the sour cream with the mayonnaise and the salt. Put dollops of the mixture on top and carefully spread them together. Use as much as it takes to make a nice layer.

Drop the lumpfish on top of the sour cream by spoonfuls, spreading it out carefully. Cover the dish with plastic wrap and refrigerate it for 4 to 6 hours.

Serve with toast points or crackers for an elegant appetizer.

Deviled Eggs

Claire Rodgers got this recipe from her best friend Jayni Bailey who used to teach second grade in Lake Eden before she moved away to California. When Claire started dating Reverend Knudson, she felt uncomfortable bringing "deviled" anything to the parsonage, but Reverend Knudson said it didn't matter what she called anything that tasted so heavenly.

When Claire asked for tips on boiling perfect eggs, Jayni said she put rubber bands around the egg cartons and tipped them on their sides in the refrigerator the night before she planned to boil them because that kept the yolks in the center of the eggs. After they were boiled, Jayni cooled them, put them in a covered bowl and refrigerated them for 24 hours before she peeled them.

To make six eggs:

Hard boil the eggs, using your favorite method. Peel the eggs. Cut the eggs in half from top to bottom. Remove the yolks and put them in a small bowl.

Mash the yolks with a fork until they're crumbled. Then add:

¼ cup mayonnaise
½ teaspoon minced onion
½ teaspoon parsley flakes
¼ teaspoon celery salt
¼ teaspoon dry mustard *(MUST be the dry kind)*

Mix thoroughly and then fill the yolk cavity, mounding the mixture a bit in the center. Place on a small platter. If you want to garnish the eggs, sprinkle them with a bit of paprika or parsley. You can also garnish them with a slice of ripe or stuffed olive.

Yield: Makes 12 halves

Fiesta Dip Platter

Sally Laughlin serves this out at the Lake Eden Inn when her customers watch football games in the bar.

16-ounce can spicy refried beans *(I used Rosarita Spicy)*
3 large ripe mashed avocados
⅓ cup salsa ranchero *(I used La Victoria Salsa Ranchero labeled "hot")*
1 finely chopped onion
1 cup sour cream *(½ pint)*
1 can *(4 ¼-ounces)* chopped black olives, drained
1 cup finely grated cheddar cheese
1 cup finely chopped lettuce
1 cup finely chopped tomatoes

You can layer this in a 9 x 13 inch glass cake pan, or on a round platter.

Spread the beans on the bottom of the dish you've chosen.

Peel and mash the avocados. Blend in the hot salsa ranchero and layer it over the beans.

Sprinkle the chopped onion over the avocado mixture.

Mix the black olives with the sour cream and spread it over the chopped onions.

Sprinkle on the grated cheddar cheese.

Sprinkle the chopped lettuce on top of the cheese.

Sprinkle the tomatoes on the very top.

Press everything down with a metal spatula, cover tightly with plastic wrap, and refrigerate it for at least 4 hours so the flavors will marry.

Serve with a basket of tortilla chips and let everyone scoop up the dip.

Herring Appetizer

THIS DISH MUST BE MADE 3 DAYS IN ADVANCE

Priscilla Knudson, Reverend Knudson's grandmother, brings this herring appetizer to every potluck dinner. The one time she decided to bring something else, twenty-six people, including her grandson, made her promise never to do it again.

Glass jar that will hold one quart

2 twelve-ounce jars marinated herring fillets
¾ cup crinkle-cut frozen carrots
2 small red onions
2 teaspoons whole allspice
2 teaspoons whole yellow mustard seeds
6 to 9 small sprigs of fresh dill

Pickling Liquid:
¾ cup white vinegar
½ cup water
½ cup white *(granulated)* sugar

Bring the vinegar, water, and sugar to a boil in a saucepan, stirring constantly until the sugar is dissolved. Take the saucepan off the heat and set the liquid aside to cool to room temperature.

Open the jars of herring and drain them in a strainer. Pick out the herring fillets, rinse them in cold water, and throw everything else away.

Cook the carrots according to the package instructions, but make sure they're still firm and not soft.

Peel the red onions and cut them into thin slices.

Arrange one-fourth of the onions in a thin layer in the bottom of the 1-quart glass jar. Top them with a third of the herring. Top the herring with a third of the carrots. Place 2 or 3 dill sprigs on the top and scatter on a third of the allspice and a third of the mustard seeds. Repeat this sequence until all the ingredients have been used, ending with a top layer of onions.

Pour the cooled pickling liquid into the jar. It should just cover the contents. If there's not enough pickling liquid, top off the jar with a little white vinegar right out of the bottle.

If the jar has a cover, put it on. If it doesn't, put a double layer of plastic wrap on the top and secure it with a sturdy rubber band.

Refrigerate the herring for 3 days before serving.

Yield: Makes about 4 cups and is perfect to take to a potluck dinner. An average serving is ⅓ cup, so it will serve at least 12 people *(maybe half that if they're Scandinavian.)*

Mrs. Knudson says to tell you that she found a pretty straight-sided glass jar at a yard sale for a dime, and it's perfect for her herring. She also says to tell you that when she brings herring to a potluck, she makes a triple batch.

Misdemeanor Mushrooms

Preheat oven to 325 degrees F., rack in
the middle position

*This recipe is from Bill Jessup, Charlie Jessup's
cousin and he's a detective. Charlie says he calls these
"Misdemeanor Mushrooms," because they're so good
they ought to be illegal.*

2 pounds pork sausage
3 cloves of finely chopped garlic
2 Tablespoons ground sage
8-ounce package cream cheese
1 Tablespoon parsley
1 ounce Marsala wine *(optional)*
1 pound medium to large mushrooms
Parmesan cheese *(to sprinkle)*

In a large, non-stick skillet, combine sausage, garlic and sage. Sauté until sausage is browned and garlic
is translucent. Drain fat from skillet and add softened,
cubed cream cheese and parsley. Simmer for 10 minutes, stir in the wine *(if you want to use it,)* remove
from heat, and cover.

Wash mushrooms. Remove stems and set caps aside.
Chop the stems very fine and stir into the sausage/
cheese mixture. Brush caps with melted butter and
arrange cap-down on a non-stick baking sheet. *(Bill
says if you shave just a bit from the bottom of the cap
to make them flat, they'll sit on the pan a lot better.)*
Fill each cap with a heaping mound of warm sausage
mixture and sprinkle with Parmesan cheese. Bake in a
325-degree F. oven for 15 minutes.

Yield: Serves 15 to 20 people as an appetizer *(unless
Charlie is there and makes a whole meal out of them.)*

Seafood Bread Dip

Preheat oven to 300 degrees F., rack in
the middle position

*This is a recipe from Carrie Rhodes. She loves to
make appetizers.*

4 eight-ounce bars of softened cream cheese
    (32 ounces in all)
½ pound chopped crab meat and/or chopped
    shrimp
4 green onions, cleaned, peeled and chopped,
    including 3 inches of the stems
1 teaspoon garlic salt
1 teaspoon black pepper
¼ cup dried chopped onions
⅓ cup mayonnaise
2 teaspoons lemon juice

Round loaf of bread, unsliced, 10 to 12 inches in diameter *(I used squaw bread)*
1 egg, beaten

Unwrap cream cheese, put it in a large microwave-
safe bowl, and heat it for 40 seconds on HIGH in the
microwave. Turn the bowl and keep heating it in
20-second increments until it's soft and you can stir it.

Add the remaining ingredients and stir it all up.

Cut the top off the loaf of bread and set it aside to
use later. Hollow out the bread with a spoon, but be
careful to leave at least a half-inch of bread on the bottom and the sides. Brush the inside of the loaf with the
beaten egg and pop it in the oven for 5 to 10 minutes
until the egg has dried. Then fill the loaf with the seafood
mixture and put the top back on.

Wrap the loaf tightly in two layers of foil, keeping the top up. Set the loaf on a cookie sheet and bake for 2 hours at 300 degrees F. *(This can hold in the oven for an hour if your guests are late.)*

To serve, take off the top and invite your guests to dip bread squares, crackers, or vegetable sticks.

Spinach Quiche

Preheat oven to 375 degrees F., rack in
the middle position

*This is my recipe. It can be served as an appetizer if
you cut it into thin slices and arrange them on a platter. It can also be served as an entrée.*

One 9-inch unbaked pastry shell
1 beaten egg yolk *(reserve the white in a small
    dish)*
10-ounce package frozen chopped spinach
½ teaspoon salt
½ teaspoon pepper *(freshly ground is best)*
3 Tablespoons horseradish sauce
2 ounces shredded Jarlsberg *(or good Swiss
    cheese)*
4 eggs
1½ cups Half & Half *(or light cream)*
⅛ teaspoon salt
⅛ teaspoon cayenne pepper
⅛ teaspoon nutmeg *(freshly ground is best)*

Beat the egg yolk in a glass with a fork. Brush the
inside of the unbaked pastry shell with the yolk. Set
the shell aside to dry.

Cook and drain the spinach. Squeeze out as much
moisture as you can and then blot with a paper towel.

In a bowl, combine the spinach with the salt, pepper, and horseradish sauce. Spread it in the bottom of
the pastry shell.

Sprinkle the top with the grated cheese.

Beat the 4 whole eggs with the reserved egg white.
Add the Half & Half, salt, and cayenne pepper. Mix
well and pour on top of cheese.

Sprinkle the top with nutmeg.

Bake at 375 degrees F. for 40 minutes, or until a knife inserted one inch from the center comes out clean.

Let cool for ten minutes and then cut into wedges and serve.

This quiche can be served warm or at room temperature. I've even been known to eat it cold, straight out of the refrigerator. It's perfect for a fancy brunch or a lazy, relaxed breakfast on the weekend.

Yield: Serves from 12 to 18 as an appetizer. Serves six as an entrée if they only have one piece.

Spinach Rollups

This recipe is from my friend Susan Zilber. Susan moved away to New York, but I bet she still makes these.

5 to 8 flour tortillas *(the large burrito size)*
16-ounce package frozen chopped spinach
¼ cup mayonnaise
½ cup softened cream cheese
¼ cup sour cream
⅛ cup dried chopped onion
¼ cup bacon bits
1 Tablespoon Tabasco sauce

Cook the spinach and drain it, squeezing out all the moisture. *(Cheesecloth inside a strainer works well for this.)* Mix together all ingredients except the tortillas.

Spread small amount of spinach mixture out on the face of a tortilla. Roll it up and place it in a plastic freezer bag. Continue spreading and rolling tortillas until the spinach mixture is gone.

Fold the plastic bag over when all the rollups are inside to make sure they stay tightly rolled. Refrigerate for at least 4 hours. *(Overnight is best.)* Slice with a sharp knife, arrange on a platter, and serve as appetizers.

Susan says to tell you that once she started to make these and found that she was out of sour cream. She used all cream cheese instead, and they were delicious.

Hannah's Addition to Susan's Rollups

5 to 8 flour tortillas *(the large burrito size)*
6 ounces chopped smoked salmon *(or lox)*
1 cup *(8 ounces)* softened cream cheese
¼ cup dried chopped onions
1 teaspoon freshly ground black pepper
1 teaspoon dill weed *(of course fresh is best)*

Mix all the ingredients except the tortillas together in a bowl.

Spread small amount of the salmon mixture out on the face of a tortilla. Roll it up and place it in a plastic freezer bag. Continue spreading and rolling tortillas until the salmon mixture is gone.

Fold the plastic bag over when all the rollups are inside to make sure they stay tightly rolled. Refrigerate for at least 4 hours. *(Overnight is best.)* Slice with a sharp knife, arrange on a platter, and serve as appetizers.

I made Susan's Spinach Rollups too, and after I cut them the next day, I arranged both kinds on the platter in contrasting rings. It looked gorgeous.

Soups

Quick Irish Chili

This recipe is from Bridget Murphy. It came from her sister, Patsy, who got it from a cousin who got it from her next-door neighbor, a man named John Brady.

2 pounds hamburger *(don't use lean—it needs some fat in it)*

2 minced garlic cloves *(or one Tablespoon of jarred, chopped garlic)*

1 large onion, finely chopped

8-ounce can tomato sauce

3 whole cooked tomatoes, skins removed and cut into large pieces *(you can use canned)*

1 bottle Guinness Stout *(12 ounces)*

3 teaspoons chili powder

¾ teaspoon ground red pepper *(cayenne)*

2 teaspoons ground cumin

2 teaspoons whole green peppercorns

1 teaspoon salt

1 Tablespoon brown sugar

Brown the hamburger in a large skillet. Add the garlic and onion and stir until the onion pieces are translucent.

Add the tomato sauce and the tomatoes. Stir well.

Add remaining ingredients and heat everything up over medium heat, then cover, turn heat to low, and simmer for 20 minutes.

Toppings:

chopped celery sautéed in oil, but still a bit crunchy

chopped green onions

shredded cheese

chopped black olives

sour cream
chili beans *(but only if you must—real chili
    doesn't have beans)*

Fill bowls with chili and top with any or all of the above.

This chili is especially good served with Bridget's Soda Bread.

Bridget says to tell you to back off a bit on the red pepper if your family doesn't like things spicy. A generous dollop of sour cream mixed into your bowl will also work to cut the heat from the pepper.

This chili will hold for hours in a crock-pot and it's perfect for halftime at football games—just make it the night before and refrigerate it in the crock. Four to five hours before you want to serve it, just put the crock in the slow cooker and turn it to LOW.

Sally's Radish Soup

This is the soup I always order when I go out to the Lake Eden Inn. Sally says you need a blender to make this soup. She also says that if you don't have one, borrow one.

4 bunches red radishes *(approximately 12 radishes per bunch)*
2 medium onions, cut into large pieces
42 ounces chicken broth *(about 5½ cups)*

6 Tablespoons butter
6 Tablespoons flour
4 cups Half & Half *(or light cream)*

6 Tablespoons Worcestershire sauce
1 teaspoon salt
½ teaspoon white pepper
3 Tablespoons horseradish sauce *(I used Heinz)****

*** If you can't find horseradish sauce, mix 1 Tablespoon ground horseradish with 2 Tablespoons mayonnaise.

Clean the radishes *(cut off the tops and the bottoms and wash them)* and place them in a large saucepan. Add the onions. Pour the chicken broth over them and simmer for 35 minutes.

Let the contents of the saucepan cool slightly and then puree in a blender. *(You'll have to do this in batches—it won't all fit at once.)* Transfer the puree to a large bowl and cover it to keep it warm.

Put the large saucepan back on the burner. Melt the butter on medium heat and then sprinkle in the flour. Stir until bubbles appear. Keep stirring and cooking for one minute. Add the Half & Half *(or light cream)* and cook, stirring frequently, until mixture has thickened. This should take about 5 minutes or so.

Add Worcestershire sauce, salt, white pepper, and horseradish sauce. Then add the radish puree and stir thoroughly. Return to the heat and stir until heated through.

If you want to get fancy, get a few extra radishes, slice them very thinly, and float them on top of the soup bowls. You can also add fresh, minced parsley for color.

Sally has a tip for you. If you want to bring this soup to a buffet dinner, don't return the saucepan to the heat after adding the spices at the end. Instead, transfer the soup to a slow cooker sprayed with Pam or other non-stick cooking spray. When you get to the potluck dinner, plug in the crock-pot, set it on LOW, and go off and enjoy yourself. Sally says to tell you that this soup will hold for at least 3 hours on LOW and maybe even longer.

Summer Gazpacho

Vera Olsen contributed this recipe. It's called "Summer" Gazpacho, because she only makes it when tomatoes are in season.

1 cucumber, peeled and seeded
1 medium sweet onion, cut into chunks
6 medium tomatoes, peeled and seeded
½ cup flavorful olive oil
¾ teaspoon chili powder
1 teaspoon garlic powder
3 Tablespoons wine vinegar or sherry vinegar
1 teaspoon kosher salt
2 cans Spicy Hot V-8 Juice *(for a total of 23 ounces)****

*** Vera says if you don't have Spicy Hot V-8 Juice, you can use Bloody Mary mix, or regular tomato juice spiced up with a little hot sauce.

Chop the cucumber and onion in small chunks and put them in a blender.

Peel the tomatoes by dipping them, one at a time, in boiling water for a few seconds until the skin cracks, and then into a bowl of ice water. This will make the peel come right off.

Seed the tomatoes by cutting them in quarters and poking out the seeds with your finger. Once that's done, chop the tomatoes up a little and put them in the blender with the onion and cucumber.

Blend the chopped cucumber, onion, and tomato on the lowest speed as you add the olive oil, chili powder, garlic powder, vinegar, and kosher salt. Pour contents into a large pitcher and add the V-8 Juice. Stir well and refrigerate for at least 6 hours. *(Overnight is fine, too.)*

When you're ready to serve, stir the gazpacho a final time and check for seasoning, adding more salt if needed. Pour the gazpacho into small bowls. Top with a generous dollop of sour cream and sprinkle with minced chives.

Salads

Dilly Onion Rings

This is Ellie Kuehn's recipe. She tried serving it on a sausage pizza out at Bertanelli's and it was really good!

One large mild or sweet onion *(a red onion is nice—more colorful)*
⅓ cup white *(granulated)* sugar
2 teaspoons salt
1 teaspoon fresh baby dill *(it's not as good with dried dill weed)*
½ cup white vinegar
¼ cup water

4 large ripe tomatoes as an accompaniment *(optional)*

Cut the onion in thin slices. Separate the slices into rings and put them in a bowl.

Combine the sugar, salt, dill, white vinegar, and water.

Pour the liquid over the onion rings.

Cover the bowl and refrigerate for at least 5 hours, stirring every hour or so.

Serving suggestions: Slice large ripe tomatoes and arrange on a platter. Lift the onion rings out of the brine and sprinkle them on top of the tomato slices. Garnish with fresh, chopped parsley leaves if desired.

You can use these onion rings to garnish cooked carrots, cooked green beans, even mashed potatoes. They're also a wonderful garnish for a mixed green salad.

Covered tightly and stirred a couple of times a day, these marinated onion rings should last for at least a week in the refrigerator.

French Dressing

Claire Rodgers contributed this recipe. She got it from one of her mother's friends, Mabel Drager.

1 can *(10¾ ounces)* condensed tomato soup
   (Claire used Campbell's Classic Tomato)
⅓ cup wine vinegar
¾ cup olive oil
2 Tablespoons Worcestershire sauce
1 teaspoon paprika
1 teaspoon salt
½ teaspoon garlic powder
½ cup brown sugar

Dump all ingredients in a quart jar. Put on the top and shake vigorously. Refrigerate.

Use to dress a nice green salad. You can put a few Dilly Onion Rings on the top, if you like.

Ginger Ale Jell-O

From my sister Andrea, the Queen of Jell-O. She got this recipe from Immelda Griese, Father Coultas' housekeeper. The original recipe used canned green grapes, but Andrea couldn't find them at the Red Owl unless she bought a huge can of fruit cocktail and picked them out, grape by grape. Since she didn't want to do that, she substituted pears, and Immelda says she likes it even better this way.

One 6-ounce package lemon or peach Jell-O
1 ½ cups boiling water
¼ teaspoon salt
½ teaspoon paprika
2 cups cold ginger ale *(Andrea uses Vernor's)*
2 cups sliced canned pears, drained
two 8-ounce cans pineapple tidbits, drained
⅔ cup sliced almonds

Dissolve Jell-O in boiling water. Add salt and paprika. Let cool to room temperature.

Add cold ginger ale. Refrigerate until partially set. *(Andrea's instructions are: "It should look like jelly on hot toast.")*

Stir in sliced pears, pineapple tidbits, and sliced almonds. Pour into a 2-quart mold and refrigerate overnight.

Dressing:
1 cup mayonnaise
¼ cup heavy cream
1 Tablespoon honey

Mix up the mayonnaise, cream, and honey. Put them in a little dish with a spoon next to the Jell-O on the table.

To serve Jell-O, turn out on a platter and invite people to take a slice and top it with a little dressing.

Holiday Jell-O Mold

Andrea's recipe again. She collects Jell-O recipes.

Spray a Bundt cake pan *(8 cups)* or other 2-quart mold with Pam or other non-stick spray. Set aside.

1 large package *(6 ounces)* lime Jell-O
1 cup boiling water
¾ cup cold water

Stir Jell-O powder into boiling water until dissolved. Add cold water and set aside to let cool.

1 teaspoon salt
2 Tablespoons fresh lemon juice
2 medium-sized ripe avocados, mashed
⅓ cup sour cream
2 to 3 drops green food coloring

Combine salt, lemon juice, mashed avocados, and sour cream. Stir until smooth. Add food coloring and mix thoroughly.

Stir avocado mixture into cooled lime Jell-O and pour into Bundt cake pan. Refrigerate until firm. *(2 to 4 hours—overnight is fine, too.)*

1 and ⅓ cups boiling water
1 large package *(8 ounces)* cranberry or raspberry Jell-O
One 8 ½-ounce can crushed pineapple with juice
Two 16-ounce cans whole-berry cranberry sauce *(2 ¼ cups)*
1 Tablespoon prepared horseradish

Dissolve Jell-O in boiling water. Add pineapple, cranberry sauce, and horseradish. Mix thoroughly. Refrigerate until syrupy. *(Approximately one hour.)*

Spoon cranberry mixture carefully over the avocado mixture. Refrigerate until firm. *(At least 4 hours—overnight is fine, too.)*

Unmold on a pretty platter to serve.

Andrea complains that this recipe is too complicated for her, but if we beg, she makes it every year for Thanksgiving and it's wonderful with turkey. She does the lime Jell-O layer the night before and the cranberry Jell-O layer on Thanksgiving morning.

Pretty Coleslaw

This is what Andrea calls "Green Jell-O." She makes it for special occasions.

2 large *(6 oz.)* packages lime Jell-O *(we like it
  with Lemon, too)*
4 cups boiling water
2 cups mayonnaise
1 teaspoon salt
½ cup vinegar *(Andrea uses raspberry vinegar)*
2 cups cold water

4 cups finely shredded cabbage *(Andrea buys it
  pre-shredded)*
2 cups finely diced celery
¼ cup finely diced onion

In a large bowl, dissolve Jell-O in boiling water. Let cool slightly. Add mayonnaise, salt, and vinegar. Stir until blended. Then add cold water and refrigerate until mixture is syrupy, but not completely set. *(This will take an hour to an hour and a half.)*

Spray Jell-O mold(s) with non-stick cooking spray. *(Andrea uses one Bundt cake pan that holds 8 cups and one small 2-cup mold.)*

Beat partially set Jell-O mixture until fluffy. Then mix in the shredded cabbage, diced celery and diced onion.

Pour or ladle the mixture into the molds you've chosen and refrigerate them for another 2 hours. Then cover the tops with plastic wrap and refrigerate at least another 4 hours before unmolding.

To unmold, you have two choices. Andrea sets the molds in the back of her Volvo and drives around town

Breads

Aunt Grace's Breakfast Muffins

Preheat oven to 400 degrees F., rack in
middle position

*This recipe is from my friend, Terry Sommers (no
relation to Becky Summers.) These muffins are just incredible. When we tested them at the Christmas potluck,
we came very close to putting them on the dessert
table.*

1 ½ cups flour
2 teaspoons baking powder
½ teaspoon salt
½ teaspoon nutmeg *(freshly ground is best)*

½ cup sugar
⅓ cup melted butter

1 beaten egg
½ cup milk
1 ½ cups cored, peeled, and then shredded ap-
    ples *(measure after shredding)*

Stir together the flour, baking powder, salt, and nutmeg. Set aside.

In another bowl, blend the sugar and melted butter
together. Let the butter cool to room temperature.

Add the egg, milk, and shredded apples to the butter and sugar mixture. Stir well. Then mix in the dry
ingredients you've set aside.

Fill well-greased muffin tins ⅔ full with batter.
Bake at 400 degrees F. for 20 to 25 minutes. Let the
muffins cool in the tins for 10 minutes and then turn
them out.

Topping:
½ stick melted butter *(¼ cup, ⅛ pound)****
½ cup sugar
1 teaspoon cinnamon

*** Use a whole stick if you really want to be sinful! It's wonderful!

Melt the butter and pour it into a shallow bowl. Mix the sugar and cinnamon together in another shallow bowl. Roll the muffins in the melted butter and then in the sugar and cinnamon mixture.

Yield: 12 muffins

These muffins are wonderful warm, but they're also good at room temperature, or even refrigerated! There is no way to serve them that's not good. To borrow an advertising slogan, "Nobody doesn't like Aunt Grace's Breakfast Muffins."

Can Bread

Do not preheat oven—bread has to rise
for several hours before baking

This bread recipe is from Cheryl Coombs. She says it's almost foolproof even for somebody who's never had the nerve to bake bread from scratch before.

½ cup butter *(1 stick, ¼ pound)*
2 cups boiling water
1 teaspoon salt
½ cup brown sugar
1 cup oatmeal *(I used Quaker Oats Quick
    1-Minute)*
two ¼-ounce packages dry yeast *(any type)*
2 eggs
4 ½ cups flour *(approximate measure)*

Melt butter in a saucepan with the boiling water. Pour it in a bowl. Add the salt, brown sugar, and oatmeal. Stir it all up.

Add the yeast quickly, before the mixture cools.

Crack the eggs in a glass and beat them up with a fork. Add them to the bowl and stir thoroughly.

Add the flour, one cup at a time, until it feels about right for bread dough. *(That's a moisture level midway between muffin batter and cookie dough.)*

Turn the dough out of the bowl and onto a floured breadboard, or table top. Let it rest a couple of minutes. *(It doesn't need to rest, but you probably do.)*

Knead the dough, adding flour as it becomes too sticky to work. *(Kneading is just punching it down, and turning it over and folding it a bunch of times. You'll like it—it's therapeutic.)* There's no need to knead *(that's a terrible pun!)* any longer than five minutes . . . just until dough is no longer sticking to your hands like stringy glue.

Wash your hands, wash the bowl, dry the bowl, and then spray the inside of the bowl with a non-stick spray. Dump the dough inside the bowl and cover it with a moist towel. Set it in a warm *(but not hot)* place to rise until doubled in bulk. *(This will take from one to two hours.)*

IMPORTANT NOTE: If you don't want to bake your bread today, don't let the dough rise. Cover the bowl with plastic wrap and put it in the refrigerator. It can wait up to 12 hours. Then just take it out in the morning, remove the plastic wrap, cover the dough with a damp towel, and set it in a warm place to finish rising.

Once the dough has doubled in bulk, turn it out onto a floured board again and punch it down. Divide the dough and shape it into loaves, rounds, rolls, little animals, braids, or whatever. Place free-form breads on greased cookie sheets. Place loaves in greased loaf pans. You can even use greased metal coffee cans for rounds and amaze your friends when you give them round sandwiches.

Cover whatever you've used to contain your dough with the moist towel again and let your creations rise for approximately 45 minutes.

Preheat the oven to 350 degrees F., rack in the middle position for cookie sheet loaves and loaf pans, or lower for the taller coffee cans.

If you want a glaze on the top of your bread, brush the tops with egg yolk mixed with a little water before you bake.

Bake large loaves and coffee cans for approximately 60 minutes, 45 minutes for smaller loaves or rounds. Rolls take about 30 minutes.

Let cool in pans *(or on cookie sheet)* on top of wire rack for 15 minutes, then turn out of pans and cool directly on the wire rack.

Cheesy Spicy Corn Muffins

This recipe is from Danielle Watson. She argued that it really isn't a recipe since it's not made from scratch, but we told her that didn't matter.

1 package corn muffin mix, enough to make 12 muffins
4-ounce can well-drained diced green chilies *(Danielle uses Ortega brand)*
½ cup finely shredded sharp cheddar cheese *(or Monterey Jack)*

Preheat oven according to the directions on the corn muffin package.

Prepare the corn muffin mix according to package directions. Add the green chilies and the shredded cheese, and stir well.

Line muffin pans with a double layer of cupcake papers and spray the inside with Pam.

Spoon the batter into the cupcake papers.

Bake according to corn muffin package directions.

Danielle says to tell you that if you have visiting relatives who don't like any spice at all, you can substitute a half can of well-drained whole-kernel corn for the peppers.

Yield: Whatever it says on the package and a little more.

Cranberry Muffins

Preheat oven to 375 degrees F., rack in
the middle position

*These are from Becky Summers. They're perfect to
serve for a Thanksgiving dinner.*

¾ cup melted butter *(1½ sticks)*
1 cup white *(granulated)* sugar
2 beaten eggs *(just whip them up with a fork)*
2 teaspoons baking powder
½ teaspoon salt
1 cup dried cranberries
2 ¼ cups flour *(no need to sift)*
½ cup milk
½ cup cranberry sauce *(use whole berry, not
    jellied)*

Crumb Topping:
½ cup sugar
⅓ cup flour
¼ cup softened butter *(½ stick)*

Grease the bottoms only of a 12-cup muffin pan *(or
line the cups with double cupcake papers—that's what I
do at The Cookie Jar.)* Melt the butter in a bowl with the
dried cranberries and set them aside to plump up and
cool. Measure out the sugar in a large bowl and add the
beaten eggs, baking powder, and salt. Mix thoroughly.

Stir in the cooled butter and plumped dried cranberries. Add half of the flour to your bowl and mix it in
with half of the milk. Add the rest of the flour and the
milk and mix thoroughly. Then add ½ cup cranberry
sauce to your bowl and mix it in.

Fill the muffin tins three-quarters full and set them
aside. If you have dough left over, grease the bottom

of a small tea-bread loaf pan and fill it with your remaining dough.

The crumb topping: Mix the sugar and the flour in a small bowl. Add the softened butter and cut it in until it's crumbly. *(You can also do this in a food processor with chilled butter and the steel blade.)*

Fill the remaining space in the muffin cups with the crumb topping. Then bake the muffins in a 375 F. degree oven for 25 to 30 minutes. *(The tea-bread should bake about 10 minutes longer than the muffins.)*

While your muffins are baking, divide the rest of your cranberry sauce into half-cup portions and pop it in the freezer. I use paper cups to hold it, and freeze them inside a freezer bag. All you have to do is thaw a cup the next time you want to make a batch of Cranberry Muffins.

When your muffins are baked, set the muffin pan on a wire rack to cool for at least 30 minutes. *(The muffins need to cool in the pan for easy removal.)* Then just tip them out of the cups and enjoy.

These are wonderful when they're slightly warm, but the cranberry flavor will intensify if you store them in a covered container overnight.

Gina's Strawberry Bread

Preheat oven to 350 degrees F., rack in
the middle position

*This recipe is from Gina, Father Coultas' cousin,
and she always brings a loaf when she comes to Lake
Eden to visit. She says to tell you that if you keep this
bread in an airtight container, it'll taste even better
the second day. It's also wonderful if you toast and
butter it.*

½ cup butter *(1 stick, ¼ pound)*
1 cup white *(granulated)* sugar
½ teaspoon strawberry flavoring *(or vanilla, or
   almond)*
2 eggs, separated
1 teaspoon baking powder
1 teaspoon baking soda
1 teaspoon salt
2 cups flour *(no need to sift)*
1 cup crushed or chopped fresh strawberries *(or
   a 10-ounce package of frozen strawberries,
   thawed and well drained, then chopped.)*

Melt butter. Mix with sugar and strawberry flavoring. Set aside and let cool.

Separate the eggs, reserving the whites for later.
When the butter/sugar mixture is warm but not hot to
the touch, add the egg yolks one at a time, stirring
thoroughly after each addition.

Stir in baking powder, soda, and salt.

Stir in half of the strawberries. Stir in half of the
flour. Add the second half of the strawberries, then the
second half of the flour.

Beat the egg whites until stiff, but not dry. Fold them into the strawberry mixture.

Spray a loaf pan *(bread pan—9 x 5 inch)* with non-stick cooking spray, then line it with wax paper and spray it again.

Turn the batter into the pan and smooth the top with a spatula.

Bake at 350 degrees F. for 50 to 60 minutes, or until a wooden skewer inserted in the center comes out clean.

Cool the bread in the pan on a wire rack for 15 minutes, then remove the loaf pan and continue to cool on the rack. Wait another 10 minutes or so before removing the wax paper.

Sally's Banana Bread

Preheat oven to 350 degrees F., rack in
the middle position

*Regina Todd got this recipe from her cousin, Sally
Hayes, who got it from her brother's neighbor, Connie.
Regina tried to teach Andrea to bake it, but that was a
lost cause and she gave up.*

¾ cup softened butter *(1½ sticks)*
1 ½ cups white sugar *(granulated)*
2 beaten eggs *(just whip them up in a glass with
    a fork)*
1 ½ cups mashed bananas *(3 or 4 overripe ba-
    nanas, the ones with lots of black spots on
    the peel)*
2 cups flour *(no need to sift)*
1 teaspoon baking soda
1 teaspoon salt
½ cup buttermilk
½ cup chopped walnuts or pecans *(optional)*

Mix the butter and sugar together until they're nice
and fluffy. Add the beaten eggs and stir it all up.

Peel and mash the bananas. *(You can do this with a
fork, if they're ripe enough.)* Measure out 1½ cups of
mashed banana and add it to your mixing bowl. Stir
well.

In another bowl, measure out the flour and mix in
the baking soda and salt.

Add half of the flour to your mixing bowl. Stir well.
Add half of the buttermilk *(you don't have to be exact)*
and mix that in. Add the rest of the flour, stir well, and
then mix in the rest of the buttermilk. Stir thoroughly.

Mix in the nuts at this point, if you decided to use them.

Coat the inside of a loaf pan *(the type you'd use for bread)* with non-stick cooking spray. Spoon in the banana bread batter and bake at 350 degrees F. for approximately one hour, or until a long toothpick or skewer inserted in the center comes out clean.

You can also bake this in 3 smaller loaf pans, filling them about half full. If you use the smaller pans, they'll need to bake approximately 45 minutes.

Cool on a wire rack in the pan, loosen the edges after 20 minutes, and turn the loaf out onto the wire rack.

Regina usually sends this banana bread home with Bill. *(I guess she figures it's the only way her son will get anything homemade.)* Andrea likes it sliced, toasted, and buttered for breakfast.

Soda Bread

Preheat oven to 375 degrees F., rack in
the middle position

*This recipe is from Bridget Murphy. She makes it
every year on St. Patrick's Day and many times in-
between.*

½ stick butter, at room temperature *(¼ cup,
   ⅛ pound)*
1 cup flour

In a large bowl, with a fork, cut the butter into the
cup of flour.

Add the following ingredients to the bowl:

3 more cups flour
1 teaspoon salt
3 teaspoons baking powder
1 teaspoon baking soda
¼ cup white sugar *(granulated)*
½ teaspoon cardamom *(or coriander)*

In a separate bowl, mix the following:

1 and ¾ cups evaporated milk *(or buttermilk)*
2 beaten eggs
2 cups golden raisins *(optional)*

Add the milk and eggs *(and the optional raisins)* to
the bowl with the flour and stir thoroughly. Turn out on
a floured board.

*Bridget says to make sure this step doesn't scare
you off. Anyone can knead bread. Just put some wax
paper on your counter, and sprinkle it with flour.*

Knead the dough *(punch it down, roll it around, and fold it over on itself like you're playing with clay and mashing it down)* for 2 to 3 minutes. If the dough becomes too sticky for you to handle, sprinkle it with more flour. When your 2 or 3 minutes are up, shape it into a ball and cut it in two with a knife you've sprayed with Pam or other non-stick cooking spray. Shape each half into something resembling something round.

Spray two 9-inch pie plates with non-stick cooking spray. Put the dough inside the pie plates, press it down, and use a sharp knife to cut an "X" on the tops a half-inch deep. *(Bridget says you might have to spray the knife first to keep it from sticking.)*

Bake the soda bread at 375 degrees F. for 40 minutes. Let cool on a wire rack to room temperature, turn out onto a breadboard, and slice to serve.

This soda bread is especially good with John Brady's Quick Irish Chili, or Irish Roast Beast.

Entrees

Baked Fish

Preheat oven to 350 degrees F., rack in
the middle position

Geraldine Goetz contributed this recipe. Her husband goes fishing with Lisa's dad, Jack Herman.

9 to 12 fillets of fish *(any firm white fish will do)*
juice of one lemon
2 teaspoons Season Salt *(see Mrs. Knudson's recipe on page 365)*
2 teaspoons pepper *(freshly ground is best)*
2 cloves garlic, minced or mashed *(you can also use jarred garlic)*
½ cup dry white wine
2 Tablespoons chopped parsley
2 Tablespoons chopped green onion
2 Tablespoons dry breadcrumbs
4 Tablespoons melted butter *(½ stick, ¼ cup, ⅛ pound)*

Rinse and dry fish fillets with paper towels. Rub with lemon juice and sprinkle with salt and pepper.

Sprinkle or spread minced or mashed garlic in the bottom of a greased baking pan *(a 9 x 13 inch cake pan will do fine.)*

Place the fillets in the pan and pour the wine over the top. Sprinkle with parsley, green onion, and breadcrumbs. Melt the butter and spoon it on.

Cover the pan loosely with foil.

Bake at 350 degrees F. for 50 minutes. Take off the foil and bake 15 minutes longer.

Pour off most of the liquid before serving. This fish is wonderful served with crusty bread and a tangy green salad.

Barbecued Anything

Preheat oven to 400 degrees F., rack in
the middle position. Spray a 5-quart or
6-quart crock-pot with Pam

*Norman Rhodes says this is the easiest barbecue
anyone could ever dream up. I've tasted his barbecued
ribs and they're absolutely delicious.*

4 to 5 pounds ribs, cut up into 2-rib servings

Barbecue Sauce:
½ cup catsup *(Norman uses Heinz)*
2 Tablespoons *(⅛ cup)* firmly packed brown
   sugar
¼ cup bottled steak sauce *(Norman uses Heinz
   57)*
¼ cup prepared mustard *(Norman uses honey
   mustard)*
2 Tablespoons *(⅛ cup)* wine vinegar *(or apple
   cider, or plain white)*
½ teaspoon Season Salt *(see Mrs. Knudson's
   recipe on page 365)*
½ teaspoon liquid smoke
½ onion, minced *(if Norman's in a hurry, he
   uses dried chopped onion)*

Place the ribs on a rack in a baking pan and brown
them at 400 degrees F. for 15 minutes. Turn them over
and brown them on the other side for an additional 15
minutes. Drain off the fat.

Combine the sauce ingredients in a large bowl.
Place the ribs in the crock-pot and pour on the sauce.
Cover and cook on LOW for 6 to 8 hours.

These ribs are great cooked entirely in the slow
cooker. If you want to use your grill, pre-cook them in

the crock-pot for 5 hours, refrigerate them, and finish them up outside on the grill.

Norman says to tell you that this barbecue sauce also works for chicken or sausage cooked entirely on the grill. For chicken, it's even better if you leave out the steak sauce and increase the mustard to ½ cup.

Norman also says that if you're pressed for time, you don't have to make the barbecue sauce. Just use a good bottled sauce. The secret is slow cooking the meat in the crock-pot—that's what makes it so tender and tasty.

Chicken Paprikash

(You can do this in a 5-quart slow cooker,
or a 325 degree F. oven)

*This is Janice Cox's recipe, and Eleanor and Otis
swear it's going to land them a son-in-law soon.*

12 skinless, boneless chicken breasts *** *(or
    the equivalent)*
2 cans Cream of Mushroom soup undiluted
    (one can is 10 ¾ ounce net weight)
1 can Cream of Chicken soup undiluted *(10 ¾
    ounces net weight)*
1 cup sour cream
2 Tablespoons paprika
¼ teaspoon ground red pepper *(cayenne)*
½ teaspoon onion powder
salt to taste
one-pound package wide egg noodles, cooked

***You can also use boneless skinless thighs,
chicken tenders, or a combination of the three.

Spray the inside of a 5-quart slow cooker or a large
roasting pan with non-stick cooking spray. Put the
soups, the sour cream and the seasonings in the pan
and stir them around to combine them. Add the chicken
and make sure it's covered with the soup mixture.

For the slow cooker: Cook on LOW for 5 to 6
hours. If you're in a hurry, cook on HIGH for 4 hours.

In the oven: Bake in a tightly covered roaster for 4
hours at 325 degrees F. Then take off the cover and
bake for an additional 30 minutes or so.

Serve over cooked egg noodles.

Yield: Feeds at least 8, unless you're talking about
a threshing crew that's been working the fields all day.

Country Ham Casserole

Preheat oven to 325 degrees F., rack in
the middle position

*This is Loretta Richardson's recipe. Her daughter,
Carly, makes it every time she gets together with her
old high school friends.*

4 slices of bread, cut into one-inch cubes
1 pound leftover ham, cut into small pieces *(or
    thinly sliced deli ham)*
24 spinach leaves, roughly chopped
12 eggs *(that's a dozen, not a misprint)*
1 cup sour cream *(or ½ cup sour cream and
    ½ cup cream cheese)*
1 cup Half & Half *(light cream)*
1 teaspoon ground pepper
½ teaspoon onion powder
½ teaspoon garlic powder
½ cup chopped green onion
1 cup grated Swiss cheese *(or Cheddar, or
    Monterey Jack)*

Grease a 9 x 13 inch cake pan. Sprinkle bread
cubes over the bottom. Cover the bread cubes with the
ham. Cover the ham with the spinach leaves.

Whisk together eggs, sour cream, Half & Half, pepper, onion powder, and garlic powder in a large bowl.
Set aside.

Sprinkle the chopped green onions in the casserole.
Add the cheese on top. Pour the egg mixture on top of
that, cover the pan with foil, and let it sit in the refrigerator for 20 minutes.

Take off the foil and bake, uncovered, at 325 degrees F. for approximately one hour or until a knife inserted near the center comes out clean.

Let stand 10 minutes before serving.

Yield: Serves 6 to 8 people for brunch.

E-Z Lasagna

Mother says to tell you she has to give credit where credit is due. She got this recipe years ago from her friend Lois Meister.

 8-ounce package lasagna noodles *(NOT cooked!)*
 32-ounce jar plain spaghetti sauce *(approx. 3 ½ cups) (Mother uses Ragu)*
 1 cup milk
 1 pound ground beef
 2 Tablespoons dried chopped onion *(or one small onion, finely chopped)*
 1 teaspoon salt
 ½ teaspoon pepper

 6 ounces sliced mozzarella cheese

 2 cups cottage cheese
 ½ cup grated Parmesan cheese
 2 beaten eggs *(just mix them up with a fork)*
 1 teaspoon garlic powder
 2 teaspoons freshly ground rosemary *(or oregano if you can't get rosemary)*

Fry the ground beef until it's brown and drain it. *(If you're using the small chopped onion instead of the dried onion, you can fry that in the same pan and drain it with the ground beef.)*

Dump the drained ground beef into a large bowl. Add the onions, spaghetti sauce, milk, salt and pepper. Mix it all together.

Grease *(or spray with non-stick cooking spray)* a 9-inch by 13-inch rectangular cake pan. Layer half of the dry uncooked noodles in the bottom of the pan.

Cover with one-half of the sauce mixture. Top that with one-half of the mozzarella.

In a separate bowl, mix together the cottage cheese, grated Parmesan, eggs, garlic powder, and rosemary. Fresh herbs are best, but if you can't get fresh rosemary in your area, you can use dried.

Spread the cottage cheese mixture in the pan next, put the rest of the dry noodles on top of that, cover with the remainder of the sauce mixture, and spread out the rest of the cheese slices on top.

Bake, uncovered, at 350 degrees F. for one hour.

Mother sometimes puts this together in advance. She covers it and refrigerates it for six to eight hours before baking. If it's chilled, allow an extra 20 to 30 minutes of baking time.

Festive Baked Sandwich

Luanne Hanks made this for the last potluck, and we all fell in love with it. It would be perfect for one of Mayor Bascomb's tailgate parties.

3 packages cold cuts, 10 or 12 slices per package
 (ham, turkey, roast beef, pastrami, whatever)
3 packages sliced cheese, 8-10 slices per package *(Cheddar, mozzarella, Swiss, whatever)*
2 cups loosely packed fresh spinach leaves
 (rinsed and blotted dry with a paper towel)
2 teaspoons prepared mustard *(stone ground
 Dijon, honey mustard or whatever)*
½ cup dried chopped onions
1 loaf frozen bread dough *(or mix up your own
 if you want)*
8-inch round pan with 3-inch tall sides *(you can
 get by with 2-inch tall sides, but it's trickier)*
9-inch glass pie plate
cookie sheet with sides *(this can be a disposable if you like)*

Let the bread dough rise according to package directions, but do it in a greased bowl instead of a bread pan.

When the dough has doubled in bulk, fold it in half
and roll it out like a piecrust on a floured board. Spray
the 8-inch round pan with non-stick cooking spray, set
it on the cookie sheet, and drape the bread dough over
it with the sides hanging down on the outside.

Put a layer of cheese in the bottom of the pan. Follow
that with a layer of dried onions *(the onions soak up
the moisture from the meats)*. Put a layer of meat on
top of the onions and brush it lightly with mustard.
Follow this with a layer of fresh spinach leaves. Keep
layering cheese, meat, onions and spinach leaves until

your layers reach the top of the pan. End with a layer of cheese if you can, so it's slightly rounded on top.

Bring up the bread dough that's draped over the sides and carefully stretch it to cover your layers. Work from opposite sides, pinching it together so it doesn't pull back. Think of a clock—pull 12 and 6 together and pinch them, then do 2 and 8, and finally 4 and 10. It doesn't matter if the dough separates and there are some holes on the top. The bread dough will rise slightly during the baking, and all will be forgiven.

Spray the inside of your glass pie plate with non-stick cooking spray and invert it over the top of your pan like a little hat. This will help keep your dough from pulling apart and also provide weight so the dough doesn't rise too much at the top and leave a hollow. Let the sandwich rest while you pre-heat your oven.

Make sure your rack is in the middle position and preheat the oven to 350 degrees F. Bake your sandwich for 50 minutes, and then take off the pie pan hat. Bake it for an additional 15 minutes, or until it's nicely browned on top.

Let your sandwich cool in the pan for at least 45 minutes to an hour before serving. It has to set so the cheese is no longer runny. Tip it out of the pan by placing your hand on the top with your fingers spread out to hold it and then inverting it. Place the sandwich on a cutting board or a large serving plate. Cut a pie-shaped wedge to start and then let your guests cut the size of wedge they want to eat. You can serve it with ketchup, horseradish sauce, pickles, coleslaw, and potato salad on the side.

This sandwich is wonderful cold or warm and it's great for picnics. Just leave it in the pan until you're ready to serve it. The wedges can also be heated in the microwave for those who like things hot. It sounds like a lot of work, but it's not, and it's definitely worth it.

Hawaiian Pot Roast

Spray the inside of a 4-quart slow cooker
with non-stick cooking spray
OR
Preheat oven to 325 degrees F., rack in
the middle position

⅓ cup cornstarch

2 cups firmly packed brown sugar

½ teaspoon powdered ginger *(or 2 teaspoons
finely diced fresh ginger)*

½ cup red wine vinegar

20-ounce can drained pineapple chunks
(reserve the liquid for later)

⅓ cup soy sauce

2 cups chopped green bell pepper *(or one
16-ounce package frozen tri-colored bell
peppers)*

⅓ cup dried minced onions

4 to 5 pound boneless chuck roast *(or any similar cut of boneless beef)*

4-ounce can of mushrooms *(stems and pieces
are fine)* OR 1 cup fresh, sliced mushrooms
from the grocery store

1 or 2 packets *(.88 ounces per packet)* beef
gravy mix *(Mother uses Lawry's Brown
Gravy mix)*

Mix the cornstarch, brown sugar, and ginger in a
bowl. Stir in the pineapple liquid. Add the vinegar and
soy sauce, and stir until smooth. Add the pineapple
chunks, onions, and the finely diced green pepper. *(If*

you decided to use the tri-colored bell peppers, just cut open the bag and dump them in still frozen.)

Prepare your slow cooker by spraying it with Pam or another non-stick cooking spray. Put a bit of the mixture in the bottom and then set the meat on top. Pour the rest of the mixture over the top, put on the lid, turn the control to LOW, and let it cook for eight to ten hours.

One hour before you're ready to serve, add the mushrooms.

(Mother puts this in the crock-pot before she goes to work and when she comes home, it's ready.)

If you're late putting this up in the slow cooker, you can cook it at HIGH for the first two hours and then switch it to LOW. Using this method, it should take only six hours or so.

If you choose to do this in the oven: Grease the inside of a roasting pan. Follow the directions above and once your pot roast is in the pan, cover it tightly with heavy-duty foil.

Bake at 325 degrees F. for five to six hours, or until the meat is easily pierced with a fork. *(I don't think you can over-bake this—if it falls apart, that's good, too.)* Then take off the foil and let it brown in the oven for another 45 minutes to an hour.

Once the meat is ready, take it out of the pan or crock-pot and let it cool for fifteen minutes.

Sprinkle one packet of gravy mix in the liquid and stir until it's thickened. Add another packet if the sauce isn't thick enough. Keep the sauce warm in the oven or the slow cooker.

Slice the meat, transfer the slices to a deep platter, pour the thickened liquid over the top artistically *(Mother's description, not mine,)* and serve.

Hot German Potato Salad with Bratwurst

This is Trudi Schumann's recipe. She says to tell you that "hot" means heated, not spicy. If you do want it spicier, use a spicier sausage and that should do it.

4 large potatoes *(or 6 medium)*
6 slices of bacon, diced
¼ cup flour
2 Tablespoons brown sugar
2 teaspoons salt
2 teaspoons dry mustard
2 teaspoons black pepper
⅔ cup vinegar *(white, red wine, or even balsamic)*
⅔ cup water
2 teaspoons celery seed
2 teaspoons onion powder
2 teaspoons garlic powder
1 large onion, chopped
6 to 10 large bratwurst *(or dinner franks, or Polish sausage, whatever)*

Grease *(or spray with non-stick cooking spray)* the inside of a 4-quart slow cooker.

Wash the potatoes, pierce them with a knife, and cook them on HIGH in a microwave for 15 minutes. You should be able to pierce the cooked potatoes with a fork, but the inside should be just a little too raw to eat at this point. *(You can do this step the night before and refrigerate the potatoes.)*

Let the potatoes cool, peel them and slice them. Put them in the bottom of the greased crock-pot.

Chop up the bacon and put it in a one-quart microwave-safe measuring cup. Microwave it on HIGH for 3 minutes, stirring midway through. Fish out the bacon with a slotted spoon and add it to the potatoes in the crock-pot. Pour off all but approximately 2 Tablespoons of the bacon grease.

Mix the reserved bacon fat, flour, brown sugar, salt, dry mustard, black pepper, vinegar, water, celery seed, onion powder, and garlic powder in the same container you used to microwave the bacon. Stir it thoroughly and heat for one minute in the microwave on HIGH. Add the chopped onion, stir it around and heat for an additional minute on HIGH.

Add this to the potatoes and bacon in the crock-pot. Cook for one hour on LOW.

Stir the warm potato salad, top it with the bratwurst you've pierced with a fork, *(so they won't explode,)* and cover.

Turn the crock-pot to HIGH and cook for an additional hour or two, or until the potato salad and the bratwurst are hot.

Hunter's Stew

Grease or spray the inside of a 5-quart
slow cooker with Pam

*This recipe is from Winnie Henderson. She says her
second husband was a hunter and she used to make
this for him all the time.*

2 pounds cubed beef *(cut into roughly one-inch
    cubes)*
1 pound other cubed meat *(venison, pork,
    turkey, chicken, more beef, even sausage as
    long as it's not too fatty)*
2 medium onions, roughly chopped
4 stalks celery, cut in ½-inch pieces
2 cups baby carrots *(or one-inch chunks of
    carrot)*

1 teaspoon garlic powder
1 teaspoon onion powder
1 teaspoon paprika
1 teaspoon pepper *(freshly ground is best)*
¼ cup brown sugar *(that's 4 Tablespoons)*
14-ounce can stewed tomatoes *(with peppers,
    with garlic, plain, any type is fine)*
three 7-ounce cans mushroom stems and pieces
    (NOT drained!)
2 medium-size potatoes, peeled and cut into
    one-inch cubes
two .88-ounce packets beef gravy mix *(I used
    Lawry's Brown Gravy Mix)*

Put the chopped onions in the bottom of the slow
cooker. Lay the chunks of meat on top of that. *(If you
plan to use sausage and it's pre-cooked, don't add it at
this point—Wait until an hour or so before serving.)*

Put the carrots and celery on top of the meat, and cook on HIGH for 5 hours.

Add the garlic powder, onion powder, paprika, and ground pepper. Then add the brown sugar, the tomatoes, and the mushrooms with the mushroom liquid. Stir it all up and add the cubed potatoes.

Pour in enough water to almost cover the meat and vegetables, but not quite. Then add ONE packet of gravy mix and stir again. *(Reserve the second package of gravy mix for the gravy itself.)*

Cover and cook on LOW for an additional 6 to 7 hours. If you start this late and don't have the required 11 to 12 hours of cooking time, you can leave the crock-pot on HIGH for the entire time, and it should be ready in 8 to 9 hours.

If there's too much liquid when you're ready to serve, sprinkle in the second gravy packet and stir it in until it's thick.

Serve in big bowls with hot crusty bread. It's a perfect winter's evening meal. *(If you use venison as the second meat, don't tell Andrea. She has real reservations about eating the star of a classic Disney movie.)*

Irish Roast Beast

Grease or spray inside of 4-quart slow
cooker with non-stick cooking spray
OR
Preheat oven to 325 degrees F., rack in
the middle position

*This recipe is from Barbara Donnelly, who got it
from her mother.*

16-ounce can whole berry cranberry sauce
6-ounce can tomato sauce
12-ounce bottle stout beer *(Barbara uses
    Guinness Stout)*
2 teaspoons freshly ground rosemary *(it's so
    much better fresh!)*
1 teaspoon thyme
1 teaspoon sage
1 teaspoon sweet basil
1 teaspoon oregano
1 teaspoon ground black pepper *(again, freshly
    ground is much better)*
1 teaspoon salt

boneless chuck or rump roast, four to five
    pounds in weight *(or any similar cut of
    boneless beef)*

.88-ounce packet beef gravy mix.

Mix all ingredients except the meat and the gravy
mix in a bowl. Put a half-cup of the mixture in the bottom of the slow cooker. Set in the meat and pour the
rest of the sauce over the top.

Turn the slow cooker to LOW and cook for 8 to 10
hours. *(If you're late putting this up in the slow cooker,*

you can cook it at HIGH for the entire time. Using this method, it should take only six to seven hours.)

When the meat is easily pierced by a fork, *(Barbara likes hers practically falling apart,)* remove it from the sauce, cut it in chunks and put it on a platter. Cover the platter with foil so it will stay warm.

Turn the slow cooker to HIGH and sprinkle in the packet of beef gravy mix. Stir until the sauce has thickened. To serve, drizzle some of the sauce over the meat on the platter. Put the rest in a gravy boat or small pitcher for the table.

If you choose to do this in the oven: Grease or spray the inside of a roasting pan with non-stick cooking spray. Follow the directions above and once your Irish Roast Beast is in the pan, cover it tightly with heavy-duty foil.

Bake at 325 degrees F. for five to six hours, or until it's easily pierced by a fork. Then take off the foil and let it brown in the oven for another 45 minutes. When it's time to make the gravy, transfer the meat to a platter and pour the liquid into a saucepan over medium heat. Sprinkle the gravy packet over the sauce and stir until it thickens.

Meatloaf

Preheat oven to 350 degrees F., rack in
the middle position

*This recipe is from Esther Gibson, Digger Gibson's
wife.*

⅔ cup cracker crumbs *(or matzo meal)*
1 cup evaporated milk *(or light cream)*
2 beaten eggs *(you can just beat them up with a
    fork)*
1 teaspoon salt
½ teaspoon garlic powder
½ teaspoon onion powder
½ teaspoon paprika
½ teaspoon pepper
½ teaspoon sage
½ teaspoon ground oregano
1 medium onion, chopped
1 ½ pounds ground beef *(or 1 pound beef,
    ½ pound ground pork)*

Grease *(or spray with non-stick cooking spray)* a
bread pan and have it ready. *(The one Esther uses is
metal and the bottom measures 4-inches by 8-inches.)*

In a large bowl, mix the cracker crumbs, beaten eggs,
evaporated milk, and seasonings. Add the chopped
onion and mix well. Here comes the messy part . . .

Add the hamburger and mix it all up with your impeccably clean hands. *(That's right, use your hands and
smoosh it all up together—this really is worth all the
mess.)*

With your hands, transfer the meat mixture to the
pan you've prepared, filling it to within ¾ of an inch of
the top, except in the middle where you should mound

it like a loaf of bread. If you have any meat mixture left over, shape it into patties, separate the patties with wax paper, stick them in a freezer bag and pop them in the freezer. They make wonderful hamburgers.

PIQUANT SAUCE MEATLOAF TOPPING:

Esther says this piquant sauce is the reason her family loves having meatloaf. It's really good!

3 Tablespoons brown sugar
¼ teaspoon nutmeg *(freshly grated is best)*
1 teaspoon dry mustard
¼ cup catsup

In a small bowl, mix the brown sugar, nutmeg and dry mustard. *(Esther uses a fork to do this.)* Mix in the catsup and then spoon the sauce over the top of your meatloaf.

Put a drip pan *(Esther has an old cookie sheet with raised sides)* under the meatloaf pan and bake it at 350 degrees F. for one and a half hours.

Let cool in the pan for fifteen minutes, then turn it out on a carving board. Let it cool for another five minutes, and then slice.

Everyone says no one makes meatloaf better than Esther!

Minnesota Hotdish

Ruel moved to Minnesota from California to teach at a local college. He says that there are more "hot-dish" variations in Minnesota than there are mosquitoes at a shore lunch. Essentially, hotdish is a comfort food concept, not a hard-and-fast recipe. Feel free to substitute and make your own variations. Some people in other more fancy parts of the country call this dish a "casserole."

    2 large onions, chopped
    1 pound of hamburger *(or ground pork, or a
        combination of the two)*
    ½ cup butter *(1 stick, ¼ pound)*
    1 pound of any cooked, leftover meat *(beef,
        pork, ham, chicken, or sausage)*
    ⅓ cup honey
    ½ cup soy sauce
    1 teaspoon garlic powder
    1 teaspoon Season Salt *(see Mrs. Knudson's
        recipe on page 365)*
    1 teaspoon ground black pepper *(freshly
        ground is best)*
    hot sauce to taste *(optional)*
    2 pounds cooked medium-size shrimp without
        tails
    2 one-pound packages of mixed frozen vegeta-
        bles *(use your favorites)*
    2 four-ounce cans sliced mushrooms, drained
    6 cups of cooked rice *(white, brown, or a mix-
        ture)*

In your largest stovetop pan and over medium heat, fry the hamburger and onions together until the hamburger is crumbly and the onions are translucent. Drain off the fat.

Add the butter and stir it around until it melts. Chop the leftover meat into bite-size pieces and add them. Then add the shrimp, honey and soy sauce. Simmer for 10 minutes to marry the flavors. This should be on the wet side. If it's not, add a little more soy sauce or your favorite flavored vinegar. *(I like raspberry vinegar.)*

Season with garlic powder, season salt, black pepper, and hot sauce to taste *(if you like it on the hot side.)*

Steam, boil, or microwave the vegetables. Drain them and add them, along with the mushrooms.

Add the cooked rice. If there's not enough room in the pan, combine the meat mixture with the rice in a large roasting pan you've sprayed with non-stick cooking spray. Mix it well.

If you're not ready to serve yet, you can keep it warm in a 325 degree F. oven, uncovered for up to an hour and a half.

Yield: Serves at least ten hungry eaters, maybe more.

Not So Swedish Meatballs

Edna Ferguson used to make her meatballs by hand, until she came up with this really good mushroom sauce and discovered that no one could really tell the difference. She likes to make hers in the slow cooker because they'll hold for a couple of hours that way, and they're really easy to take to a potluck dinner.

1 five-pound bag cooked, frozen meatballs *(about 120 meatballs)*

1 restaurant-sized can cream of mushroom soup undiluted *(50 ounces)*

1 cup whole milk, Half & Half, or cream *(depending on how rich you want it)*

⅓ cup dried onions *(or one large onion, finely chopped)*

1 teaspoon Seasoned Pepper *(or freshly ground black pepper)*

1 teaspoon garlic powder

1 teaspoon onion powder

1 envelope *(.88 ounce)* brown gravy mix *(just in case you need it)*

Cooked egg noodles, fettuccine, mashed potatoes, or rice

Spray a 5-quart slow cooker or a large roasting pan with Pam or other non-stick cooking spray. Combine everything except the frozen meatballs in the bottom of the slow cooker or the roasting pan. Mix in the frozen meatballs, making sure the tops are covered with the sauce.

Cook in the slow cooker on low for 6 to 7 hours, or in a tightly covered roasting pan at 350 degrees F. for 5 to 6 hours.

Check meatballs a half hour before the end of the cooking time. If there's too much liquid, sprinkle some brown gravy mix over the top and stir it in. If there's not enough liquid, add more milk or cream. Check for salt at this time and add it if needed.

Finish cooking and serve over egg noodles, fettuccine, potatoes, or rice.

These can also be served as appetizers if you cut back on the liquid. Present directly from the slow cooker or roaster, and provide food picks and small plates for your guests.

Rose's Restaurant Turkey

Preheat oven to 275 degrees F., rack in
the bottom position

*This is the turkey that Rose uses at the café for her
hot turkey sandwiches with the mashed potatoes and
gravy on top, and her turkey salad.*

*Note: DO NOT put stuffing in this turkey!!! The
cavity must be empty except for gizzard, neck, & liver
if you want to use them.*

One uncooked *(doesn't that sound better than
    "raw?")* turkey, thawed, rinsed, and patted dry
A roaster big enough to hold the turkey
A meat rack big enough to hold the bird &
    small enough to fit in the roaster

If you want to roast the gizzard, liver, or neck,
sprinkle them with salt and pepper and place them inside the largest cavity of the turkey.

Spray the rack and roaster with Pam or other non-
stick cooking spray.

Spray the turkey with non-stick cooking spray. Salt
and pepper the outside of the turkey. Place the turkey,
BREAST DOWN, *(Rose knows this is unusual, just do
it)* on the rack in the roaster.

Roast turkey at 275 degrees F., uncovered, for 23
minutes per pound.

Remove the turkey from the oven. Cover it loosely
with foil and let it sit for at least 30 minutes.

Carve in the kitchen.***

****Rose say this turkey doesn't at all resemble that
gorgeous brown centerpiece turkey that wives carry*

*out and place on the table for their husbands to carve.
This turkey must be carved in the kitchen, and you'll
find the meat practically falls off the bone. You'll also
find that the meat is moist and delicious and much better than meat from a bird that looks gorgeous.*

Salmon Loaf

Preheat oven to 350 degrees F., rack in
the middle position

*This recipe is from Stan Kramer's sister Kitty. (When
they were growing up, Stan used to tease that she was
fated to marry a man named Katz.) Kitty says you can
use pink salmon, but the loaf turns out looking a little
gray. Red salmon's more expensive, but it's worth it if
you're serving this for company.*

2 cans red salmon *(I used two 14.75-ounce
    cans)*

1 cup finely ground bread crumbs *(or cracker
    crumbs or matzo meal)*
1 cup evaporated milk *(or light cream)*
2 beaten eggs *(you can just beat them up with a
    fork)*
1 teaspoon salt
½ teaspoon pepper
½ teaspoon onion powder
½ teaspoon sage
½ teaspoon ground oregano
¼ cup melted butter *(½ stick, ⅛ pound)*
¼ cup dried chopped onions *(or ½ small onion,
    finely chopped)*
8-ounce package frozen green peas

Spray a bread pan with non-stick cooking spray.
*(The one Kitty uses is glass and the bottom measures
4-inches by 8-inches.)*

Drain the salmon in a strainer. Prepare it by taking
out the bones and removing most of the silver skin.
Let it continue to drain while you mix up the rest of
the loaf.

In a large bowl, mix the ground breadcrumbs, evaporated milk, beaten eggs, and seasonings. Add the melted butter and dried chopped onions, and mix well.

Add the salmon and the frozen peas, and mix it all up with a big wooden spoon. *(You may have to get in there with your hands to make sure it's thoroughly mixed.)*

Transfer the salmon mixture to the pan you've prepared, filling it to within a half-inch of the top. If you have any salmon mixture left over, shape it into patties, separate the patties with wax paper, stick them in a freezer bag and pop them in the freezer. They make wonderful salmon patties. Just thaw them and fry them in butter.

Bake at 350 degrees F. for 1 to 1 ½ hours. If the top starts browning too rapidly, tent a piece of aluminum foil over the top.

Let cool for ten minutes and then slice and serve. This is especially good with dill sauce.

Dill Sauce:

This sauce must be made at least 4 hours in advance (overnight is even better.)

2 Tablespoons heavy cream
½ cup mayonnaise
1 teaspoon crushed fresh baby dill *(if you can't find baby dill, you can make it with ½ teaspoon dried dill weed, but it won't be as good)*

Mix the cream with the mayonnaise until it's smooth and then mix in the dill. Put the sauce in a small bowl, cover it with plastic wrap, and refrigerate it for at least 4 hours.

Smothered Chicken

Laura Jorgensen got this recipe from her friend, Dee Appleton, who lives in Texas. It's wonderful!

1 package boneless chicken breasts *(skinless is fine—my bag was 4 pounds and contained 7 large boneless skinless chicken breasts)*

½ cup butter *(1 stick, ¼ pound)*

½ cup flour

1 Tablespoon Season Salt *(see Mrs. Knudson's recipe on page 365)*

1 teaspoon ground black pepper

1 teaspoon paprika

½ teaspoon ground oregano

½ teaspoon ground thyme

½ teaspoon garlic powder

½ cup dried chopped onion

1 Tablespoon parsley flakes

1 teaspoon sweet basil *(not absolutely necessary, but adds a lot)*

1 teaspoon chervil *(not absolutely necessary, but adds a lot)*

1 cup dry white wine *(or water with a Tablespoon of red wine vinegar)*

Take out your largest frying pan and melt the butter on medium heat. Mix the flour, salt, pepper, paprika, oregano, thyme and garlic powder in a bowl. Dredge the chicken in the flour mixture and brown it in the butter. *(If there's any flour left in the bowl, just dump it in on top.)* Do the underside of the chicken breasts first, so that when you're finished browning both sides, the right side is up. *(This should take about five minutes per side.)* When the chicken is browned, sprinkle the dried onion, parsley, sweet basil, and chervil over the top. Then dump in the wine, turn the heat down to simmer, and cover the pan. Let it cook for 45 minutes or until the chicken breasts are fully cooked.

Laura serves this with egg noodles and makes a sauce. After removing the chicken to a platter with sides, I pour in a little more white wine or water and cook the pan drippings for 2 or 3 minutes until they're the right consistency. Laura serves this separately so folks can pour it over their noodles and chicken.

Sides

Apple 'N Onion Dressing Balls

Lisa's Aunt Ida used to say that if it was inside the turkey, it was stuffing. If it was outside the turkey, it was dressing. This dressing recipe is from her.

1 cup minced onion
1 cup finely chopped apple with the peel on
    (cored, of course)
1 chicken bouillon cube dissolved in ¼ cup hot
    water *(or ¼ cup chicken broth)*
½ teaspoon sage
½ teaspoon ground Mexican oregano
½ teaspoon thyme
½ teaspoon ground black pepper
2 beaten eggs *(just whip them up with a fork)*
1 six-ounce package herb seasoned stuffing mix

1 stick butter *(½ cup, ¼ pound)*

Grease *(or spray with non-stick cooking spray)* the inside of a 4-quart slow cooker.

In a large mixing bowl combine the onion and apple.

In a small bowl, dissolve the bouillon cube *(or measure out the chicken broth.)* Add the sage, oregano, thyme, and black pepper. Mix everything up and then add it to the onion and apple in the large bowl. Mix well.

Add the eggs and then the stuffing mix, stirring until everything is moistened.

Shape the mixture into 8 balls and place them in the crock. Melt the butter and pour it over the top.

Cover and cook on LOW for 3 to 4 hours.

Sprinkle the stuffing balls with paprika or chopped parsley before serving.

You can use the crock-pot for any dressing. Just grease it, turn it to LOW, sprinkle the top with parsley or paprika and dot it with butter, and it'll be ready in 3 to 4 hours.

If your guests are late, the way Aunt Ida's grandchildren always are, she says to tell you that the dressing will hold for at least an hour longer.

Corn Pudding

Grease or spray the inside of a 4-quart
slow cooker with cooking spray

Kathy Purvis gave us this recipe. She says her family has been serving it for Thanksgiving dinners for as long as she can remember. She also says there's probably a way to make it in the oven, but no one remembers how to do it.

One package *(8 ½ ounces)* corn muffin or cornbread mix
2 beaten eggs *(whip them up in a glass with a fork)*
⅓ cup brown sugar
8-ounce package cream cheese *(regular, not whipped)*
16-ounce can cream-style corn *(14.5 ounce can will work, too)*
2 ⅓ cups frozen sweet corn kernels *(a 16-ounce package)*
1 cup frozen tri-color peppers, chopped
1 cup whole milk *(evaporated will do fine, or light cream will work also)*
½ stick *(¼ cup, ⅛ pound)* melted butter
1 teaspoon Season Salt *(see Mrs. Knudson's recipe on page 365)*
1 teaspoon pepper *(freshly ground is best)*
½ teaspoon nutmeg *(freshly grated is best)*

Soften the cream cheese in the bottom of a microwave-safe bowl on HIGH for 30 seconds. Stir it up with a spoon. Let it cool until it's warm to the touch.

Add the beaten eggs and brown sugar. Mix thoroughly.

Add the corn muffin or corn bread mix. Stir to incorporate.

Add the can of cream-style corn, the frozen corn kernels, and the tri-color peppers.

Stir everything up and add the milk and the melted butter. Stir in the Season Salt and the pepper.

Spray the crock of a 4-quart slow cooker with Pam. Put in the corn pudding mixture. Grate ½ teaspoon of nutmeg on the top.

Put the cover on the slow cooker, turn it to HIGH, and let the corn pudding cook for 3 to 4 hours.

Serves 10 to 12 people as a side dish.

Green Bean Classic With a Twist

Preheat oven to 325 degrees F., rack in
the middle position

*Eleanor Cox made up this variation on the classic
green bean casserole. She always brings two casseroles
to our potluck dinners, but they're gone in a big hurry.*

16-ounce bag frozen cut green beans
16-ounce bag frozen yellow wax beans
One can *(10¾ ounces)* cream of mushroom soup
One can *(10¾ ounces)* cream of chicken soup
1 cup shredded cheese *(Cheddar or Jack)*
¼ cup dried chopped onions
½ teaspoon garlic powder
1 six-ounce can French-fried onions *(I used
    French's)*
salt and pepper to taste *(I used 1 Tablespoon
    salt, and 2 teaspoons pepper)*

Spray a disposable half-size steam table pan with
non-stick cooking spray. Set it on a cookie sheet so the
bottom will be supported.

Thaw the beans in the microwave, but don't cook
them. Dump them in the pan. Pour the two soups over
the top, add the cheese, dried onions, and garlic powder. Add salt and pepper, and half of the French-fried
onions. Mix it all up right there in the pan.

Cover the pan tightly with two layers of foil, and bake
it at 325 degrees F. for one hour. *(An hour and a half is
fine, too—this dish holds well for guests who come late.)*

Take the foil off the top and dump on the other half
of the French-fried onions. Bake uncovered for an additional half hour or until the onions are brown and
crispy.

Holiday Rice

Preheat oven to 350 degrees F., rack in
the middle position

*This recipe is from Pam Baxter, Jordan High's
Home Economics teacher. She gives it to all her students.*

1 pound *(approximately 2 and ⅔ cups)*
      uncooked mixed rice***
3 and ⅓ cups boiling chicken stock *(or beef
      stock)*
one envelope dry Onion Soup *(1-ounce, I use
      Lipton's)*
⅓ cup dried onions
1 sixteen-ounce package frozen tri-color bell
      peppers *(or a sixteen-ounce package of
      frozen corn & peppers, or one cup fresh
      chopped bell peppers)*
2 teaspoons ground black pepper

½ cup butter *(one stick, ¼ pound)*

*** Pam uses a one-pound package of Trader Joe's
California Rice Trilogy. If you can't get that, use 1 cup
long-grain brown rice, 1 cup wild rice, and ⅔ cup
brown Basmati rice. *(Or any other combination you
wish, as long as it adds up to 2 and ⅔ cups of dry rice.)*

Rinse off the rice in a strainer and pat it dry. Mix
rice and all ingredients except butter together in a large
bowl. Transfer mixture to a greased casserole dish.
Cut the butter into 8 pieces and put it on top of the
casserole. Cover the casserole with heavy-duty foil if
it doesn't have a cover. Bake at 350 degrees F. for 2
hours. Take off the foil and bake for another 20 to 30
minutes.

Make-Ahead Mashed Potatoes

This is a slow cooker recipe, but you can
also do it in the oven

*Edna Ferguson contributed this recipe. She says
every new bride should be presented with it, right
along with her wedding ring.*

Approximately 8 pounds potatoes, peeled
3 packages *(8-ounces each)* cream cheese
½ cup heavy cream
salt
pepper
1 cup dried, chopped onions
1 stick cold butter
parsley and/or paprika to garnish

a packet of dry instant mashed potatoes *(just in
case you need them)*
more cream or milk *(just in case you need it)*

Boil the potatoes in salted water until they're tender
enough to mash. Drain them. Soften the cream cheese
in a bowl in the microwave. Then mash the potatoes
with the cream cheese and the cream. *(A hand masher
works just fine—Edna says you want a few small chunks
so people can tell they're homemade.)*

Mix in salt and pepper to taste. Mix in any other
seasonings you'd like *(garlic powder, onion powder,
etc.)* Add a cup of dried onions and mix them in.

Spray the inside of a 5-quart slow cooker with Pam
or other non-stick cooking spray. Spoon in the potatoes. Garnish with parsley or paprika. Cut the stick of
butter into eight pieces and press the pieces down a little on top of the potatoes. Put the cover on the crock-
pot. You're all done.

Plug in the slow cooker and set it on LOW. Cook for a minimum of 4 hours, but as long as 5 or 6 hours. Check a half hour before serving to see if they're the right consistency. If there's too much liquid, sprinkle in some instant mashed potatoes and stir them in. If there isn't enough liquid, add more cream and stir it in. When the potatoes are perfect, you can add a little cholesterol by cutting another stick of butter into chunks and putting them on top, if you wish. Even if you don't, the potatoes will be delicious when you serve them. *(I put mine up around noon for an evening dinner.)*

Edna says that if you don't have a slow cooker and you're too cheap to buy one to make your life easier, you can put these in a pan, cover them tightly with two layers of foil, and heat them in a 300 degree F. oven for 3 hours. She also says to tell you that they'll hold in the oven for another hour if your guests are late.

them cool for about ten minutes so that the eggs and cheese hold them together, cut them into serving-size squares, *(you can get about 12 from a pan,)* transfer the squares to a platter, and top each one with a generous dollop of sour cream and a sprinkling of caviar *(or crumbled bacon for those who don't like caviar.)*

Scandinavian Red Cabbage

This recipe is from Minnie Holtzmeier and she says it's so easy, no one can possibly get it wrong. (She obviously forgot about Andrea!)

6 slices bacon, diced
¼ cup brown sugar
⅛ cup flour *(2 Tablespoons)*
2 teaspoons salt
1 teaspoon pepper
¾ cup dry red wine
¼ cup butter, melted *(½ stick, ⅛ pound)*
1 head red cabbage, roughly shredded *(6 to 8 cups)*
1 chopped onion

Dice the bacon, put it in a 2-cup microwave bowl and cook for 2 minutes on high, stirring midway through cooking time. Pour off the bacon fat and set the bacon pieces aside.

Grease *(or spray with non-stick cooking spray)* the inside of a 4-quart slow cooker.

Combine bacon pieces, brown sugar, flour, salt, pepper, red wine, and butter in the bottom of the crockpot. Stir it all up.

Shred the red cabbage and chop the onion. Add them to the crock and toss them with the liquid. Cover and cook on LOW for 3 to 4 hours.

Either drain some of the juice before serving, thicken it with a bit of flour and water, or use a slotted serving spoon.

Silly Carrots

Irma York contributed this recipe. She got it from her friend, Ginnie Redalje.

2 pounds carrots, peeled, cooked and sliced***
10 ¾-ounce can condensed tomato soup *(Irma uses Campbell's)*
¾ cup white *(granulated)* sugar
¾ cup wine vinegar
¼ cup olive oil
2 teaspoons prepared mustard *(Irma uses Dijon)*
2 cups diced celery
1 teaspoon salt
½ teaspoon pepper

*** or two 16-ounce packages frozen, sliced carrots prepared according to package directions

Combine all ingredients except carrots in a saucepan. Heat to boiling. Turn down heat and simmer for 10 minutes. Pour over the cooked carrots.

Serve hot, or cold. If you choose to serve them cold, these can be made in the morning and refrigerated until dinner.

Spinach Soufflé

If you're going to bake this right away,
preheat oven to 350 degrees F., rack in
middle position.

*This is Michelle's recipe. It's very good and I'm
proud of her.*

Assemble:
½ cup butter *(one stick)*
2 Tablespoons grated onion *(you can also use
    dried and add them with the spinach)*
⅔ cup flour *(no need to sift)*
2 cups Half & Half *(or cream, or milk)*
2 cups grated Cheddar
2 cups cooked, well-drained chopped spinach
2 teaspoons Season Salt *(See Mrs. Knudson's
    recipe on page 365)*
¼ teaspoon white pepper
6 eggs, separated

Melt butter in large saucepan. Throw in onions and
sauté. Then dump in flour and stir around for at least
two minutes. *(They say it should bubble, but mine
never does.)* Add Half & Half and stir until it thickens
into a thick sauce. Take off heat.

Stir in: spinach *(and the onions, if you used dried,)*
cheese, salt & pepper. Beat egg yolks *(by hand is fine)*
and add them.

At this point you can stick the whole thing in a
bowl and refrigerate it until later. Overnight is okay,
too. Keep egg whites refrigerated in a separate covered
bowl.

Preheat oven to 350 degrees F., while you wait for
the concoction and the egg whites to warm to room

temperature. Beat egg whites until soft peaks form *(not hard peaks)*. Fold into spinach mixture. Dump in a greased oven dish.

Bake at 350 degrees F. for an hour *(mine took an extra 15 minutes)* until the top is nicely browned. This soufflé doesn't fall when you take it out of the oven, so you can take it to a potluck dinner.

Sweet Potato Casserole

Preheat oven to 350 degrees F., rack in
the middle position

*Lucille Rahn contributed this recipe. She got it
from her friend Meryl in New York, who got it from her
friend Hazel. Lucille asked Meryl to ask Hazel, but
Hazel's not sure where she got it in the first place.*

3 cups cooked, mashed sweet potatoes or
    yams***
⅔ cup white *(granulated)* sugar
¼ cup melted butter *(½ stick, ⅛ pound)*
1 teaspoon vanilla extract
½ cup whipping cream
2 beaten eggs

1 cup brown sugar, firmly packed
1 cup chopped pecans
½ cup flour
½ cup softened butter *(1 stick, ¼ pound)*

*** It's better with freshly cooked sweet potatoes
or yams, but you can also use well-drained canned
sweet potatoes or yams. It'll take one 29-ounce can
and one 15-ounce can to make a scant 3 cups of mashed
sweet potatoes. Two 29-ounce cans will yield almost
4 cups, but you can use them and things will still turn
out just fine.

Spray a 9-inch by 13-inch baking dish with non-
stick cooking spray.

In a large mixing bowl combine sweet potatoes,
sugar, melted butter, vanilla, and cream. Mix in the
beaten eggs and stir thoroughly. Pour the mixture into
the baking pan you've prepared.

Rinse out the bowl you used and dry it with a paper towel. Combine the brown sugar, chopped pecans, and flour, mixing them up with a fork. Add the butter and mix with the fork until it's crumbly.

You can also do this in the food processor with the steel blade and cold butter cut into 8 pieces. If you do this, add the chopped pecans by hand after everything else is processed.

Sprinkle the brown sugar mixture over the top of the sweet potato mixture. Bake, uncovered, for 30 to 45 minutes. If the rest of the dinner's not ready, cover the pan with foil, turn off the oven, and leave the casserole inside. When the guests arrive, take out the casserole and serve.

Desserts: Cakes

A note from Hannah: When you page through the dessert section, you may wonder why you don't see Shawna Lee Quinn's Brownies, especially since you know that they were accepted by the Lake Eden cookbook committee.

To make a long story short, Lisa happened to be paging through her mother's copy of "Joy of Cooking," and she came across a brownie recipe that sounded wonderful. She started to make it and that's when she realized that it was EXACTLY the same as the brownie recipe that Shawna Lee had submitted, right down to the amounts and the method and everything. The cookbook committee thought it was only right to attribute the previously printed source, "Joy of Cooking," but Shawna Lee didn't like that idea and she told us to just leave her brownies out if that's the way we felt about it.

Christmas Date Cake

Preheat oven to 325 degrees F., rack in
the middle position

*This recipe is from my Grandma Ingrid. She used to
make this cake every Christmas.*

2 cups chopped pitted dates *(you can buy
    chopped dates, or sprinkle whole pitted
    dates with a bit of flour and then chop them
    in a food processor.)*
3 cups boiling water
2 teaspoons baking soda

Pour the boiling water over the dates, add the soda
(it foams up a bit) and set them aside to cool. While
they're cooling, cream the following ingredients together in a large mixing bowl:

1 cup *(2 sticks)* soft or melted butter
2 cups white *(granulated)* sugar
4 eggs
½ teaspoon salt
3 cups flour *(you don't have to sift it)*

Once the above are thoroughly mixed, add the
cooled date mixture to your bowl and stir thoroughly.

Butter and flour a 9-inch by 13-inch rectangular
cake pan. *(This cake rises about an inch and a half, so
make sure the sides are tall enough.)* Pour the batter
into the pan. Then sprinkle the following on the top, in
this order, BEFORE baking:

12 oz. chocolate chips *(2 cups)*
1 cup white *(granulated)* sugar
1 cup chopped nuts *(use any nuts you like—I
    prefer walnuts or pecans)*

Bake at 325 degrees F. for 80 minutes. A cake tester or a long toothpick should come out clean one inch from the center when the cake is done. *(If you happen to stick the toothpick in and hit a chocolate chip, it'll come out covered with melted chocolate —just wipe it off and stick it in again to test the actual cake batter.)*

Let the cake cool in the pan on a wire rack. It can be served slightly warm, at room temperature, or chilled.

Chocolate Fruitcake

Preheat oven to 300 degrees F., rack in
the middle position

*These cakes pack a punch, especially if you have
more than one piece.*

If you're planning to give them as Christmas gifts,
bake them at least 3 weeks ahead of time, preferably
right after Thanksgiving.

3 sticks melted butter *(1 ½ cups, ¾ pound)*
4 cups white *(granulated)* sugar
8 beaten eggs *(just whip them up with a fork)*
2 teaspoons baking powder
1 teaspoon baking soda
1 teaspoon salt
1 teaspoon ground nutmeg
½ teaspoon cardamom *(or 1 teaspoon cinnamon, but cardamom's better)*
½ cup unsweetened baking cocoa
½ cup molasses
1 cup milk *(or light cream)*
4 ½ cups flour *(you don't have to sift it)*
1 cup brandy or rum*** *(you'll need an additional cup or two for the wrapping)*
1 cup chopped dried apricots *(or any chopped
dried fruit)*
2 ½ cups chopped nuts
1 cup chocolate chips
1 ½ cups coconut flakes
cheesecloth to wrap cakes

***If you don't want to use alcohol, use a cup of
fruit juice instead of the brandy, do not wrap in cheesecloth, and either give the cakes as gifts within a day or
two of baking, or wrap them tightly in foil and freeze
them in freezer bags.

Spray 8 baby loaf pans with Pam or other non-stick cooking spray. *(My pans are stamped 5 ¾ x 3 x 2 ⅛ on the bottom.)* Line the pans with wax paper by cutting a strip to extend over the width of the pan, leaving "ears" on the side. You don't have to worry about the ends of the pans—they'll be okay unlined. Spray the whole thing again with Pam or other non-stick cooking spray, dump in some flour, and swish it around *(over the wastebasket or sink)* so that all the inner surfaces of the wax paper and the pan are dusted with flour. Knock excess flour out.

Melt butter in a large microwave-safe bowl. Add the sugar and mix it up. Allow it to cool slightly while you beat the eggs in another bowl.

When the butter and sugar mixture is no longer hot to the touch, mix in the beaten eggs. Then add baking powder, baking soda, salt, nutmeg, and cardamom, and cocoa, stirring after each addition. Mix in molasses and milk.

Add the flour cup by cup, stirring after each addition. Then add the cup of brandy and mix some more. Dump in the apricots, nuts, chocolate chips and coconut and stir until everything is thoroughly mixed.

Fill the baby loaf pans ¾ full with batter. This batch should make eight or nine mini-cakes.

Bake at 300 degrees F. for 1 hour. Remove from oven, place pans on rack and let them cool for 10 minutes. Gently lift out cakes, put them back on the rack, and allow them to cool for another 10 minutes. Peel off the wax paper and finish cooling.

Open a window near your work surface. This sounds silly, but you can get pretty light-headed doing the next step, as it involves some powerful fumes.

Pour a cup of brandy into a bowl. Fold the cheese-cloth over so it's double thick and cut lengths that are long enough to wrap around the cakes. Dip lengths of cheesecloth in the brandy, one at a time. Spread the cheesecloth out on a breadboard or on wax paper on your counter, wrap the cake in the cheesecloth, and place it in a gallon freezer bag. *(I put 2 cakes in each bag.)* Seal the bags and store them in the bottom of the refrigerator for at least 3 weeks, taking them out every week to add more brandy to the cheesecloth. *(I use a small bulb baster so I don't have to unwrap them.)*

If you give these cakes for Christmas, just take them out of the refrigerator, leave the cloth on, and wrap them in Saran Wrap. Then wrap them again in foil and stick a bow on top. These cakes are wonderful sliced and topped with ice cream!

NOTE: Cheesecloth has gotten really expensive. If you can't find any on sale, I've substituted one thickness of unbleached muslin from the fabric store. Just wash the muslin in hot water with NO SOAP and dry it in your dryer. Cut it into lengths AFTER washing and drying (it'll shrink in the washer and dryer,) and it'll work almost as well as the cheesecloth.

Coffee Cake

Preheat oven to 350 degrees F., rack in
the middle position

*Note: Some coffee cake is more like sweet bread.
Regina Todd's is really a cake, so the cookbook committee decided to put it in the cake section.*

1 cup soft butter *(2 sticks, ½ pound)*
1 and ¾ cup white sugar *(granulated)*
1 teaspoon salt
2 teaspoons vanilla
1 ½ teaspoons baking powder
6 eggs
3 cups flour *(no need to sift)*

The Filling:
3 cups chopped fruit *(or crushed berries—the
    fruit can be fresh, frozen, or canned***)*
⅓ cup white sugar *(granulated)*
⅓ cup flour

The Crumb Topping:
½ cup brown sugar *(tightly packed)*
⅓ cup flour
¼ cup softened butter *(½ stick, ⅛ pound)*

***If you choose to use drained canned fruit, make
sure it's been canned in its own juice or in water.

Grease the inside of a 9-inch by 13-inch rectangular cake pan, or spray it with non-stick cooking spray.

Mix the cup of soft butter with the white sugar until
it's fluffy. Add the salt, vanilla, and baking powder.
Mix thoroughly.

Add the eggs one by one, mixing after each addition.

Add the flour in one-cup increments, mixing thoroughly after each addition.

Spoon one-half of the batter in the cake pan and spread it out with a rubber spatula. Leave the rest in the bowl for later.

The filling: In another bowl, mix the fruit, sugar, and flour. *(If you've used chopped apples, peaches, or pears, add ½ teaspoon cinnamon to the mix.)* Spoon the fruit mixture on top of the batter.

Drop spoonfuls of the remaining batter on top and spread them carefully with a rubber spatula. *(The fruit doesn't have to be covered completely—the batter on top will fill in as it bakes and the crumb topping will cover the rest.)*

The crumb topping: Mix the brown sugar and the flour in a small bowl. Add the softened butter and cut it in until it's crumbly. *(You can also do this in a food processor with chilled butter and the steel blade.)*

Sprinkle the crumb topping over the pan as evenly as possible.

Bake at 350 degrees F. for 45 to 60 minutes. Remove the pan from the oven and let the coffee cake cool on a wire rack.

Andrea, Bill, and Bill's father like this served warm, right from the pan. Regina likes it thoroughly cool.

Regina told me that one time she wanted to make this coffee cake, but she didn't have anything in the pantry except a can of cherry pie filling. Instead of mixing the ingredients for the filling, she just dumped in the whole can of pie filling and it worked just fine.

Jell-O Cake

Preheat oven to whatever it recommends
on the cake mix box.

*This recipe is from Andrea, who makes it for Tracey's
birthday every year. Tracey's friends love it because
it's colorful. Andrea loves it because it's easy and she's
the undisputed Jell-O Queen of Lake Eden.*

1 package white cake mix *(1 pound 2.25
    ounces)*
The ingredients called for on the cake mix box
2 three-ounce packages dry Jell-O in contrast-
    ing colors

1 small tub of Cool Whip, or one can of
    whipped cream

Preheat the oven to the temperature it recommends
on the cake mix box.

Grease and flour a 9-inch by 13-inch rectangular
cake pan.

Mix up the cake using the directions on the box.
Bake the cake for the required amount of time. Let the
cake cool to room temperature.

When the cake has cooled, dump one package of
Jell-O into a small bowl. Add one cup boiling water to
the Jell-O and stir until it's dissolved *(about one minute.)*

Poke holes in the top of the cake with a fork,
punching it all the way to the bottom of the cake pan.
Make about 30 punches.

Pour the Jell-O evenly over the top of the cake. Give
it a minute or two to sink down into the holes you
punched.

Refrigerate the cake for an hour.

Prepare the second package of Jell-O, mixing the contents with 1 cup boiling water and stirring for one minute, or until it's dissolved.

Punch more holes in the top of your cake, crisscrossing the first holes. Pour the second bowl of Jell-O liquid over the top of the cake. Give it a minute or two to sink down and then cover it with plastic wrap or foil. Refrigerate the cake for at least 4 hours. Overnight is fine, too.

Andrea says to warn you that the top is going to look ugly and that's why you'll frost it with Cool Whip or whipped cream.

When it's time to serve, "frost" your cake with Cool Whip or whipped cream and cut into square pieces.

To Make A Layer Cake:

For a truly gorgeous cake, divide the batter into two 8-inch round pans and bake it according to the package directions. Then divide the Jell-O between the two pans.

To frost, remove the cakes from the pans, use Cool Whip or whipped cream between the layers and to frost the sides and top. Everyone will ooh and ahh when you slice the cake.

Andrea made a confession to me the night of the Christmas potluck dinner. She said she doesn't bake the cake. She buys an unfrosted sheet cake at the Red Owl, does the part with the Jell-O, and frosts it with Cool Whip. I thought about this for a few minutes and decided it's probably a good thing.

Lady Hermoine's (Hannah's) Chocolate Sunshine Cake

Preheat oven to 325 degrees F., rack in
the middle position

4 one-ounce squares unsweetened baking
    chocolate
1 cup frozen orange juice concentrate, melted
    and at room temperature
½ cup soft butter *(1 stick, ¼ pound)*
2 ½ cups white sugar *(granulated)*
2 teaspoons baking powder
½ teaspoon salt
½ teaspoon orange extract *(or ½ teaspoon
    vanilla)*
2 eggs
2 cups flour *(no need to sift)*
½ cup milk
1 cup chopped pecans *(or walnuts)*

Grease *(or oil, or spray with non-stick cooking spray)*
the inside of a Bundt pan. Dust with flour, or cocoa,
knocking out the excess.

Put the chocolate and the orange juice concentrate
in a microwave-safe bowl and heat it for one minute
on high. Stir it and then heat it on high for another
minute. Stir until the chocolate has melted. Set the
bowl aside to cool. *(You can also do this in the top of a
double boiler.)*

The following steps are a lot easier if you use an
electric mixer: Combine the butter and sugar, and mix
until fluffy. Mix in the baking powder, salt, and orange
extract. Add the eggs, one at a time, mixing after each
addition.

Add half of the flour to the bowl. Mix thoroughly. Mix in the milk, and then add the rest of the flour.

When the chocolate mixture is cool enough to touch, add it to your bowl. Mix thoroughly. Scrape down the bowl with a rubber spatula and then add the nuts. Give a final mix.

Let the batter rest for several minutes, and then pour it carefully into the prepared Bundt pan.

Bake at 325 degrees F., for 60 to 70 minutes, or until a cake tester inserted in the center of the ring comes out clean.

Remove to a wire rack and let cool for 25 minutes. Loosen the cake around the outside and inside edges with a sharp knife and tip it out onto the wire rack.

Let the cake cool completely and then glaze. *(Or, if you don't feel like making a glaze, just dust the cool cake with confectioner's sugar.)*

Chocolate Glaze:
1 cup chocolate chips
⅓ cup cream
1 teaspoon vanilla

Combine in a microwave-safe bowl. *(I use a one-quart glass measuring cup.)* Microwave on HIGH for one minute. Stir until chocolate chips are melted. If the glaze is too thick, add a little more cream. If the glaze is too thin, add a few more chips.

Drizzle the hot glaze over the crest of the cake and let it drip down the sides.

Poppy Seed Cake

Preheat oven to 350 degrees F., rack in
the middle position

This recipe is from Shirley Dubinski.

1 box yellow cake mix *(1 pound, 2.25 ounces)*
One package *(4.3 ounces)* lemon pudding & pie
    filling *(NOT sugar free)****
4 Tablespoons poppy seeds
½ cup lemon juice
½ cup water
½ cup vegetable oil
4 eggs

*** You can substitute a 3.4 ounce package of
Jell-O Lemon Instant Pudding and Pie Filling if you
can't find the kind of pudding you have to cook.

Grease and flour a Bundt pan.

Dump the dry yellow cake mix in a large bowl. Mix
in the dry lemon pudding and pie filling. Add the poppy
seeds, lemon juice, water, and oil. Mix until well-blended.

Add the eggs one at a time, mixing after each addition.

Beat 2 minutes on medium speed with an electric
mixer or 3 minutes by hand.

Pour the cake batter into the Bundt pan.

Bake at 350 degrees F. for 45 to 50 minutes or until
a cake tester inserted into the center of the cake comes
out dry.

Cool on a rack for 15 minutes. Loosen the outside
edges and the middle, and tip the cake out of the pan.
Let the cake cool completely on the rack.

When the cake is cool, drizzle Vanilla Glaze in ribbons on the top and down the sides. *(Or, if you don't feel like making a glaze, just let the cake cool completely and dust it with confectioner's sugar.)*

Vanilla Glaze:
1 cup powdered *(confectioner's)* sugar
1 teaspoon vanilla
6 Tablespoons cream

Measure powdered sugar into a small bowl. Stir in vanilla and cream. Stir until thoroughly mixed. The glaze should be the proper consistency to drizzle over the cake. If it's too thick, add a bit more cream. If it's too thin, add a bit more powdered sugar.

Drizzle the glaze over the crest of the cake and let it drip down the sides.

Refrigerate until serving.

Rose's Famous Coconut Cake

Preheat oven to 325 degrees F., rack in
the middle position.

*A note from Hannah: Rose McDermott called to
give me this recipe the day before I had to turn everything in to our editor. This has come close to convinc-
ing me that the man in the red suit with the sleigh is
real. Tracey asked for seven things in her letter to
Santa, and she got three of them. If she gets that puppy
she wants, I'm a believer.*

  1 ½ cups softened butter *(3 sticks)*
  2 cups white *(granulated)* sugar
  4 eggs
  1 cup sour cream*** *(you can substitute plain
      yogurt for a lighter cake)*
  ½ teaspoon baking powder
  1 teaspoon coconut extract *(if you can't find it,
      you can use vanilla)*
  1 ¾ cups flour *(not sifted)*
  2 cups flaked or shredded coconut *(pack it
      down when you measure it—more is better
      in this case)*

*** Measuring sour cream is messy—it's easier
just to buy the one-cup *(half pint)* container and use
the whole thing.

Generously grease *(or spray with non-stick cooking
spray)* a Bundt pan. Dust it liberally with flour and
knock off the excess.

Cream softened butter and sugar in the bowl of an
electric mixer. *(You can mix this cake by hand, but it
takes some muscle.)* Add the eggs, one at a time, and
beat until they're nice and fluffy. Then add the sour
cream, baking powder and coconut extract.

Put the flour and the coconut in a food processor. Process with the steel blade until the mixture looks like fine cornmeal. *(You don't have to do this if you don't have a food processor, but most folks like it better.)*

Add half of the flour/coconut mixture to the bowl. Mix thoroughly. Add the rest of the flour/coconut combination and mix until the batter is smooth.

Let the batter rest for five minutes or so. Then pour it into the Bundt pan, smoothing the top with a rubber spatula.

Bake at 325 degrees F. for 60 to 70 minutes. The cake should be golden brown on top and a wooden skewer inserted in the center of the cake ring should come out clean.

Cool in the pan on a rack for 25 minutes. Run a knife around the inside edges of the cake to loosen it and don't forget to loosen it around the funnel in the middle of the pan. Turn the cake out on the rack and let it cool completely.

When the cake is completely cool, glaze it with Coconut Glaze.

Coconut Glaze:
1 cup powered sugar *(confectioner's sugar)*
¼ cup heavy cream
1 teaspoon coconut extract *(or ½ teaspoon coconut, ½ teaspoon vanilla)*
¼ cup coconut flakes

If the powered sugar has big lumps, sift it. Otherwise, use it as it is. Put the powered sugar in a small bowl. Add the heavy cream and the coconut extract. Stir until smooth. *(If you can't get it smooth, you may need to heat it for thirty seconds or so in the microwave on HIGH, and then stir again.)*

If the glaze is too thick to pour over the cake, thin it with a little more cream. If the glaze is too thin, thicken it with a bit more powdered sugar.

Drizzle the glaze over the crest of the cake and let it drip down the sides. Sprinkle the cake with the coconut before the glaze dries.

Mother's been after Rose for years to use my Chocolate Glaze on this cake. (You can find it in Lady Hermoine's (Hannah's) Chocolate Sunshine Cake recipe.) She even took Rose the recipe. Rose liked it a lot, and now she offers two cakes, one with Coconut Glaze and the other with Chocolate Glaze.

Desserts: Pies

Coconut Green Pie

Preheat oven to 350 degrees F., rack in
the middle position

*Note: Bridget Murphy makes this green pie every
year for St. Patrick's Day dinner. She says that if green
food doesn't spark your appetite, either cover the top
with whipped cream, or shut your eyes when you eat it.*

You'll need a blender to make this pie. It makes its
own crust.

In the blender container combine:
1 ½ cups water
one can sweetened condensed milk *(14 ounces)*
½ cup Bisquick *(biscuit baking mix)*
3 eggs
¼ cup *(½ stick)* melted butter
2 teaspoons vanilla
3 or 4 drops green food coloring *(optional—
    don't tell Bridget I said this, but you can
    leave out the green food coloring if you'd
    rather.)*

Blend on low speed for 3 minutes.

Spray a 10-inch pie plate with Pam or other non-
stick shortening. Pour the contents of the blender container into the pie plate and let it stand, uncovered, at
room temperature for 5 minutes. *(The Bisquick settles
to the bottom and that's what makes the crust.)*

Sprinkle 1 cup of flaked coconut over the top of the
pie.

Carefully place the pie in a 350 degree F. oven.
*(This takes steady hands! I set my pie plate on a bak-
ing sheet before I fill it, just in case it spills on the way*

to the oven.) Bake pie for 40 to 45 minutes or until a knife inserted one inch from the edge comes out clean.

Cool on a wire rack.

This pie can be served slightly warm, room temperature, or chilled. Bridget says to remind you that it's wonderful with strong Irish coffee, and to be sure to refrigerate leftovers.

Pecan Pie For A Holiday Crowd

Preheat oven to 350 degrees F., rack in
the middle position

For First Step:
2 cups flour *(no need to sift)*
1 cup softened butter *(2 sticks, ½ pound)*
¾ cup loosely packed brown sugar

For Second Step:
5 beaten eggs *(just whip them up with a fork)*
1 cup brown sugar
½ cup melted butter
1 and ½ cups white corn syrup *(I use Karo)*
¾ teaspoon salt
1 ½ cups roughly chopped pecans
⅛ cup flour *(that's 2 Tablespoons)*

First Step: Cream softened butter with brown sugar
and add flour. Mix well. Spread 3 cups of this mixture
in a greased 9 by 13 inch cake pan and pat it down
with your hands. Reserve the rest for a crumb topping.
*(You can use cold butter if you divide each stick into
8 pieces and zoop everything up with the steel blade of
your food processor.)*

Bake the crust at 350 degrees F. for 15 minutes.
Remove from oven. DON'T TURN OFF THE OVEN!

Second Step: Beat the eggs and mix them with the
brown sugar. Add the melted butter and stir it all up.
Then mix in the white corn syrup, salt, and pecan
pieces. Now add the flour and mix thoroughly.

Pour this mixture over the crust you just baked.
Sprinkle the reserved crust mixture from the first step
on top. *(At this point you can carefully decorate the*

*top with a few half pecans, if you want to make it fancier.
I don't bother. With something this good, you don't
need decoration.)*

Bake at 350 degrees F. for another 30 to 35 minutes. Remove pan from the oven and cool on a wire rack. Once the pan is cool to the touch, refrigerate it until ready to serve.

To serve, cut the Pecan Pie into 16 pieces. You can top these with whipped cream if you like, but they don't really need it.

Bill likes to eat this cold, right out of the refrigerator. Andrea likes it best at room temperature. Carrie loves it when it's still warm, served with a scoop of vanilla ice cream on top. Mother also likes it warm, but with chocolate ice cream. I like it any way at all, anytime.

Pumpkin Pie For A Thanksgiving Crowd

Preheat oven to 350 degrees F., rack in
the middle position

1 ½ cups flour *(no need to sift)*
¾ cup butter *(1 ½ sticks)*
½ cup powdered *(confectioner's)* sugar *(don't
    sift unless it's got big lumps)*

4 eggs
1 ½ cups white *(granulated)* sugar
1 teaspoon salt
½ teaspoon nutmeg *(freshly ground is best)*
½ teaspoon cardamom *(or 1 teaspoon cinna-
    mon, but cardamom's better)*
3 ½ cups plain canned pumpkin, no spices
    added *(29-ounce can)*
2 cans evaporated milk *(12-ounce cans)* or
    3 cups light cream

Cut chilled butter into 12 pieces. Layer them between the flour and the powdered sugar in the bowl of
a food processor. Process until the mixture has the
consistency of corn meal. *(You can also do this by cutting softened butter into the dry ingredients.)*

Coat a standard 9 x 13 inch cake pan with non-stick
cooking spray. Pour the mixture inside, shake it until
it's evenly distributed on the bottom, and press it down
a bit with a metal spatula.

Bake at 350 degrees F. for 15 minutes. Let it cool
while you prepare the pumpkin pie filling, but DON'T
SHUT OFF THE OVEN.

Beat the eggs in a large bowl *(or use an electric
mixer.)* Mix in the sugar, salt, nutmeg, and cardamom.

Add the pumpkin and blend. Then add the evaporated milk and mix thoroughly.

Pour this over the crust you just baked. Stick it back in the oven and bake it for another 60 or 70 minutes, or until a knife inserted near the center comes out clean.

Chill overnight, cut into 16 squares, and serve each with a generous dollop of sweetened whipped cream.

Desserts: Cookies

Cherry Bomb Cookies

Preheat oven to 350 degrees F., rack in
the middle position

*This is my Grandma Ingrid's recipe. She used to
make these for special occasions.*

3 cups flour *(no need to sift)*
½ teaspoon baking powder
½ teaspoon baking soda
¼ teaspoon salt
1 cup *(2 sticks, ½ pound)* softened butter

2 beaten eggs
1 cup white *(granulated)* sugar

2 jars *(16-oz. each)* maraschino cherries WITH
    STEMS *(about 65 cherries)*
Small bowl with powdered *(confectioner's)*
    sugar for dipping

Open the jars of cherries and drain the cherries.
Leave them in the strainer while you make the cookie
dough.

Put flour, baking powder, soda, and salt in a mixing
bowl. Stir with a fork until thoroughly mixed. Cut in
the softened butter with two forks, continuing to cut
until the mixture looks like coarse corn meal. *(You can
also do this in a food processor with the steel blade,
using cold butter cut in half-inch chunks.)*

Beat the eggs in a medium-sized bowl and combine
them with the sugar.

Add the egg and sugar mixture to the rest of the ingredients and stir until thoroughly mixed.

Extract small bits of dough with your fingers and wrap them around each maraschino cherry, leaving the stem sticking out. Press the bottoms of the dough-wrapped cherries down slightly on a greased baking sheet, 16 to a standard-sized sheet. *(4 rows of 4 cookies works nicely.)*

Bake at 350 degrees F. for 10 minutes. *(Cookies will be white—if they start to brown, reduce the baking time.)* Let the cookies cool on the cookie sheet. Then dip them in the powdered sugar so that the entire cookie part is covered, but not the stem.

Yield: 5 to 6 dozen cookies.

Kids love these, probably because they can pick them up by the stem, pop the whole cookie in their mouths, and pull off the stem.

For Christmas, I make these with one jar of red maraschino cherries and one jar of green. Once they're arranged on a platter lined with a paper doily, they're really pretty.

Christmas Sugar Cookies

Do not preheat oven—this dough must
chill before baking

*I came up with the cookie recipe and Lisa did the
frosting.*

1 ½ cups melted butter *(3 sticks, ¾ pound)*
2 cups white *(granulated)* sugar
4 beaten eggs
2 teaspoons baking powder
1 ½ teaspoons salt
1 teaspoon flavor extract *(lemon, almond,
    vanilla, orange, rum, whatever)*
5 cups flour *(no need to sift)*

Mix the melted butter with the sugar. Let cool. Add
the beaten eggs, baking powder, salt, and flavoring.

Add the flour in one-cup increments.

Refrigerate dough for at least two hours. Overnight
is fine, too.

When you're ready to bake, preheat the oven to 375
degrees F., rack in the center position.

Divide the dough into four parts for ease in rolling.
Roll out the first part of the dough on a floured board.
It should be approximately 1/8 inch thick.

Dip the cookie cutters in flour and cut out cookies,
getting as many as you can from the sheet of dough. *(If
you don't have cookie cutters, you can cut free-form
cookies with a sharp knife.)* Use a metal spatula to remove the cookies from the rest of the sheet of dough
and place them on an UNGREASED cookie sheet.
Leave at least an inch and a half between cookies.

If you want to use colored sugar or sprinkles to decorate, put it on now, before baking. If you'd rather frost the cookies, wait until they're baked and cooled.

Bake at 375 degrees F. for 8 to 10 minutes, or just until delicately golden in color. Leave them on the sheet for a minute or two and then transfer them to a wire rack to complete cooling.

Icing:
2 cups sifted confectioner's sugar *(powdered sugar)*
pinch of salt
½ teaspoon vanilla *(or other flavoring)*
¼ cup cream

Mix up icing, adding a little more cream if it's too thick and a little more powdered sugar if it's too thin.

If you'd like to frost the cookies in different colors, divide the icing and put it in several small bowls. Add drops of the desired food coloring to each bowl.

Use a frosting knife, or a brush to "paint" the cookies you've baked.

Heavenly Tea Cookies

DO NOT preheat oven—this dough must
chill before baking

1 ½ cups melted butter *(3 sticks, ¾ pound)*
2 cups firmly packed brown sugar
2 beaten eggs *(just whisk them up in a glass
    with a fork)*
2 teaspoons baking powder
1 teaspoon vanilla *(or other flavoring—I used
    lemon extract)*
1 ½ cups dried mixed fruit chopped
    with 2 Tablespoons flour *(measure fruit
    after chopping)*
3 cups flour

Melt the butter in a microwave-safe bowl on HIGH
for 2 ½ minutes. Add the brown sugar and mix it up.
Let it cool for several minutes. When the mixture is
warm to the touch, but not hot, add the beaten eggs,
baking powder and vanilla.

Chop the dried mixed fruit. This is easy with a food
processor and the steel blade. Just drop in the fruit *(I
used peaches, apples, pears, and apricots)* and sprinkle the 2 Tablespoons of flour on top. Pulse until the
fruit is finely chopped, adding a bit more flour if it
starts to "gum" up. Measure out a cup and a half of
chopped fruit.

Add the fruit to your mixing bowl and stir it in.
Then add the flour, one cup at a time, stirring after
each addition.

Place the dough in the refrigerator for 20 minutes
to firm up. Then divide it into 4 parts. Using waxed
paper, roll each part into a log approximately 2 inches

in diameter. *(If the dough is too sticky, return it to the refrigerator and let it chill for another ten minutes.)* Wrap the logs in fresh sheets of waxed paper, stick them in a plastic bag, and store them in your refrigerator for at least 4 hours. *(Overnight is fine, too—Heavenly Tea Cookie dough will keep up to a week in your refrigerator.)*

When you're ready to bake, preheat the oven to 375 degrees F., rack in the center position.

Take out a roll of dough, *(just one—it's easier to work with when it's chilled)* unwrap it, and roll it on the counter again if the bottom has flattened in the refrigerator. Cut quarter-inch thick slices with a sharp knife and place them on a greased cookie sheet, 12 to a standard-sized sheet. Return the unused dough to the refrigerator. Bake the cookies at 375 degrees F. for 10 minutes or until nicely browned.

Cool one or two minutes on the sheet and then transfer the cookies to a wire rack to cool completely.

Yield: 6 to 7 dozen cookies.

Note: These cookies are not very sweet—if you prefer a sweeter cookie, dust the tops with powdered sugar before serving.

Lisa's Pieces

Preheat oven to 350 degrees F., rack in
the middle position

1 cup regular semi-sweet chocolate chips
1 cup melted butter *(2 sticks, ½ pound)*
¼ cup strong coffee
1 cup chopped pitted dates *(you can buy
    chopped dates, or sprinkle whole pitted
    dates with a bit of flour and then chop them
    in a food processor.)*
1 ½ cups white *(granulated)* sugar
2 beaten eggs *(just whip them up with a fork)*
1 teaspoon vanilla
1 teaspoon baking soda
1 teaspoon salt
1 cup chopped walnuts or pecans *(measure
    after you chop them)*
1 cup milk chocolate chips
3 ½ cups flour *(no need to sift)*

Put the semi-sweet chocolate chips, butter and
coffee in a microwave-safe bowl and microwave until
they're melted. *(Approximately 2 minutes on high.)*
The chips may maintain their shapes, so stir until
they're smooth. Add the chopped dates, mix them in,
and set the bowl aside.

Measure the sugar into a large mixing bowl, and
stir in the beaten eggs. Add the vanilla, baking soda,
and salt. Mix thoroughly.

Add the melted chocolate mixture to your bowl and
then mix in the chopped nuts and the milk chocolate
chips. Add the flour in half-cup increments, mixing
after each addition.

Let the dough sit for ten minutes or so, then drop dough by teaspoons onto a greased cookie sheet, twelve cookies to a standard sheet. Flatten the dough balls slightly on the sheet with the heel of your impeccably clean hand. *(If the dough is too sticky, chill it for a few minutes.)*

Bake at 350 degrees F. for 10 to 12 minutes. Let the cookies sit on the cookie sheet for a minute or two and then transfer to a wire rack to complete cooling.

Yield: Approximately 8 dozen cookies, depending on cookie size.

Blueberry Shortbread Bar Cookies

Preheat oven to 350 degrees F., rack in
the middle position

*This is Betty Jackson's recipe. She says to tell you
they're the best bar cookie to eat if you're on a diet,
because they have only three-quarters of a cup of powdered sugar. (That's true, but she's forgetting about all
the sugar in the can of pie filling.)*

3 cups flour *(no need to sift)*
1 ½ cups softened butter *(3 sticks, ¾ pound)*
¾ cup powdered *(confectioner's)* sugar *(don't
   sift unless it's got big lumps)*
1 can *(21 ounces)* blueberry pie filling

FIRST STEP: Cream butter with powdered sugar
and add flour. Mix well.

*(You can also do this in a food processor using cold
butter cut into chunks and the steel blade.)*

Spread HALF of this mixture *(approx. 3 ½ cups)*
into a greased 9-inch by 13-inch pan. *(That's a standard size rectangular cake pan.)*

Bake at 350 degrees F. for 15 minutes. Remove the
pan from the oven. DON'T TURN OFF THE OVEN!

Let the crust cool for 5 minutes.

SECOND STEP: Spread the pie filling over the top
of the crust you just baked. Sprinkle it with the other
half of the crust mixture you reserved and gently press
it down with a metal spatula.

Bake the cookie bars for another 30 to 35 minutes, or until the top is lightly golden. Remove the pan to a wire rack.

Cool thoroughly and then cut into brownie-sized bars. If you like, sprinkle the bars with a little extra powdered sugar.

Desserts: Other Sweet Treats

Candied Pecans From Lois

Preheat oven to 325 degrees F., rack in
the middle position

*Sally Laughlin's mother, Francine, got this recipe
from her friend Lois Melin.*

2 pounds pecan halves

2 egg whites
dash of salt
1 cup white *(granulated)* sugar

½ cup melted butter *(1 stick, ¼ pound)*

Spray two 9-inch by 13-inch cake pans with non-stick cooking spray. Divide pecans and put half in one pan, half in the other. Toast them at 325 degrees F., for 5 minutes.

Beat the two egg whites with the dash of salt until stiff but not dry. Fold in the sugar and then the toasted pecan halves.

Pour half of the melted butter in one pan and half in the other. Divide the nut mixture and put half in each pan. Fold the mixture into the melted butter with a wooden spoon or spatula.

Bake at 325 degrees F., uncovered, for 10 minutes. Stir.

Bake another 10 minutes. Stir.

Bake an additional 10 minutes. Stir.

Remove pans from the oven and spread the contents out on wax paper. Let cool slightly, and then separate. Cool completely.

Sally puts these in little tins and gives them as Christmas presents. They're so good, you won't be able to resist them.

Chocolate Fruit Platter

This recipe is from Bonnie Surma, who says this is about as fancy (and easy) as she ever gets when it comes to desserts.

2 cups *(16-ounce package)* chocolate chips

Dried fruit *(apricots, peaches, dates, figs, and pears work best)*

Melt the chocolate chips in the top of a double boiler and stir them until smooth.

Spread the fruit out on cookie sheets lined with wax paper.

Dip the fruit into the chocolate, coating half of the piece. Once dipped, place the fruit on the waxed paper. *(Pears look best if you dip the bottom half.)*

Once all the fruit is dipped, refrigerate the cookie sheets for at least an hour. Take them out 30 minutes before you're ready to serve. *(The chocolate is tastier if it's not too cold.)* When it's time to serve, arrange the fruit on a platter and serve with strong coffee for an elegant dessert.

Bonnie says to tell you that you can dip fresh strawberries in chocolate by this method. If you buy strawberries with the stems on, you can dip the whole berry. Otherwise, just pierce the top half of the berry with a toothpick and dip the bottom half.

Mother reports that Bonnie made a lovely platter for the Lake Eden Regency Romance Readers group last summer. It had strawberries dipped in milk chocolate, semi-sweet chocolate, and white chocolate.

Beverages

English Eggnog

This recipe was contributed by Winthrop Harrington II. Even though Winthrop isn't from Lake Eden, Mother is so it's in.

1 dozen eggs
¼ cup white sugar
1 quart whole milk
1 pint Half & Half *(light cream)*
1 pint whipping cream
2 cups brandy *(or rum, or whiskey of your choice)*

Separate the eggs. Beat the egg whites until they form soft peaks. Set aside.

Beat the whipping cream until it forms soft peaks. Fold it into the egg whites. Set the mixture aside.

Beat the egg yolks until light-colored and fluffy. Mix in the sugar, milk, Half & Half, and brandy. Fold into the cream/egg white mixture.

At this point, the eggnog can be refrigerated in a tightly covered pitcher for up to 12 hours.

To serve, stir the pitcher and then pour the eggnog into glass cups, if you have them. Dust the tops with freshly grated nutmeg, or cinnamon.

This is English Eggnog and it's not as sweet as American Eggnog. Taste it after you've made it. If your family would like it sweeter add more sugar to taste.

To make the non-alcoholic version, add 2 additional cups of milk and 2 teaspoons of rum extract or vanilla extract.

Dimpled Duchess

Bertie Straub contributed this recipe. She told me she serves these drinks when her best customers stay late for a "hen party" at the Cut 'n Curl. Mother says she certainly wouldn't swear this on a stack of Bibles, but there's a rumor going around that one too many Dimpled Duchess could be responsible for Donna Lempke's bright orange hair.)

Use a blender to make these drinks. For each person served you will need:

1 ounce *(2 Tablespoons)* amaretto liqueur
4 ounces *(½ cup)* strawberry ice cream

Zoop up the ice cream and the liqueur in the blender and pour into a fancy stemmed glass.

Bertie says to make certain that anyone who's had more than two Dimpled Duchesses gets a ride home with someone who hasn't.

Extras (that didn't fit anywhere else)

Baking Conversion Chart

These conversions are approximate, but they'll work just fine for Hannah Swensen's recipes.

VOLUME:

U.S.	Metric
½ teaspoon	2 milliliters
1 teaspoon	5 milliliters
1 Tablespoon	15 milliliters
¼ cup	50 milliliters
⅓ cup	75 milliliters
½ cup	125 milliliters
¾ cup	175 milliliters
1 cup	¼ liter

WEIGHT:

U.S.	Metric
1 ounce	28 grams
1 pound	454 grams

OVEN TEMPERATURE:

Degrees Fahrenheit	Degrees Centigrade	British (Regulo) Gas Mark
325 degrees F.	165 degrees C.	3
350 degrees F.	175 degrees C.	4
375 degrees F.	190 degrees C.	5

Note: Hannah's rectangular sheet cake pan, 9 inches by 13 inches, is approximately 23 centimeters by 32.5 centimeters.

Index Of Recipes

APPETIZERS

SOUPS

SALADS

BREADS

BEVERAGES

EXTRAS (that didn't fit anywhere else)

With The Cookie Jar, Hannah Swensen has a mouthwatering monopoly on the bakery business of Lake Eden, Minnesota. But when a rival store opens, tensions begin to bubble. . . .

As she sits in her nearly empty store on Groundhog Day, Hannah can only hope that spring is just around the corner—and that the popularity of the new Magnolia Blossom Bakery is just a passing fad. The southern hospitality of Lake Eden's two Georgia transplants, Shawna Lee and Vanessa Quinn, is grating on Hannah's nerves—and cutting into her profits.

At least Hannah has her business partner Lisa's wedding to look forward to. She's turned one of Lisa's favorite childhood treats into a spectacular Wedding Cookie Cake. But Hannah starts to steam when she finds out that Shawna Lee has finagled an invitation to the reception—and is bringing the Magnolia Blossom Bakery's Southern Peach Cobbler for the dessert table.

Hannah doesn't like having the Georgia Peach in the mix, especially when both Shawna Lee and Hannah's sometime-boyfriend, Detective Mike Kingston, are no-shows to the wedding. Hannah has suspected that Mike is interested in more than Shawna Lee's baking abilities. So when she sees lights on at the Magnolia Blossom Bakery after the reception, she investigates—and finds Shawna Lee shot to death.

Everyone in town knew The Cookie Jar was losing business to the Magnolia Bakery—a fact that puts Hannah at the top of the initial list of suspects. But with a little help from her friends, Hannah's determined to prove that she wasn't the only one who had an axe to grind with the Quinn sisters. Somebody wasn't fooled by the Georgia Peaches and their sweet-as-pie act—and now it's up to Hannah to track down whoever had the right ingredients to whip up a murder. . . .

**Please turn the page for an exciting sneak peek at
PEACH COBBLER MURDER
coming in paperback in February 2006!**

Hannah glanced at the clock. She'd unloaded her cookie truck in only ten minutes. The earliest that Norman could arrive was five minutes from now and that was probably optimistic. She went back to her favorite table, but she couldn't seem to relax. There was something about the bright lights glaring in the interior of the Magnolia Blossom Bakery that made her nervous.

Perhaps there'd been a robbery. The moment the idea occurred to Hannah, her imagination was off and running. If the robbery had happened during the day, the robber might not have realized that all the lights were on. At this very moment, the cash drawer could be open and the Magnolia Blossom Bakery could be minus the day's receipts. A good citizen of Lake Eden, one who could put aside petty jealousy and hold the welfare of a neighboring business paramount, would check to make sure the cash register at the Magnolia Blossom Bakery was intact.

Hannah groaned. The last thing she wanted to do was put on her boots and her coat, and walk across the street to make sure no burglar had invaded her competitor's bakery. But basic decency demanded she do so, and she liked to think of herself as a basically decent person. Hannah stuffed her still-aching feet into her boots and slipped into her parka coat, zipping it up all the way. She scrawled a note to Norman: *Across the street at Shawna Lee's—maybe a burglary?* and taped it to the outside of the back door. And then she hurried around the side of her building to see if there was a problem with the Magnolia Blossom Bakery.

The wind had teeth, and shards of ice pelted Hannah's face as she left the protection of her building. She turned up the collar of her parka coat and held her hand up to shield her eyes as she dashed across Main Street. She ducked under the pseudo-Jeffersonian portico of Lake Eden Realty and peered in the plate glass window of her cobbler challenger.

Andrea's description hadn't done the Magnolia Blossom Bakery justice. It was gorgeous and Hannah would be the first to admit it. The magnolia tree mural the Minneapolis artist had painted was spectacular, all the tables and chairs matched, and everything was new and shiny. The color scheme was incredibly appealing and everything Hannah saw fit in perfectly. The homemade decorations at The Cookie Jar couldn't hold a candle to the decorator embellishments at Shawna Lee and Vanessa's Bakery.

Hannah sighed. She didn't like feeling second-rate, even in the category of decorations. Comforting herself with knowledge that at least her baked goods were better, she took another, less envious and more appraising look, and came to the conclusion that absolutely nothing was out of place. The cash register drawer was pushed in, there were no signs of vandalism, and everything looked ready and set to go for business in the morning. But something about the bright lights really bothered her, and she felt she should check further. Even though there wasn't much petty crime in Lake Eden, it was possible that a group of teenagers had waited until Shawna Lee had left and then broken in to steal whatever pastry they could find in the kitchen. The lights were on in there, too. She could see them blazing through the diamond-shaped window in the swinging door.

Hannah wished that Norman were with her, but no cars had driven past and he was probably still doing what they not so jokingly called "mother duty." She didn't relish going inside to check out someone else's kitchen, but she couldn't just stand here and do nothing. She tried the front door, hoping it would save her a trip around to the back, but it was locked securely. If pastry bandits were to blame for turning on the lights, they must have entered and left by the back door.

"Shawna Lee?" Hannah called out, knocking loudly on the front door. When that didn't work, she balled up her fists and hammered loudly, doing her best to wake anyone who might be sleeping upstairs. No one was home. She was certain of it. Only the dead could sleep through the racket she'd made. Hannah pushed that very unwelcome thought aside and decided she'd have to go around to the back.

Keeping a sharp eye out for broken or pried windows, or any other signs of unauthorized access, Hannah walked around the side of the building. Everything looked secure, but a glance in the kitchen window made her frown. There was a colorful pink and green box on the counter and the label read, *Betty Jo's Frozen Peach Cobbler, a division of Macon Foods.* Shawna Lee had claimed that her Southern Peach Cobbler was made from an old family recipe. Maybe that was true, but it was Betty Jo's family recipe, not Shawna Lee's.

Hannah's gaze moved toward the ovens and what she saw made her frown deepen. A pan of peach cobbler was upended next to the open oven door. It was a mess, a jumble of sliced peaches and biscuit topping strewn over a puddle of sticky juice on the white tile floor. Had Shawna Lee simply dropped the pan as she was taking it from the oven? Or was there a more sinister reason for the baking disaster?

A glance at the other kitchen window gave Hannah an unwelcome answer to her question. There were two round holes in the glass, and each hole was surrounded by a spider web of cracks. She was no expert, but they looked like a couple of bullet holes to her!

Hannah swallowed hard as she pressed her nose against the glass and held her breath so it wouldn't fog up. Was that a shoe she saw peeking out from behind the work counter?

There was the wise thing to do and the foolish thing to do. Hannah knew the wise thing would be to call for help, or wait for Norman, or do anything other than go into the kitchen to check it out by herself. But the time it took to do the wise thing could spell the difference between life and death for whoever was wearing that shoe.

Maybe the best thing to do is nothing at all, the not-so-nice side of Hannah's psyche whispered in her ear. *What difference would it make if you just went back to The Cookie Jar and pretended you hadn't seen that shoe? Who would know?*

"I'd know," Hannah answered out loud, accepting the burden of her own good character. It didn't matter what she thought of Shawna Lee personally. If her cookie competitor was hurt or in trouble, Hannah had a responsibility to do what she could to help.

Once she'd made up her mind, Hannah moved quickly. She raced to the back door, fully prepared to kick it in if that's what it took, but when she turned the knob she found it unlocked. She pushed the door open, praying that the two holes she'd seen weren't bullet holes, the shoe behind the counter had no foot in it, and the peach cobbler on the floor meant nothing more than a slip of an oven glove. But where was Shawna Lee? And why hadn't she shut the oven door and cleaned up the mess?

"Uh-oh," Hannah gasped, skidding to a stop as she rounded the corner of the kitchen counter. Shawna Lee was down on her back on the tile floor and there was a huge blossom of what looked like dried strawberry syrup on the bib of her white chef's apron. There was also a neat hole in the middle of the blossom and Hannah knew that there was no point in continuing to contaminate what was surely a crime scene. Shawna Lee had been shot in the chest and anyone with an ounce of brains could see that she was dead.

Carnival Pride℠
April 2 - 9, 2006.

7 Day Exotic Mexican Riviera Itinerary

DAY	PORT	ARRIVE	DEPART
Sun	Los Angeles/Long Beach, CA		4:00 P.M.
Mon	"Book Lover's" Day at Sea		
Tue	"Book Lover's" Day at Sea		
Wed	Puerto Vallarta, Mexico	8:00 A.M.	10:00 P.M.
Thu	Mazatlan, Mexico	9:00 A.M.	6:00 P.M.
Fri	Cabo San Lucas, Mexico	7:00 A.M.	4:00 P.M.
Sat	"Book Lover's" Day at Sea		
Sun	Los Angeles/Long Beach, CA	9:00 A.M.	

ports of call subject to weather conditions

TERMS AND CONDITIONS

PAYMENT SCHEDULE:
50% due upon booking
Full and final payment due by February 10, 2006

Acceptable forms of payment are Visa, MasterCard, American Express, Discover and checks. The cardholder must be one of the passengers traveling. A fee of $25 will apply for all returned checks. Check payments must be made payable to **Advantage International, LLC and sent to: Advantage International, LLC, 195 North Harbor Drive, Suite 4206, Chicago, IL 60601**

CHANGE/CANCELLATION:
Notice of change/cancellation must be made in writing to Advantage International, LLC.

Change:
Changes in cabin category may be requested and can result in increased rate and penalties. A name change is permitted 60 days or more prior to departure and will incur a penalty of $50 per name change. Deviation from the group schedule and package is a cancellation.

Cancellation:

181 days or more prior to departure	$250 per person
121 - 180 days or more prior to departure	50% of the package price
120 - 61 days prior to departure	75% of the package price
60 days or less prior to departure	100% of the package price (nonrefundable)

US and Canadian citizens are required to present a valid passport or the original birth certificate and state issued photo ID (drivers license). All other nationalities must contact the consulate of the various ports that are visited for verification of documentation.

<u>We strongly recommend trip cancellation insurance!</u>

For complete details call 1-877-ADV-NTGE or visit www.AuthorsAtSea.com

For booking form and complete information
go to **<u>www.AuthorsAtSea.com</u> or call 1-877-ADV-NTGE**

Complete coupon and booking form and mail both to:
Advantage International, LLC,
195 North Harbor Drive, Suite 4206, Chicago, IL 60601

BOOK YOUR PLACE ON OUR WEBSITE AND MAKE THE READING CONNECTION!

We've created a customized website just for our very special readers, where you can get the inside scoop on everything that's going on with Zebra, Pinnacle and Kensington books.

When you come online, you'll have the exciting opportunity to:

- View covers of upcoming books
- Read sample chapters
- Learn about our future publishing schedule (listed by publication month *and author*)
- Find out when your favorite authors will be visiting a city near you
- Search for and order backlist books from our online catalog
- Check out author bios and background information
- Send e-mail to your favorite authors
- Meet the Kensington staff online
- Join us in weekly chats with authors, readers and other guests
- Get writing guidelines
- AND MUCH MORE!

Visit our website at
http://www.kensingtonbooks.com